Exit Row

By Judi Culbertson

Exit Row

DELHI LAINE MYSTERIES

An Illustrated Death
A Photographic Death
A Bookmarked Death

Exit Row

JUDI CULBERTSON

WITNESS
IMPULSE
An Imprint of HarperCollinsPublishers

EPub Edition MARCH 2016 ISBN: 9780062365163

Print Edition ISBN: 9780062365170

RRD 10 9 8 7 6 5 4 3 2 1

To my father, H. R. Chaffee,
who watched the sun rise all over the world
and passed his love of travel to his family.

Chapter One

IT WAS A beautiful day to fly.

The plane dipped toward the terra cotta cliffs, then recovered, and Jackson imagined the sun face on its tail fin righting itself. Although the rain had dried in instant streaks on the plane's windows, Jackson could envision it glistening on the pinion trees and Indian paintbrush far below. A stand of aspen would be swaying in the breeze.

He navigated the beverage cart up the aisle, careful not to bump the edges of the luxurious blue seats. Coffee, orange juice, and a miniature jalapeño corn muffin, and the flight would be over. It lasted less than two hours. Most domestic airlines had abandoned food service years ago, but Day Star promised "a spa experience" and did everything but offer a hot tub.

But that was for show. In Denver, he and Karleen would dart around the empty plane, replacing magazines, wiping down the bathroom sinks, and vacuuming up crumbs. Larger airlines hired servicing agents to go over their planes between flights, but at a small company you did everything yourself. Karleen called

Jackson "Drone 1" and herself "Drone 2," as in "Drone 2 has cramps today."

After three weeks, he was getting her humor. His first morning, she had said, "Today's coffee flavor is arsenic."

At his startled expression, she had bumped her hip against his mischievously. "Airplane humor. But you'll soon be ready to poison them all."

Jackson already was. Not that he had anything against the passengers personally, but when Day Star summoned him to their offices in Santa Fe a month earlier, he'd assumed they were finally going to let him fly. He had dreamed of being a pilot since his first plane trip to Albuquerque for the state baseball playoffs. Since the air force demanded a college degree even before training, he had gotten his BAAS in Roswell two years ago to qualify. It was a good time to be Native American, with lots of government education grants and incentives.

Day Star, flying out of Taos, had been his first choice. When they hired him, they explained he would have to do other work first, and he understood that. They had started him off in ticketing in Denver, then put him on phone sales, always with small bonuses. But he was getting impatient, and when he was summoned to Santa Fe in July, he assumed his apprenticeship was over.

Instead, Will Dunlea, the CEO, told him he was being "promoted" to flight attendant. "Jackson, you're so good with people. And we need a body temporarily. As soon as we can get one of these air force guys to retire, you're in."

"But that's crazy!"

Will spread his hands sadly. "We're a small company. You always knew that."

He'd give them three months—no more.

And then what will you do? Move to some place you've never been before? Sabotage the plane out of spite?

For today, he would just do his job.

"Something to drink? Coffee, tea, water?" he asked a man in a blue-checked shirt and rose-tinted glasses. The man looked up from a mountain of fashion magazines. Jackson had noticed him studying the photographs, blotting out the models with his hand to better see the background. Who looked at the scenery instead of the girls?

"Nothing stronger?" The man had an accent, like that actor who had played Harry Potter.

"Afraid not."

He grinned. "Coffee's fine, black. Are those the Rockies so soon?" He gestured at the window with a yellow felt marker. "Short trip!"

"No, not yet." Jackson ducked his head until he could see out of the small glass oval, then twisted his arm to look at his watch, shocked at the unfamiliar mountains. What... "It's supposed to be the Sangre de Cristo," he managed to blurt out.

His hand shook a little as he poured coffee into a white paper cup. He wanted to investigate, but his cart was ahead of him and Karleen close behind him, ready to pass out muffins and napkins. They worked well together; after the first week she had told him the secret of the oxygen canisters in the hold.

But why were they flying a different route?

"Yoo hoo! Do you have any Yoo-hoos?"

Fighting the shock of what was happening outside, Jackson stared at the little girl in the next seat. She was pixieish and giggling, her face pressed against her seatmate's arm as if she had said something daring. The older girl grinned too. A collection of trolls with wild purple hair stood on the tray tables. Were they popular again? Jackson had heard the older girl entertaining the younger one by making up situations between the dolls. "If you don't do something about that hair, I'll never sleep with you again!"

He hadn't been able to keep from laughing.

No Yoo-hoo. "How about a Sprite?" he coaxed.

The plane gave a swoon then, and without waiting to hear her answer, Jackson abandoned his cart in the aisle, squeezing painfully around it. He had to get to the cockpit and find out what the trouble was. What if both pilots were unconscious in there? Thank God he knew how to fly!

Shouldering people aside, he bumped hard against a radiant young woman with a large baby bump. Her smile turned puzzled as he grabbed her by the shoulders and sat her down. Other passengers—an old man clutching the seat back for support, a handsome athletic type in a Dodgers baseball cap—had to be removed from the aisle as well.

"Yo!" the athlete protested.

Jackson ignored him.

As he passed Clayton, his younger friend from the reservation, Clayton gave him a goofy grin. He was so excited to be going off to college, to be taking his first plane ride, that Jackson didn't think he had stopped smiling since takeoff.

Jackson grinned back and kept moving quickly.

The cockpit door was locked, of course. As he pressed the numbers on the keypad he felt another swoon, this one a dip that twisted his stomach. Hadn't any of the passengers felt it? Perhaps they thought that this was what riding in a little plane was all about. Would he know what to do? He hadn't flown a plane as large as this since college.

Expecting that he might have to take over the controls, as the door opened, Jackson was shocked to see both pilots seemingly alert.

"What's going on?" He gasped.

The copilot, in his sixties with a gray crew-cut, turned, startled, and then looked back at the instrument panel. "Fuel's acting wonky," he said over his shoulder. "Not feeding properly. We're checking it at the Ranch."

The captain, a man in his late fifties whom Jackson knew by sight, was speaking into the voice control. "Day Star 113, Day Star 113. How do you hear me? Irregularities, we're taking it down to check." He sounded professional, calm, but at the same time he was yanking on the yoke as if to gain altitude.

Irregularities? Could they make it to the Ranch?

The captain stayed hunched over, a squawking coming into his headset that Jackson could not decipher as the plane banked shockingly to the right. Through the open door behind him, Jackson could hear faint, surprised cries like the voices on a roller coaster on a summer day, rising in a delicate wave, then cutting off abruptly. His early-morning breakfast of eggs and muffins jammed in his throat.

The captain finally noticed him. "Get out of here, you! Go do your job!"

Furious and embarrassed, Jackson slammed the metal door. *If you weren't so selfish, I'd be doing* your *job, old man!*

The nose of the plane dipped suddenly and held there. This time there were screams. Jackson heard a clatter and saw his cart rattling down the aisle toward him as if it were alive, angrily spewing cans of soda and juice. Grabbing a handhold to keep from falling backward, he watched the silver coffee pitcher bounce off the cart's top and heard someone scream—had it landed over some-one, liquid splashing and burning? He never should have abandoned the cart!

The cart stopped moving as the plane stabilized.

Then the captain was on the intercom, his voice reassuring. "We're experiencing some turbulence; it happens here in the mountains sometimes. I've deployed the oxygen masks. The attendants will help you fit them on."

Jackson sprang into action, helping the terrified passengers around him place the masks over their noses and mouths.

"Stay in your seats!" he called frantically. "Fasten your seat belts—but not too tight. And take off your shoes!"

Everything Karleen had told him came back to him. But where was she? Then he caught sight of her golden curls in the back of the plane. She was strapped into the jump seat, her eyes squeezed shut, hands pressed against her face.

He felt suddenly sick, gagging on the food in his throat. Around him a sweet, cloudy haze was gathering, the spillover from the oxygen masks. But this wasn't just oxygen, it had nitrous oxide mixed in as part of the Day Star mystique. It was supposed to relax passengers during turbulence. And they were calmer now, many with their eyes shut.

Then he saw Clayton moving down the aisle toward him, hands out, his eyes euphoric. His varsity baseball cap was skewed to one side. Jackson had to get to him, get him belted in. But the beverage cart, snagged on a seat, created a barricade between them.

Sit down, Jackson wanted to shout. But he couldn't say anything.

There was a rocking from side to side, the sweet odor nightmarishly oppressive now, mixing with the smell of his own vomit. Jackson dropped to his knees, his limbs tingling, fingers scrabbling against the stiff wool carpet. He clutched at the steel stanchion of a seat as the plane started to roll over, overhead compartments opening and raining down luggage.

There was a steady rush of air like the hiss of an angry kachina, and Jackson shut his eyes, bracing as the plane hit the mountain with a metal scream.

But he was too happy to care.

Chapter Two

From the open car window, Fiona could hear the hum of a departing plane and smell the exhaust riding on the August air. Soon that plane would be in a high arc above the Long Island Expressway, rising above farms and beaches. It reminded her of the picture she had stolen from her social studies book, an illustration that showed all modes of transportation at once—a plane over a busy highway, next to a train being raced by a horse. On the horizon an ocean liner sailed.

From her earliest moments, all she had wanted to do was get away.

After smuggling the picture home, she had taped it into the scrapbook she kept hidden under her bed. The scrapbook, her lifeline to a larger world, had started life as a hymnal with ornate leather tooling, but Fiona had covered "Amazing Grace" with pictures of Japanese pagodas. She planned to visit all those places when she left Lamb's Tongue, Iowa, and was no longer Emma Lou Jensen.

By eleven she had mined the old *National Geographic* magazines in her adoptive aunt and uncle's shed and was augmenting the travel pictures with glamorous couples sipping champagne on balconies beside the sea. And her dreams had come true, at least some of them.

Fiona locked the Toyota and crossed the asphalt to the Islip-MacArthur terminal. It was originally designed in the 1940s to look like a flying saucer, with a round upper story and oval windows overlooking the runways. Subsequent additions and expansions lessened its charm. In her short career as a travel writer, she'd written about more beautiful airports. Her favorites were in Seoul and Dubai.

Quickly glancing at her watch, she saw that Lee's plane from Denver should be just touching down. He had been gone only four days, but it seemed like longer. It was the first time in the seven months they had been together that they had been apart. And they had a special reason to celebrate. Just before he left, they decided it was time for them to find an apartment together.

Tomorrow the search would begin.

Chapter Three

As FIONA MOVED through the automatic glass doors and found the arrivals board, she saw that the flights were listed as "On Time" except for one: Voyager Flight 886 out of Denver was marked "Delayed."

Well, it was still only four thirty in the afternoon. Around her, the small airport was jammed with sunburnt vacationers, especially teenagers laboring under backpacks and poster tubes. It was the last Sunday in August, and people were heading wearily home. Infected by their mood, she decided she needed black coffee while she waited.

The woman behind the Starbucks counter had a harried, defensive look—a look Fiona had come to know well during her brief foray as a lawyer. Had this woman spawned Billy, her first case in juvenile court, who stole only luxury cars? Or Gina, who had stuck a knife in her enemy in gym class as easily as slicing into butter?

Thank God those days were behind her, that she had saved enough money to travel and write her blog. Only…She looked around her and then carried her coffee to a dark gray upholstered chair in the waiting area from where she could see the arrivals board. Balancing her cup on the armrest, she pulled several papers out of her bag. For the last few months, she had been writing feature articles for *Gusto!* This month's was titled "How Being Beautiful Can Kill You!" and was supposed to highlight the dangers of cosmetics. The risks of plastic surgery were well known, but Fiona was writing about how tinted contact lenses could make you blind and unsanitary manicures leave you with infected fingers. She still had to research deadly lotions.

Mitzi, the articles editor, demanded to know Fiona's own beauty routine. "Your hair is so shiny! Your skin is flawless!"

Fiona didn't have a beauty routine. Moisturizer with SPF in the mornings, shampoo, and conditioner—whatever was cheap— several times a week. Lipstick from the dollar store. Growing up, her looks had not been valued. She had been too thin, with odd coloring—black hair, but light gray eyes and olive skin, which her aunt said sadly came from "that Indian."

Skimming what she had written so far, Fiona realized the magazine would be pushing her for more experts' quotes. She sighed. Could she invent a couple of cautionary doctors? A temptation, but probably not; the magazine fact-checked everything.

She glanced again at the monitor and saw that Flight 886 had arrived.

Thank God! Fiona walked over and stood at the back of the crowd in the waiting area. She waited next to a half-sized model of a famous Long Island dinghy and watched as the passengers funneled through the swinging doors. They were soon engulfed in tiny explosions of love. She knew Lee wouldn't be elbowing people out of his way to get off the plane; he was too relaxed for that. After five days in Indian country, she imagined him wearing jeans and a wrinkled cotton shirt with the sleeves rolled up. He cared even less about clothes than she did.

As the people in front of her drifted off, Fiona moved closer to the doorway. But the trickle from the plane was drying up, flight attendants now wheeling navy canvas bags with the Voyager logo of red feet. The women were chatting and shepherding the last of the stragglers through the double doors.

Fiona approached a pretty black woman with elegant corn-rowed hair. "Excuse me. I'm supposed to be meeting someone flying in from Taos, but he hasn't come through."

The woman gave her an exhausted smile. "People with checked luggage sometimes exit through there." She pointed toward another door.

"He didn't check anything." Lee kept his expensive camera equipment in his navy backpack, cushioned by a few changes of clothes. "He was on the shuttle out of Taos to Denver and then on Flight 886."

"Did you say from Taos?" An older man in a tan Western shirt with a bolo tie spoke up from behind the flight attendant. Something about his silvery mustache reminded her of an actor. Had she seen him before? "I was on that flight. We were late leaving Taos and had to change planes midflight, so the Denver plane had to wait for us. But the shuttle from San Diego was late too. Guess they got smogged in."

"Do you remember anyone on the plane with light hair and tinted sunglasses? An English accent? He had a navy backpack and maybe had his camera out." *He was born in South Africa. He has an unforgettable face.*

But the man blinked apologetically. "I'm afraid I don't remember him. I fly so much, I don't pay much attention to anyone else."

"Really? I look at everybody." *I try to imagine what their stories are.*

The man touched his Stetson and moved on past her, the scent of his cologne making her nose wrinkle. She did not wear perfume—it gave her headaches—but this man's aftershave seemed expensive. He was headed for the Hamptons, she decided.

When the double doors finally stayed shut, Fiona took out her phone. She must have missed the text from Lee explaining what had happened. She hadn't heard a beep, but sometimes she didn't notice.

Nothing.

Quickly she texted him: *Where r u?* She knew he would not have been able to contact her from the plane, and when she'd heard nothing from Denver, she'd assumed he'd been rushed onto the connecting flight with no time in between. But if he had missed Flight 886, where was he?

Chapter Four

FIONA HEADED IMMEDIATELY for the Voyager counter. There was a lull in check-ins and she walked right up to the agent, a stocky blond with long comb-over strips of hair and the white company shirt of red feet. Looking past him she noticed the smaller logos of Day Star, Dakota, and WestAir on the back wall.

"Any luggage?" He bestowed a welcoming smile on her, enhanced by two front teeth outlined in gold.

She smiled back. "No. I'm here to meet someone who was supposed to be on Flight 886. But he wasn't, and he hasn't texted me or called."

He tilted his head up like a squirrel sensing danger. "Where was he originating?"

"Taos. Someone from that shuttle *did* make the plane; he told me it got to Denver late."

The agent considered. "Your passenger might not have gotten to the boarding gate fast enough. Or gone off in the wrong direction by mistake. Or stopped to pick up lunch. Was he waiting for a wheelchair? When they're holding the plane to begin with, they don't hang around."

"Wonderful." She reminded herself not to take her annoyance out on this man and added moderately, "What happens if he did miss it?"

"Nothing. He'll get put on the next plane to Islip."

"Really? Even if it was his fault?"

"We honor the Flat Tire Rule." He winked at her, leaning his elbows on the counter. "One of the industry's best-kept secrets. If you miss a flight, but show up at the counter within two hours, the government says we have to honor your ticket."

"That's still in effect?"

"Not all airlines honor it anymore," he agreed. "We do, though. The next flight from Denver is due in forty minutes. He'll probably be on that."

"That's not too bad." They'd have to hurry to make their dinner reservation in Brooklyn, but it was still possible.

He looked pointedly past her and she moved away, realizing that other people were now waiting. Away from the queue, she stopped and took out her phone again. There had been no beep signaling a text. Was the server down? The server must be down.

BACK IN THE waiting area, she saw several people sitting in the circle of gray seats nearest the arrivals door. They were carefully ignoring each other, and especially avoiding a woman with a boy in a tray-table wheelchair and a beautiful little girl with red-gold curls. Around the trio was the evidence of their sojourn: plastic toys, used napkins, crushed paper cups, upside-down books.

Waiting for Daddy? The woman, her pleasant face heavy with freckles, was paging through a *Madeleine* book.

As soon as Fiona stepped into the circle, several of the people looked up hopefully. "If you're waiting for someone who was supposed to be on Flight 886, they'll probably be on the next Voyager flight. It's due in about thirty minutes," she said.

A man about twenty-five with dark hair slicked back into a narrow ponytail stared up at her. One muscular arm hugged a red JanSport backpack, and the other hand was cradling a phone. "*Thirty minutes?* Are you kidding? How do you expect us to make the connection to Portland that's leaving in ten? Answer me that!"

"Sounds hard," she agreed. "You're flying to Oregon from here?"

"*Duh.* Try Maine. You airline people don't know shit."

Airline people? "You think I work for Voyager?" She was astonished. "I don't work for the airline."

"Oh, right." He closed his eyes and settled back in his seat as if he couldn't be bothered talking to her anymore.

Who is this jerk? Fiona looked at the others and spread her arms. "You think black bicycle shorts and a chartreuse T-shirt are the airline's uniform? I'm just here to meet someone."

The freckled mother gave her a commiserating smile. "I'm glad you told us about the next flight. My father was supposed to be on the one that just came in, and when I didn't see him I got worried. He gets so confused since my mother died."

Fiona made a sympathetic sound.

"The last time he was here and read stories to my kids, he skipped whole pages." She rolled large green-speckled eyes. "He didn't even notice when it didn't make sense. I'm Maggie, by the way. And Derek and Brenda."

She looked desperate for human contact.

"I'm Fiona." She finally let herself look at the boy. He had the same dark-red hair and attractive features as his mother, but his mouth stayed permanently open. He was slumping forward in the chair now, his leg twitching. Did he know he was at an airport?

"Does he have cerebral palsy?" In her travels, Fiona had found that most people liked to answer questions.

"No. Car accident. My husband was driving." No smile now.

Life's arbitrary spoilers, waiting in the shadows to strike out. Had the husband died?

"Mom-mee!" The little girl slid off her seat and faced them, stomping a tiny pink sneaker with a mermaid's face on the toe. "I want to go home! You said we could go home. You know what? You lied!"

Maggie sighed and raised an eyebrow at Fiona. "Brenda's my little devil." Then she bent over to straighten Derek in the chair and wipe the drool from his face, and Fiona looked around at the others before sitting down. A stocky, dark-haired man in a red Planet Fitness T-shirt was paging through the *National Enquirer*, chuckling to himself. It was the first time Fiona had ever seen someone read the paper outside of a supermarket line.

She knew she should work on her column but felt too restless to concentrate. The other people felt intrusive, in her way, though they seemed absorbed in what they were doing. The woman across from her, whose wiry black-and-silver hair haloed her elegant face, was circling titles in the *New York Times Book Review*. She had on a silky white T-shirt and a skirt of giant red poppies, with red sandals on her narrow feet.

The woman looked up suddenly to glare at Brenda, who was rhythmically kicking her feet and hitting the underside of her seat. "Don't do that, little girl! You're giving me a headache."

Brenda squinted at the woman and kept kicking.

"Brenda, stop, or no watching *Frozen* when we get home." Maggie made a grab for her daughter's feet, but Brenda squirmed away.

"You know what? You're the meanest mommy I know!" But the kicking slowed, then finally stopped.

The woman gave her a syrupy smile. "Thank you, honey. It's just that I'm on a tight schedule, and this delay is not helping."

"Here." The man with the *National Enquirer* held it out to her. "You'll enjoy this."

The woman stared at him, as if trying to decide whether she had been insulted. "Thank you, but I don't read tabloids." Her tone was dismissive, and Fiona was surprised to see the man's mouth turn up in a secret grin.

It made Fiona laugh. "I read it when I'm in line at the check-out and there's a headline I can't resist," she told him. "My favorite is 'Titanic Survivor Found on Iceberg in Norway.'" When she read stories like that, she tried to figure out how they could somehow be true.

"It was here when I came," the man added, distancing himself from the offending paper. He took out his phone and, after a moment, the woman picked up the *Book Review* again. She continued circling items.

Fiona checked for messages on her own phone, then glanced at her watch. Fifteen minutes to go. "Are you a librarian?" she asked the woman.

"A librarian? No."

"An editor?" she persisted. Who else would be analyzing the *Book Review*?

"You can tell?" The woman seemed to relax and tossed her silver-black hair as if pleased. "They'd love to get rid of me, but I'm hanging in. It's not the money, of course; my husband was a well-known dentist."

"Lucky you."

The backpacker snorted, but the woman's dark eyes were amused. "What do you do besides ask questions?"

"I write. I had my own blog that was syndicated in a lot of newspapers—*The Eccentric Traveler*. Now I'm freelancing." *And trying to pick up the pieces of my professional life.*

Fiona expected the usual polite smile, but the woman tilted her head, amazed. "Really? That's you? I loved that column! Hang-gliding over Cairo. Getting Greek cab drivers to take you home to dinner. Getting lost wherever you went. Why ever did you stop?"

Because something so terrible happened that I had to come home. For a moment she felt overcome by that dark terror again. *Stop! I'm sitting in an American airport. Lee is almost here, and we'll have a wonderful evening. Tomorrow we'll find our dream apartment, and I'll be safe.*

Realizing the woman was still waiting for an answer, she said, "You know how the economy is. Newspapers can't afford outside writers anymore, and the Internet thinks everything should be free."

"I'm waiting for one of my writers." The woman was suddenly animated. "She's just wonderful!"

Fiona tamped down a feeling of rivalry. "What does she write?"

"True crime. She's reading at a mystery bookstore tonight and doing *Good Morning America* on Tuesday."

"Wow." Her competitiveness gave way to awe. "What's her name?"

"Susan Allmayer. She was an investigative reporter in Phoenix, but moved to Santa Fe. I think *Examination in Blood* will be her breakout book." She included the whole circle in her glance. "It's a terrific story! All about a college professor who kills a pregnant student and mails her body parts to universities around the country. Unfortunately—for him—she was the college president's daughter at the school where he mailed her head."

The backpacker, who had been scowling at his phone, looked up at that. "Does that kind of writing pay?"

She studied him severely. "Yes, but it's hard work. You have to do a lot of research and be able to understand the human heart. You need to interview people skillfully and write well. And you've got to have sympathetic victims, women or children, preferably from the middle class or above. Or at least with aspirations. People need to be able to identify with them." Her hand crept into her white straw bag as if looking for something, then retreated. "Don't tell me you're a writer too. What are the odds?"

"Nah, computer science. But I'm looking to retire."

The editor choked on a laugh. "Retire?"

"What's so funny about that? I'm almost thirty. All it takes is one great idea, and you're set for life."

"That's what your generation thinks, isn't it?"

"Well, good luck to you," the man with the *Enquirer* said. "I don't think I'll ever be able to retire."

"What do you do?" Fiona asked.

"Pool maintenance. I have my own outfit. But my daughter's only twelve. She's who I'm waiting for."

At that moment, the "Arrivals" notice flashed on the monitor, and there was a garbled loudspeaker announcement.

The editor stuffed her *Book Review* in her bag and pushed up from the navy worsted chair, giving an unselfconscious groan. "Lordy, these seats are excruciating!"

The rest of the group stood up too. Then, except for the backpacker, who was biting a knuckle, they smiled politely at each other.

Their voyage together was over.

Chapter Five

LEE WAS NOT on the plane. Fiona joined the group of people waiting and watched as the stream of exiting passengers once again slowed and then stopped. This time, she did not stop the flight attendants in their navy uniforms to question them. After several minutes, the lounge was empty again except for the people she had been waiting with. It was as if a giant wave had swept over a beach and left only them—flotsam—behind.

"Shit, shit, shit!" The backpacker pounded his fist against the back of a seat. "Where is he?"

"Where was he coming from?" But Fiona dreaded the answer.

"Taos. Where else?"

"Maybe this flight was already booked up," the pool man said. "People who had tickets would be given preference over standbys."

"Yes, but it wasn't their fault!" Fiona told herself not to catastrophize. She had too much imagination.

"It *is* the end of vacation," Maggie agreed quickly, giving Derek's wheelchair a tiny jiggle to quiet his moaning. "I should have told my father to come next week."

"He'd better be on the next flight," the backpacker threatened. *Or else what?*

"I get what you're saying," Fiona told the man. "But if they were bumped, why didn't they call to let us know?"

Maggie laughed. "My dad wouldn't."

"Coral probably forgot to charge her phone again." Her father gave a laugh. "I'm always on her about it."

"Well, I think it's very inconsiderate," the editor said. "This is going to disrupt our whole schedule! Unless—did I give Susan my new cell number? I *think* I did."

"I'm gonna find out what's going on," the backpacker announced, and stalked off.

Fiona pulled out her iPhone and retrieved a dial tone. The phone was still charged, still working. It was odd, though, that she hadn't gotten texts from anyone else. It had to be a service glitch.

She started to put the phone away when it dinged. *At last.*

It was a text from her bank, offering a new deposit app.

The backpacker returned, a messenger with an outraged scowl. "That was the last fucking flight of the day from Denver! Can you believe it? From now on they fly into LaGuardia. It doesn't matter; I've already missed the fucking connection to Portland!" He adjusted the red pack on his shoulders and stormed off.

"Well, I'm not driving all the way to Queens," the editor said. "I'll go home and wait for Susan to call me."

"That's all we can do," the other man agreed.

No, it's not! Fiona's heart was racing like a frightened child in the dark. Before the second plane landed, she'd thought that Lee might have forgotten to charge his phone or left it on the Taos plane. There would been no time to retrieve it or to call her. But if he hadn't made this flight either, he'd have found a phone.

She stood rooted to the floor by a more shocking idea. What if he had collapsed at the Denver airport and been taken to the closest hospital? No one would know to call her! If he were unconscious, he would not have been able to tell them. She pictured the paramedics trying to revive him, the wail of the ambulance siren peeling traffic out of the way, someone nestling his blue backpack beside his head.

What if he was dead?

Chapter Six

COMB-OVER HAD BEEN replaced at the Voyager counter by a woman with gray hair and a serious face. She looked up as Fiona stepped in front of her. "Name?"

"No, I'm not a passenger, I need to find out about my—fiancé. Did anything happen to one of the passengers on the morning shuttle from Taos or when it landed in Denver?"

"The Day Star plane? I haven't heard of anything."

"Can you check? *Please?* If anyone got sick?"

The representative pushed her lips into a single line as she considered it, then began typing on her keyboard. After a moment she picked up her dark blue phone. "Hi, this is Edie. Any emergencies on flights today? Specifically"—she peered at her computer screen—"Day Star 101 out of Taos?"

She listened, then said, "Uh-huh. Okay. Someone here is asking. Thanks." A pause. "You too."

She hung up and looked at Fiona. "Interesting you should ask. They had a fuel line problem and switched planes, but the flight got into Denver with no problem. It was late, of course, but so was the feeder from San Diego, so they held our flight."

"But no passengers got sick or went to the hospital?" *A relief. Of course, a relief.* But it didn't answer her questions.

Edie looked at her, blue eyes kind behind glasses. "Why don't you tell me what this is all about?"

This was what Fiona liked best about Long Island, that people cared enough to stop and talk to you. She glanced behind her, at the people and their luggage.

"Don't worry about them. I'll get someone." Edie picked up the dark blue phone again. As soon as a young man in a white shirt with the Voyager logo stepped behind the counter, she motioned Fiona to one side. Fiona could feel the curious eyes of the passengers burning her back.

"My fiancé was supposed to be on that plane out of Taos, but he wasn't. Several other passengers didn't make it either, so we just thought they'd be on the next Voyager flight. But they weren't, and somebody said it was the last flight from Denver for the day!"

Keep it together. Edie's kindness and her own desperation made her voice ragged. "The other people had reasons their people might have missed the flight, but I don't. I mean, he hasn't texted me or called. He let me know he was getting on the plane in Taos. But then…nothing!"

"And that's why you thought he might have gotten sick. What's his name, hon?"

"Lee Pienaar." Automatically she spelled it. *You may have seen his photographs in magazines.*

Edie moved away from her and picked up the phone. This time Fiona could not hear any conversation. Instead she watched the check-in progress beside her, saw the passengers produce driver's licenses and in one case a maroon passport.

Then Edie was back, looking perplexed. "I don't know what to tell you. A Lee Pienaar was scheduled for Flight 886, but he never checked in. He wasn't on the next flight either. You'll need to check with Day Star if he was actually on their shuttle. Unfortunately, they're a Western outfit; they have no presence here. And we have no way to check their manifests." She sighed. "I'm sorry."

"No, you've helped a lot. Can I call them?"

Edie's face relaxed. "Of course you can. I'll get you the number."

"Thanks." Now—*now*—she could find out where he was.

As soon as she had the number, written on a Post-it bearing the Voyager logo, Fiona retreated to a seat in the arrivals lounge. The waiting area was once again full. Evidently, flights were still arriving from other cities.

The area code she pressed in was unfamiliar, but a cheerful voice informed her that the corporate offices in Santa Fe were closed on weekends and would reopen tomorrow morning at ten o'clock.

No! I have to talk to you now! Didn't they have an emergency contact number? Maybe it was on their website. But if she sent an e-mail, would somebody read it before Monday morning?

This can't be happening. They had plans for the evening, a life to get on with. How could she wait until tomorrow morning to find anything out? But maybe she wouldn't have to. She imagined him leaving his phone on the shuttle flight, realizing it when he got to Denver, and running back desperately to retrieve it. The airline couldn't find the phone, and Flight 886 had departed in the meantime. The next flight from Denver was already full.

So now he was headed for LaGuardia Airport without his phone to let her know. And if her cell number was stored on his lost phone…he probably wouldn't know it from memory, since he had never had to dial it. He knew her apartment landline, but of course she wasn't there.

That jerked her up in her seat. There were probably messages, multiple messages, waiting for her back in Sydney Beach. She cursed herself for never bothering to learn the retrieval code to pick up her messages remotely. But between e-mails and texts to her iPhone, no calls to her apartment phone ever seemed that urgent.

Until now.

Chapter Seven

STALLED AT A traffic light in Eastport, Fiona realized she had forgotten about their dinner reservations. No chance of making those now. Would the Diligent Farmer restaurant give them a second chance later if they just didn't show up? No, they had her landline number. She had to be the one to cancel.

If Lee was landing at La Guardia, would there be enough time to shoot over to Brooklyn? But it was a large airport and she had no idea what airline they might put him on. No, it was better to go home.

As the light changed, Fiona considered something else. Lee traveled widely, both for his own photography and on assignment, and had never lived a workaday life. For the last four years, she hadn't either. If he woke up, as he had in April, and decided they should drive to Jekyll Island in Georgia, he knew that she would be happy to go too.

Was it possible that in the airport he had heard about some unbelievably beautiful place to photograph, a spot that he could not miss, especially since he was already out there? Perhaps he had rented a car and headed out impulsively, thinking he would just get a later plane. She saw him lost, running out of gas in the mountains where there was no phone service. Even now he was waiting by the side of the road, desperate, hoping that someone would come by . . .

Fiona turned onto Sunrise Highway. A year ago they hadn't even known each other, though he had read her travel writing and she had seen his photographs in magazines. They met at a reception when *Gusto!* was moving to larger quarters, and hit it off immediately. Afterward they had gone for a drink, and that had been that. Lee had been born in South Africa and sent to school in England and had a repertoire of stories. By the next morning, he had known everything worth knowing about her as well.

Fiona parked her Toyota in its numbered space. It was due for its state inspection next month, and God knew what problems might show up this year. She still had some money saved from her law firm days, money she had used to finance her travels until her blog had become successful, but now there was only the money from *Gusto!* coming in.

Fortunately, rents in Sydney Beach were low. Though the town was located on the south shore of Long Island, not far from the Hamptons, it had none of their cachet. When she'd moved into the studio at Mario's Vacation Apartments last December, the manager had warned her that prices would skyrocket in summer.

But when June came, she cajoled the manager into letting her stay on at the same price, pointing out that she was a responsible tenant and would still be there next winter when other units were vacant. Yet now she realized guiltily that she wouldn't. There would be no reason to stay here once she was settled in Brooklyn. Lee was currently subletting an apartment, and she was there much of the time. But living together would be different.

She hadn't yet broken the news to the manager.

Fiona grabbed her bag from the passenger seat and locked the doors, then clattered up the outside wooden stairs to the second floor. She had no doubt that there would be multiple messages from Lee, and as she entered the dim foyer, she saw that her machine light was blinking. *Yes.*

Quickly she pressed "Play."

The message had come in at 5:26 p.m.

"Good evening, Ms. Reina. I'm calling from the Diligent Farmer to confirm your reservation for seven o'clock this evening. If there are any changes or modifications, please let us know." The number followed.

Damn! That couldn't be all.

The Diligent Farmer could go fuck himself.

How COULD SHE make the time pass until tomorrow morning? It seemed an intolerable wait. She didn't dare leave the apartment in case Lee called; eventually, she slathered peanut butter on a handful of Triscuits and finished a bottle of cabernet sauvignon. At eleven, when the phone still hadn't rung, she took two Valium to make herself sleep.

She woke up for good at 6:20 a.m. Monday morning. Her "Via Venezia" sleep shirt was clinging to her, the day's heat already creeping into the apartment. Consciousness returned with a slap. Lee wasn't lying in bed beside her. She had no idea where he was.

She willed herself to get up and make coffee, but did not move. What was the point? She couldn't call the airline in New Mexico until noon Eastern time. On the other hand, the column for *Gusto!* was due Thursday.

Right. But how could she care about the horrors of cosmetics when her life felt upside down? Another glance at the clock. At least she should go to the gym. If she left now, she could see Karl and find out if he had any other ideas. They had been friends since her first law job; he would never soften the truth to make her feel better. A reality check was what she needed.

Besides, exercise would help fill the time. She would not do a class; she would talk to Karl and then use the machines. Quickly she made coffee, then headed out.

SHE FOUND KARL getting set up for a spin class, already wearing his narrow plastic glasses and red sweatband over his large forehead.

"I have to talk to you," she said breathlessly.

"What's up?" He abandoned the bike and followed her out of the room.

They sat down at a wire table in the small café area, not bothering to order anything.

"It's Lee. He was coming home from Santa Fe yesterday, but he wasn't on the plane. And I haven't heard from him since!"

Karl nodded. "How long have you guys been together?"

"It's not that! Things were great between us. We talked for a long time Saturday night. I'm worried that something's happened to him."

"Like what?"

"I'm not sure. He may have gotten sidetracked taking photos and gotten lost in the mountains. But it's odd; there were other people at the airport waiting for passengers who didn't get there either. And didn't text or call." She leaned earnestly across the table and told him everything that had happened, including the older man who said he had been on the shuttle but couldn't remember Lee. "It's driving me crazy!"

"Well, let's look at the facts." Karl was brisk, in attorney mode. "You've established that there wasn't a problem with the flights. At least one person who was on Lee's plane arrived in New York. For some reason, he's choosing not to communicate with you. You have to decide why."

Fiona sat silent.

Why would he stop communicating with her? He was either incapacitated and couldn't—or he was letting her know their relationship was over. Was he slipping out of her life as easily as he had moved into it? At forty-one, he had never been married. Maybe, in the months they had been inseparable, he felt that they were heading down a road he did not want to be on. Fiona had told the Voyager representative that he was her fiancé in order to be taken more seriously, but they had never talked about marriage.

But it couldn't be true! When they had talked on their phones Saturday night—using FaceTime for the pleasure of seeing each other—everything had been normal. They made jokes about what they would do to each other when he was back: love talk.

He hadn't sounded like a man about to disappear from her life.

Karl gave her the look that had calmed many clients. "It's probably not as bad as you think. There's some reasonable explanation. I bet by tonight it's all worked out."

"Really?"

"In the meantime, what about these other people waiting for passengers? Can you get in touch with any of them and see if those people ever arrived? Or contacted them? If they got here, they might know something about Lee."

"That's true. I'm sure I could find some of them. And I'll see what Day Star has to tell me when they open, about whether he was on the plane."

Karl tilted his head delicately. "If it's his way of ending things, it's better to know now." He pushed up, his large hands almost tipping the table.

"Are you in court today?" Fiona asked.

"Yes. Yes, I am. Judge Callaghan."

"Yikes."

Thank God. Thank God I never have to do that again.

"Everybody misses you, Fee. Your wonderful stories about what *could* have happened. Even the judges were amused."

"That's the trouble with law: it's so cut-and-dried. There are so many *rules*."

Karl laughed.

She wasn't sorry she had gone to law school. After her junior year at Iowa State, she was running low on funds. She had attended on scholarships, and her family, the Jensens, had ponied up the rest, but she knew she could not travel the world—still her dream—without money. Her grades were not outstanding, but she remembered her conversation with her high school guidance counselor.

Mrs. Malloy had insisted she apply for status as a Native American. The father listed on her original birth certificate, Leonard Charley, was a Chippewa Indian who had worked in Lamb's Tongue for a few months on his way east.

Fiona brought Mrs. Malloy the document. "But I never lived on the reservation or anything."

"That's hardly the point." Mrs. Malloy peered at her over her half-glasses and demanded to know what else Fiona had going for her. "You're bright enough, but so are a million other seventeen-year-olds."

"Maybe I should be a doctor." That seemed a good way to earn money fast.

The guidance counselor laughed. "With your grades? Lawyer, maybe; I could see you arguing in court. Trying to make people see things your way."

Fiona's Native American roots hadn't gotten her into Columbia or Yale, but Hofstra Law School on Long Island had given her a scholarship and enough work-study opportunities to survive. They had even helped her find a job at Legal Aid. It wasn't *their* fault that she had tired of the law.

Pressing Fiona's shoulder, Karl strode off.

Fiona went upstairs to the treadmills and set the machine for twenty minutes. Could Lee have gotten food poisoning and be too sick to phone? Maybe the planes were overbooked in Denver and he kept giving up his seat to pile on credits for future flights, embarrassed to tell her. *Right.* He was just as likely to be trapped in the Sangre de Cristo Mountains in a time-warp and surface in a hundred years, wondering if his dinner reservation was still good.

Maybe Karl's right: Lee just hates me.

Chapter Eight

BACK AT THE apartment, Fiona drank more coffee. She didn't think she could face writing about the perils of poisoned lipstick, but she reminded herself that she didn't have the financial luxury of not working. She was much too scattered to concentrate on her serious project, a series of guidebooks to destination cities. Her first, *Paris's Brightest Lights*, had already been accepted by a publisher, and she was starting work on *New York's Best Apples*.

The second book would detail the restaurant with the best cappuccino, the salon with the cheapest haircut, the friendliest Irish bar, and so on. She and Lee had planned a trip to sushi bars later this week. Living right in Brooklyn would make it easy to research the city. But how could she do it without him?

Meanwhile, Karl's idea was a good one. Fiona got a yellow-lined pad from her desk to make notes. True, there were three million people on Long Island, but like DNA, everyone had left traces of who they were.

The easiest was the editor whose author was reading at a mystery bookstore last night. How many of those could there be?

Checking her laptop, Fiona found only one in Suffolk County, over in Sayville. She could call, but she was suddenly too restless to stay in the apartment any longer. It was not that long a drive.

AT TEN O'CLOCK, Fiona reached the Black Cat Bookshop, a large Victorian house with a black wrought-iron fence and black shutters. Orange paint on the front window announced a "Back-to-Ghoul sale." *Cute.* She wondered if she should use the ghost-shaped brass knocker, but it was a store, after all, so she turned the knob and walked in, stopping in a foyer that was papered with author-signing announcements.

A bony woman in a blue-striped sundress was kneeling on the bare wooden floor, removing books from a carton. She turned and grinned at Fiona. "More goodies! On the other hand, more bills."

Fiona laughed.

Then something stirred on the counter, and she turned quickly. It was the largest cat she had ever seen, stretched out next to the cash register. Black, of course, and wearing a red collar with rhinestones. "My God!"

The woman nodded. "The owner. Twenty-eight pounds and counting. Was there something specific, or did you want to browse?"

"I'm looking for a true-crime book that just came out. It has 'blood' in the title," she said, proud that she had remembered.

The woman put back her head and laughed. "Honey, they all do. Can you tell me anything else about it?"

"How about a college professor killing a student? The president's daughter or something."

"You mean *Examination in Blood.* What a shame you weren't here last night; we had an author reading." She pushed herself up and moved toward the counter. "We may still have a few copies put aside for people who couldn't make it."

Fiona felt her heart jump. "The author was here?" Did that mean the editor had picked her up in the city after all?

"Not exactly." The woman was now fishing under the wide oak counter. "Her flight was delayed, so her editor came instead. Kind of odd, but she read from the book. A real ham! She couldn't give many details about the writing of it or sign autographs, but it was better than nothing. Aha!" Triumphantly she brought out a book with a black and red cover, a dust jacket with a photograph of a smiling family jaggedly torn in half.

Fiona hesitated. Considering her finances, she really shouldn't buy a hardcover book. But the woman felt like a kindred spirit, and the cat, who was watching her with wise yellow eyes, probably needed the money. "Okay, great. You wouldn't happen to have the editor's number, would you?"

The brown eyes narrowed. "Actually, I think I do. But why?"

"I'm getting the book for my mother. If I could arrange to have it inscribed when the author arrives, it would mean the world to her."

"Oh, of course! Let me track it down."

It was an interesting lie. Her real mother had drowned herself when Fiona was two, and her aunt—her mother's oldest sister, Karen Jensen—was not a reader. Her passions were the Lamb's Tongue Community Church and the Jasper County Fair. A tale of bloody body parts would be just the ticket. *"To Aunt Karen—Enjoy!"*

But looking down at the lurid cover, she felt a frisson of guilt. She really needed to get back to Iowa for a visit. They had tried to do their best by her. It wasn't the Jensens' fault that she had always wanted to leave.

BACK IN HER car, Fiona called the number the bookshop owner had given her.

"Hi there!" The answering machine voice was perky. "You have reached the estate of Rosa Cooper. I'm either at the gym or out doing good deeds. If you have my office number, you can reach me there. But do leave a message."

That was the woman. Fiona left a message, then wondered if she might be at the airport right now, meeting Susan's plane. Or at the gym.

What next? She decided to go back to her apartment. There was always the chance Lee had called, and it would be easier to try to reach the other people from there. With a last look at the haunted bookstore, she slipped her phone in her bag. As she did, she realized she had stopped checking it for a text from Lee.

Chapter Nine

SETTLED ON THE green velour sofa, Fiona checked her laptop for "Swimming Pool Maintenance, Suffolk County." There weren't as many results as she had feared, but far too many to call. Yellow pad in hand, she began a list. She could discount Irish names; he had definitely been Italian. She also did not bother writing down the numbers of large companies or those with cute names like Blue Enchantment or Pools-R-Us. That didn't seem like the man she had met.

Next she considered the geography. She discounted locations in the Hamptons. Too pricey for someone who thought he would never be able to retire. Too close to the Nassau County line, and he would have just used LaGuardia. But everywhere else was fair game.

She was connected mostly to voice mail asking her to leave a message and promising to call right back. She did get a receptionist once. "DiPenna Pool Service."

"Hi. I'm trying to reach someone who was at MacArthur Airport yesterday to meet his daughter. I can describe him for you."

"That's okay. Sal doesn't have any daughters."

"Okay, thanks."

An hour after she had made the last call, her phone rang.

"Hello?"

"This is Dom Basilea. You called me about being at the airport yesterday?"

Thank God. "I was one of the people waiting. Black bicycle shorts, chartreuse shirt?"

"Oh, right. Did you find out anything?"

"Did your daughter get in?"

A hesitation. "Not yet."

"Well, my boyfriend didn't either, and I'm really worried. And she didn't call?"

"No, but I think I know what happened. Coral was visiting my wife in Taos—she's staying at this artist's colony—and she was supposed to be leaving on Sunday for Mexico. I think she may have taken Coral with her."

"Would she do that? Is she Mexican?"

"Huh? No. She's just a little crazy. But she's headed somewhere I can't reach her."

"And she wouldn't let you know?"

"Like I said...Listen, I gotta get back to work."

"Okay, but will you call me if your daughter gets in? And was on that flight, I mean?"

"Sure."

As soon as she hung up, the phone rang. *Lee.* Lee, thank God! She grabbed for it. "Hi!"

"This is Rosa Cooper. You left a message?"

"Oh. Yes." She wouldn't let herself feel the terrible letdown until that call was over. "I'm Fiona Reina from the airport. *The Eccentric Traveler*?"

"Oh, yes. The pretty one."

Pretty? She supposed so. Growing in Lamb's Tongue, where Scandinavian blondes were the standard, Fiona's straight dark hair and olive skin were not valued. People thought her eyes—light gray but with a black circle around the iris—were weird. Aunt Karen had seemed unhappy when her breasts came in early and full, as if it were not quite decent.

"I was wondering if your author ever got here."

"Susan? No, she didn't. She hasn't even called, which isn't like her at all!"

The sound of drums in the background. Fiona realized it was her heart. "But what could have happened?"

"I don't know, but I can't understand it. This is something she's wanted for years. What author wouldn't? *Good Morning America*! We had to jump through hoops to—do you realize what it takes to get on a show like that? She was deliberately flying in early so she could rest up beforehand."

"And it's tomorrow morning? Maybe she'll still make it."

"Your lips to God's ears. Airlines are so crazy these days. All these hubs and layovers instead of just plain flying."

"I'm calling Day Star as soon as their offices open to see if Lee was on the flight. And I talked to that pool guy. He hasn't heard anything from his daughter either."

"Why don't you try the FAA, their offices in Denver, just to make sure? Any irregularities have to be reported to them. Let me know what you find out."

It only took a minute to find the number for the Denver office, but after she called, she was shifted to three different extensions.

"My name is Fiona Reina," she told the last voice wearily. "I'm calling from New York. I need to know if there were any problems with planes yesterday."

"I'm sure there were." The voice was male and good-humored. "What did you have in mind?"

"Well, something in your area. Between Taos and Denver. Or Denver and New York." She felt stupid. Nobody had suggested any problem with the planes.

"You're talking about a problem with a scheduled flight? Why do you want to know?"

"I'd heard something might have happened. I'm not a journalist or anything," she said quickly. As soon as she said it, she realized that was not true. Not an investigative journalist, anyway.

"I'll take a look. It's all public record. But you're not talking about a small private craft, two-seater, anything like that."

"No, more commuter sized. Like a Day Star shuttle?" My bad, leading the witness.

"Ah, Day Star. *That* bunch of cowboys. These little guys, they're a menace in the air. Buy up those old boats and don't update shit! Uh—sorry about that."

"It's okay."

"Let me see what they were up to yesterday." Silence while he checked. "Tucson and Phoenix, routine. Denver, made an emergency landing to their own airfield. Fixed whatever it was, but came in an hour late. No disasters though. If anything happened, we'd know about it right away."

But would they?

Chapter Ten

THE CALLS TO schools for disabled children in Suffolk County went rapidly. As soon as Fiona murmured something about calling from social services, people were anxious to help. Not exactly true, but she wasn't doing it for fraud or criminal purposes. She soon had a phone number for Maggie Farley, mother of Derek.

The woman who gave it to her sighed. "A really sad situation. No hope of change, but she won't give up; she keeps trying all these therapies for him that she can't afford. As I'm sure you know."

Fiona murmured something, then clicked off and pressed in the number.

"Yes, hello?" There was the sound of a plaintive wail in the background. Probably Brenda.

"Hi, Maggie? This is Fiona Reina. From the airport yesterday?"

"Yes, hi! Did your boyfriend ever get in?"

"No. What about your father?"

"Not yet."

"I talked to the FAA, and they said that the plane from Taos had a little trouble but finally landed. Late."

"Well, that's good. That it got there, I mean."

"Aren't you worried? About your father?"

"A little. But he might not even have made the plane."

"Isn't there anyone you can check with?"

"I could call the complex where he lives. But I think it will all work out."

"I hope so. I'll call you back if I find out anything else."

"You could stop by." She sounded as though she would welcome the company.

FIONA WASN'T SURE she wanted to find the backpacker. She already had three. Still, his friend might have landed and know something about Lee and the others.

The challenge would be tracking him down. All he had said was that he was into computers. No…computer science. That sounded more academic. Could he be affiliated with the university? She went to the Stony Brook University site and accessed the Computer Science Department. After scrolling down the faculty photographs to the end, she was disappointed not to see anyone who looked like him. Hard to imagine him dealing with students anyway.

She was about to leave the page when she saw other headings— Affiliated Faculty, Research Faculty, Emeritus—and clicked on those instead. She found him under "Researchers," with a smile so charming she almost passed him by. Greg Sanderson. His areas of interest were everything from algorithms to web accessibility. Once she had his name, she was able to get a phone number from whitepages.com. She hoped he hadn't decided to go off to Portland anyway.

The phone was picked up after three rings. "What?"

"Greg Sanderson?"

"Who's this?"

"I was one of the people waiting at the airport yesterday. Fiona Reina? I was wondering if your friend ever showed up."

"If he had, I wouldn't be talking to you, would I? I'd be on the face of Mt. Katahdin." Still, his tone was good-humored.

In the face of, more likely. "Did you hear from him?"

"Why are you asking me all these questions? Come to that, how did you find me? I didn't give you my name."

"The information superhighway is a wonderful thing. Why I'm calling is, no one else has heard from the people we were waiting for either. Don't you think that's odd?"

"Well, it's only been a day, Fiona."

He had glommed onto *her* name pretty fast.

"You want me to keep you posted?"

"Sure."

"DAY STAR AIRLINES. Priss speaking." The voice was warm and not young.

Fiona heard it as the voice of someone experienced, someone who would understand. "Hi, Priss. My name is Fiona Reina. I'm calling about a flight yesterday morning, a flight from Taos to Denver? I wanted to find out whether someone was actually on the flight."

"And you are? A relative?"

"Not exactly. It was my fiancé."

A perplexed silence. "But, Fiona. Surely you understand that we can't just give out information like that over the phone. We don't know who you are or why you want it. Or whether the passenger would even want you to know."

"Of course he'd want me to know! And I want it because he never arrived. I haven't heard from him since he was about to board." Yet even as she said it, she knew she sounded like a jealous lover tracking down someone who had escaped her clutches. "He texted me right before he got on the plane, so I know he was planning to fly."

"I'm terribly sorry."

"What if I came to your offices? Would you tell me then?"

A pause. "Where are you calling from?"

"New York. Is there anyone else I can speak to?"

"They'll only tell you what I just did. It's a firm company policy."

"You mean you can't even tell me if he was on the plane or not? I find that hard to believe!"

"I know what you're saying, and I'm sorry. But you could be a private detective, and he could sue us for divulging his whereabouts. And you can't fax us proof that you're a relative, because you aren't."

"Not yet." Part of Fiona knew that the law had to agree with their policy. But why were they being so inflexible? "Okay, fine. Thank you."

You haven't heard the last of me.

Her final call was to Rosa Cooper.

"Hi, it's—"

"Oh, Fiona. I'd hoped you were Susan. She was on the phone with me twice Saturday about what she should wear for the show, she was that excited. Anyway, after you called me, I called the Santa Fe police. They had someone stop by her house, though they couldn't legally enter the premises. They said the house looked normal, no break-ins, and nobody answered when they knocked."

"Did you try the hospitals?"

She laughed. "I'm very thorough. No joy there."

"I tried the hospital in Taos last night," Fiona confessed. "Just in case. But no one like Lee had been admitted."

"What did the FAA say?"

"That's what's interesting. They don't think very highly of Day Star and their equipment. Evidently it's some fly-by-night outfit. They had to stop and refuel or something in the middle of the flight! And they got to Denver late. None of the other passengers that people were waiting for have arrived or called. Something happened during that hour, I know it!"

"Like what?"

"I don't know. But maybe they wouldn't let some of the passengers get back on."

"Hmm. The fact remains, they *are* missing. Maybe we should get together and decide what to do next."

"You think so? I mean, I can't just sit around not knowing anything."

"Give me the other numbers; I'll set something up."

Chapter Eleven

THEY MET AT a sports bar near the airport, which Rosa Cooper complained had all the ambiance of an old sock. The same baseball game played on every mounted screen. Fiona was the last to arrive; she hurried over to the large corner booth under a blue-and-orange Mets banner.

Maggie shifted on the leatherette seat to make room for Fiona, her freckled face shiny in the glow of a red glass candle holder. "This is wonderful. I *never* get out." Then her expression clouded. "But there's something I have to tell everybody now that you're here."

Rosa put up a hand, her arm jingling with intricate silver bracelets. "Let her order."

Fiona glanced at Maggie, but she seemed content to keep her news to herself. What had she been going to say? Had she heard something on the news on her way to the restaurant?

Because everyone was drinking beer, she ordered a Blue Point ale.

"I still don't know why we're here," Greg Sanderson said to Rosa. "Do you always pick up people waiting for planes?"

He meant it to be funny, but nobody laughed. Fiona turned to Maggie. "What were you going to say?"

"Well, I'm not sure what it means," she said, playing with her glass. "But just before I left for here, this woman called me. She said she was from a hospital in Denver and that my father had had a slight stroke on the plane. He's okay now, and they're putting him on a flight to me in a day or two."

Fiona reacted first. "But that's wonderful!" It was, wasn't it? It was the last thing she had been expecting Maggie to say. "It means he isn't missing anymore."

"It's good news for everyone, isn't it?" Maggie's large green eyes scanned the table.

"Of course it is. It proves nothing sinister's going on," Dominick said. He was still wearing his work clothes, dark green cotton pants and shirt with his name embroidered in yellow on the pocket. "I knew there had to be a logical explanation. It's Eve playing one of her tricks."

"Wait a minute," Greg said, his voice demanding. "Did you get the name of the hospital?"

"I—no. I didn't think about that. I was so happy I didn't think about anything else."

"Of course you didn't," Fiona said in her defense. But there were still problems. In the late afternoon, she had called *Gusto!* to see if they had heard from Lee.

They hadn't. He had sent some early photos to make sure they were acceptable, but the editors needed the images directly from his camera. Once they had them, they would Photoshop the models into the Southwestern scenery. The days of flying crews to exotic places was over—at least for *Gusto!*

"He said he would stop in today," the fashion editor had told her, perplexed. "When do you think it will be?"

"Lee was supposed to take the photos to the magazine today," Fiona told the group. "Even if he was avoiding me, he wouldn't blow *them* off."

"Maybe he's just not that into them either," Greg said.

" 'Not into them either'? Not into them?" Her fury startled everyone. "How do you know what he's into or not? You don't even know him—or me!"

"Keep your shorts on, I didn't mean—"

"I'm sick of people coming up with dumb explanations. Look at the facts: Five people coming to New York get on a plane in Taos and are never heard from again. They never call with any explanation. Okay, Maggie's father," she said, conceding. "That's still four who are missing. So where the hell are they?"

"Coral's in Mexico with her mother," Dominick said.

"Dimitri's just an asshole."

But Rosa gave her head a vigorous shake. "No, she's right. This is inexplicable. Susan Allmayer would never act like this."

"I feel like I'm sitting around doing nothing while Lee's in trouble somewhere. Something happened, I know it! It's not the plane—the FAA said it landed in Denver—but are there always people missing like this? I don't think so!"

"What are you going to do?" Rosa asked.

"I don't know. But I can't do anything here. At least out there, I could get the authorities involved."

"Would you really go?"

"Flying's no big deal for me. I've got tons of miles."

"If you went, you could stop by Susan's to see if the neighbors know anything."

Greg leaned back in the booth and grinned at Fiona. "Our woman in Santa Fe."

"You want me to find your friend?"

"Sure. And stop global warming while you're at it."

They left the bar and said good night in the parking lot.

Fiona decided that the meeting had been useless.

Chapter Twelve

TUESDAY MORNING FIONA was back at Islip MacArthur Airport, arranging frequent-flyer tickets on Voyager and Day Star. The flight to Denver was full, and Voyager upgraded her to first class.

She stowed her bag in the roomy overhead compartment. It held nothing more than jeans, a sweatshirt and several T-shirts, running shoes, underwear, and a nightshirt. She was wearing her usual traveling outfit: a navy top with tailored khaki slacks and matching jacket. The heaviest things in her bag were her laptop and several books. She was bringing *Examination in Blood* by Susan Allmayer, *Out of Africa* by Isak Dinesen, and a library copy of *Beauty Can Hurt You.*

It was not until she was settled into her leather seat that she realized the irony of the Dinesen book. Karen Blixen's lover, Denys Finch-Hatton, had died tragically in a plane crash at the height of their love affair.

She had brought it because of the African connection. Lee's dream was to go back home to South Africa and photograph everything, from its staggering beauty to the poverty that remained, then publish it in a book. He and his brother had inherited their grandparents' farm north of Johannesburg, and he'd pointed out that he and Fiona could live there free.

"How long?" she asked.

"A year?"

"God, no. I grew up on a farm, remember?"

"But this is beautiful country. How long, then?"

"Two weeks?"

He'd laughed and hugged her shoulder.

But they already had a wonderful life in Brooklyn, friends to hang out with, restaurants to try, work projects they loved. When they moved in together, it would be perfect. *If* they moved in.

She'd had an odd phone call when she was packing. When her phone started playing "La Marseillaise," she'd run over to the desk, sure that it was Lee.

She saw from the caller ID that it was Dominick Basilea.

"Hi, Dominick. Listen, I'm sorry I yelled at everybody. It was just—"

"Never mind that. I'm calling to see if you'll do something for me."

"Sure."

"If I send a photo of Coral to your phone, could you swing by the house in Taos to see if she's there? I'm sure she won't be, but as long as you'll be around there... You are going, aren't you?"

"I thought her mother had taken her to Mexico."

"Yeah, well, when I got home, there was this voice-mail message from Eve. She was calling Coral to see if she'd gotten home okay. Like she *had* put her on the plane. Now I don't know what to think. I mean, I think it's still a trick, but..."

"What do you want me to do if I see her?"

"Don't do anything! Just call me. I'll take it from there."

What was this about? Why wouldn't he want her to pick up Coral and bring her home?

He gave her the address, and Fiona assured him she would do as he said.

SHE SWALLOWED A Dramamine and shifted the tiny pillow under her head. All she wanted to do was sleep. But as soon as they were in the air, flight attendants were coming by with headsets and eye shades and pouring mimosas from glass pitchers. Mimosas! Fiona no longer expected any extras on domestic flights, but first class was evidently another world. And she hadn't had her orange juice for the day.

THE DENVER STOPOVER was chaotic. The connecting Day Star flight was in a far part of the airport, down an escalator to a ground-level area where passengers were waiting for the shuttle to take them out to the plane. *No wonder Lee missed the flight,* she thought crossly, then reminded herself that he had now had two days to find the gate.

When they reached the plane in the middle of the tarmac, Fiona was shocked by how small it looked. Not as small as that flight to Key West once, when they'd asked the passengers how much they weighed and told them where to sit, but this plane could not have held more than twenty-five or thirty seats.

"I thought it would at least be a jet," Fiona said to the older woman sitting beside her on the aisle.

A flight attendant making sure their seat belts were fastened overheard her. "Taos doesn't have runways long enough for jets. And actual flight time is not much more than an hour."

"Were you on Sunday's flight?"

He touched a tiny mustache that made him look like a Mexican film hero. "Which one?"

"The morning flight from Taos to Denver?"

Why did his eyes widen? But then he smiled. "Sunday's my day off."

"How many people does this plane hold?" she persisted. She looked around at the blue seats and yellow headrests.

The attendant waited as if to see whether there was a point to her question. When she didn't say anything else, he said, "These planes are really very safe. And today's a beautiful day."

He moved past them awkwardly, as if in pain.

The grandmotherly woman, pushing out the frontiers of a peach pantsuit, leaned toward her. "Feeling nervous, hon? Want some gum?"

"Sure. Thanks."

Opening a huge black purse, the woman offered her a selection. "Wrigley's Spearmint, Dentyne, Doublemint, or Juicy Fruit. I think there's some Bubble Yum I keep for kids."

Fiona laughed. "You're a walking candy store."

The woman opened the mouth of the bag wider and turned it toward her. "Tums, Maalox, Dramamine, Kaopectate, Rolaids, aspirin, Lactaid, and breath mints. I don't cross the street without my supplies."

"Wow. I don't know, I'll take Spearmint."

The woman rooted around and handed her a white pack. "Keep it. It's not my favorite." She smiled sympathetically. "This your first flight?"

No, about my five hundredth. "It's just, you hear so much about accidents with small planes like these."

"Well, like that nice boy said, it's perfectly safe." But then she cocked her head. "I understand there was some trouble a few years ago. I don't know what happened." She looked as if she wanted to settle in and chat, as if it was how she had planned to entertain herself during the flight, but Fiona felt too exhausted to go on talking. Besides, she needed to keep watch out the window. This was the same route the plane had flown Sunday. She doubted there would be anything to see, but if there were . . .

Removing the silver foil from the piece of gum, she stared at the tarmac as the plane began to move.

"Have you ever been out West before?" her seatmate asked, persistent.

"California, of course. And to Santa Fe twice, but by way of Albuquerque. How about you?"

"Oh, gracious, I live in Phoenix. But not in the summer—no thank you! I stay up in the Rockies. I'm visiting my daughter and grandkids in Chimayo for a few days."

Fiona nodded and then turned toward the window to watch the takeoff.

When they were airborne, she waited until the surrounding buildings had faded away and then stared down at a wilderness. The plane passed over a slope with green growth that looked like the lion on a heraldic crest. The lion gave way to suede squares and tan rectangles, and then they were moving through skimpy cloud puffs.

When the clouds spread out thickly like her aunt's quilting batting, she turned away. Her seatmate had just been handed a napkin with a tiny muffin and a glass of orange juice. Fiona accepted the same and turned back to the window.

Suddenly the terrain was visible again. This earth looked baked, crossed occasionally with lines that had to be roads. A few more patches of green appeared and stretched into the stick figures of a kindergarten drawing. Gleaming bits of metal winked at her, shocking her into alertness. But what might have been debris from a downed plane was only silo tops, set in the ground like studs in jeans.

Now her seatmate was snoring softly, and Fiona felt her own eyes close. She gave her head a shake. It hurt her neck to keep looking down, but she wanted to see everything she could. A curving tan road divided into triangles looked like a variegated snake. The land was mostly empty. Flying over Long Island at this height, you would see miniature parking lots and the turquoise ovals of pools.

When they were coming in low over the Sangre de Cristos, she caught sight of a smaller aircraft moving across the parched ground. It kept pace with them exactly—a ghost plane. *Lee's plane.* Then they were descending to the ground and there was the usual rush of air, the flaps on the wings standing up to slow the momentum. As the two planes merged, she realized she had only been seeing their shadow.

But the idea of a ghost plane haunted her.

Chapter Thirteen

LANDING IN TAOS was like entering a foreign country. Mountains crowded the tiny airport. Fiona moved across the landing strip, but she could see no public transportation. Most of the other passengers were still clustered around the back of the plane where their luggage was being unloaded, and her seatmate had been joined by a young woman in jeans and a plaid shirt, holding the leash of a golden retriever puppy.

The terminal itself was no more than an afterthought, a building set in the middle of a dusty field. She made her way into a large room and looked around. A tropical fish tank, pressed against wood paneling, had nothing living inside. There was a row of several small offices: Payless Car Rental, Helicopter Mountain Trips, and Day Star Airlines.

At least she could rent a car here. There was Dominick's mission to carry out in Taos, and she had already decided to stop at the hospital, Holy Cross, to make sure Lee had not ended up there without identification. At the Payless cubicle, she rented a silver Sentra with front-wheel drive, refusing extra insurance and a GPS that cost nine dollars a day. Then, palming the car key, she went into the far cubicle that had "Day Star" painted on the window in yellow.

Again she was blindsided by fury, remembering what the FAA rep had said about Day Star's equipment. This hole-in-the-wall airline had no business risking people's precious lives by putting them in jeopardy. Why weren't there laws about companies like them?

An Indian woman—or possibly Mexican—her hair in glossy braids, looked up.

Fiona didn't smile. "I'm looking for information about a passenger. He was supposed to be on the Day Star flight between here and Denver last Sunday."

The woman, wearing a name tag that identified her as Beatriz Twelve Trees, stared back at her. Was it the same wariness verging on panic that she had seen in the flight attendant's eyes? Maybe this woman did not speak English. Fiona paged back to her rudimentary Spanish. *Hasta la vista, baby.* "*El avión. Cualquier problema?*"

The woman's mouth turned down. "Sometimes the planes run late because of the rain. But these planes run fine."

Ah. "No problems on Sunday? I know the flight was late, that they had to stop and refuel or something. That's what the cowpoke on the flight from Denver said."

"Cowpoke?"

"Never mind. I was just wondering if anything else happened on the flight. If any of the passengers got sick or anything. If anything unusual happened."

"These planes run fine." She said it firmly.

Hola? For this she'd flown two thousand miles? "Well, *gracias*."

Obviously this young woman was not in the loop—if there was a loop. She thought about asking to speak to someone else, but then decided they would only tell her the same thing.

As SHE CROSSED the waiting area in the direction of the restrooms, Fiona thought about her FaceTime conversation with Lee on Saturday evening. She had turned on her phone and there he was, sun-bleached hair tousled, blue eyes welcoming.

"I spent the day at Georgia O'Keefe's Ghost Ranch. Interesting place. I'll send you the shots I fancy."

"Did you take any inside the house?"

"A few for myself."

"Those are the ones I want to see. I've never been inside Ghost Ranch. You needed an appointment a month in advance, and I never got around to that."

He laughed. "Patience isn't your strong suit."

"Listen, I think I found the perfect apartment! It's in a brownstone—someone from the magazine is moving out. It's on the ground floor, and it's even got a garden out back. Just for us!"

"And how much is this Eden going to set us back?"

He laughed when she told him.

"We can do it," she said insistently. "Where are you eating tonight?"

"Anywhere close that doesn't take too long or cost much. What about you, my sweet?"

"A Lean Cuisine pizza," she admitted. "But I'll make up for it tomorrow night."

"You never told me where we were going. Can I guess?"

"No! I want it to be a surprise. A welcome-home surprise."

It hadn't been, of course. Something so simple as a celebratory dinner together hadn't happened.

She wondered drearily if it ever would again.

THE RESTROOM WAS basic: plain white tile, but clean. The ache that hovered around her stomach signaled the arrival of her period later this week. Her face in the mirror over the sink looked tired. Wisps of dark hair were coming loose from her braid. Was this no more than a wild-goose chase?

As Fiona crossed the room go out the back, she glanced at the Payless office and stopped dead. Standing at the counter, her back to Fiona, was Beatriz Twelve Trees. She was talking earnestly to the young woman who had handled Fiona's car rental. Heads bent together, they were looking at something on the counter between them. Fiona didn't think it was a take-out menu.

What if she went over there and walked in to see what they were doing? She could say that she couldn't find the car, couldn't get the door open, anything. She had every right to be in there. As she started toward the cubicle, the blonde looked up and froze. A moment later, Beatriz whirled around and gave her a dark stare too.

Chapter Fourteen

FIONA APPROACHED THE row of rental cars, shaken. Overhead a large black bird, its feathers splashed with white, seemed to be circling her. A magpie? That was a bird of ill omen according to legend—but so were crows, ravens, buzzards, probably the whole darker half of the avian population. She wouldn't take it as a sign, but maybe she should.

It took a while to locate the lights, the windshield wipers, and the air-conditioning button, but she was finally ready to drive south into town. Switching on the ignition, she backed out and started down the road, passing under high wires strung with suspended orange balls. The line of single-engine planes she passed seemed tiny, dwarfed by the Sangre de Cristos. She wondered if any of the planes belonged to movie stars or other celebrities who owned second homes around here.

But not right around here. As in cities around the world, the area surrounding the airport was desolate. She drove past a gravel pit, a trailer park, and a wealth of rusting farm machinery before she turned onto the larger road that led to town. Soon she was driving by a collection of weathered adobe buildings with turquoise window frames. Turquoise, she knew, was meant to keep the evil spirits away.

She paused at a blinking light to look down at the car rental street map on her lap. If she were reading it right, she should be able to take Ranchitos to San Antonio to Valverde, south of the plaza. Finally she turned onto a residential street where the houses were narrow and crowded together. She slowed to look at house numbers and stopped in front of a bungalow whose deep blue-green trim had almost peeled away. The front yard was dirt except for two patches of red geraniums in pots beside the foundation. A string of chilies hung on the battered gold door.

If it meant anything, there was no car parked in the primitive driveway.

Fiona climbed the wooden steps that protested even her weight and knocked on the door, making the chili *ristra* bounce against the wood. On a visit to San Antonio, she had been charmed by the rubbery red peppers and brought a string home. They had quickly rotted in the Long Island humidity. Even here a pungent, chalky smell puffed out at her.

When no one came to the door, she shielded her eyes and peered through the front window. Large paintings that reminded her of maps but done in fantastical pinks and oranges were standing around the floor. So Mrs. Basilea painted a little. There were two wooden chairs and a sagging couch, but no attempts at a decorating scheme.

"Eve and Coral ain't home."

She jumped at the voice. Turning, she saw a boy about ten, wearing only denim cutoffs.

"You scared me!"

"If you want Eve, she went away. We're feeding Mr. Briggs."

"Who's Mr. Briggs?"

"Cat."

"Oh." She had hoped, briefly, he was some kind of elderly relative who could give her information. "What's your name?"

"Joey." He picked a large scab off his elbow and held it between thumb and finger before popping it into his mouth.

Charming. "And Eve and Coral went to Mexico?"

"Naw." The boy watched her with knowing black eyes. "*Eve* went to Mexico. Coral went back to her dad."

Like a needle testing battery power, Fiona's mind gave a quick jump. "They didn't both go to Mexico? It's okay if they did." Better than okay.

Joey had picked up some kind of long reed and was drawing in the dirt, writing the answer. "Naw," he said finally when Fiona did not bend down to read it. "Eve went with Rafe. They didn't want to take Coral too."

"Who's Rafe?"

The eyes looked wiser. "Her power mower."

Fiona had a wild image of Eve putt-putting south along the highway, hair flying, and then she laughed. "You mean her paramour?"

"That's what I said. That's what she calls him."

Well. It put a different spin on the idea of a mother absconding across the border with her child. She wondered if Dominick knew about Rafe. Bored artistic wife off to New Mexico, where she meets the man of her dreams. Coral, a golden ball bouncing between them. Except . . .

"Do you know when Coral went home?"

He screwed up his narrow face. "Sunday. Because we went back to school Monday."

School started early out here. "How come you're not in school today?"

"I'm sick. Want to see my tongue?"

Before she could look away, she saw that it was coated a repulsive white.

"Bye, Joey. Feel better soon."

She retraced her way to the main road and considered her plan. A quick stop at Holy Cross Hospital, which showed up as a light blue rectangle on her map, then on to Santa Fe to find a place to stay. Once she found Route 68 going south, it would be less than two hours.

THE HIGHWAY WOUND south beside a river that looked brown and shallow. Every minute or two she passed a new group of rafters, and closer to the road a stand selling pottery and painted kiva ladders. To her left the cluster of mountains arched toward the sky.

Something that she first thought was a hawk descended slightly, and she saw it was a hang glider, a black silhouette against the blue. Ducking her head to see it better, she yearned to be up there herself, with nothing but the sun and wind currents on her mind. She missed those days of exploring new places, of following candlelit processions down darkened streets, of sitting in cafés to write her blog.

Why had she assumed it would go on forever? Come to that, why had she assumed that Lee would always be there, that their life could only get better?

Lee, send me a message—wherever you are.

As she drove south, the mountains crept closer to the road, their red shape restrained by fences and a mesh covering. Even here there was the familiar sign, "Watch for Falling Rocks." She wondered if falling rocks had anything to do with the wooden crosses on the edge of the road, wreathed by artificial flowers, and decided they probably marked car crashes the way they did at home. But then she saw two white crosses at the top of a cliff and wondered.

As she turned onto the larger Route 84, the mountains took a step back again, replaced by brown hills tufted with small green bushes. The sides of the road were crowded now with businesses and signs for Santa Fe. She passed a neon-tubed outline of a huge cowboy in front of the Round-Up Motel and decided she could not face a room with a bolted-down TV and venetian blinds.

The Turquoise Trail Inn was a Territorial-style building with authentic furnishings and shared bathrooms. Fiona's room had a white kiva fireplace in one corner, a red tile floor, and French doors leading to her own patio outside. Even without her own shower it had been more than she wanted to pay, but most places on the highway had "No Vacancy" signs and she was happy to be in the center of Santa Fe. Besides, what did the money matter? If she found Lee, it would be worth it. And if she didn't…who cared how much she had left in the bank?

Activating the ceiling fan, she let herself stretch out on the white bedspread. She had promised to stop by Susan Allmayer's house, but the Dramamine still in her system was compelling. It was too late to go to the Day Star corporate offices. She let herself sleep.

When she woke up, the world was dark.

Chapter Fifteen

The Day Star offices were located west of the plaza on the Paseo de Peralta in an adobe building set back from the sidewalk. Its glass windows looked black under a porch formed by brown pillars. Above the door a large brass sun face had been pressed into the clay. Junipers, cacti, and other succulents lined the entrance walk.

Fiona waited across the street under a cottonwood tree. The people approaching the building, laden down by newspapers, canvas bags, and Styrofoam cups, reminded her of her days as a lawyer. She had drunk no more coffee than usual today, but her stomach was seizing up in the same way. Why hadn't she gone to Lee's apartment in Brooklyn and photocopied his passport? It would have been a good thing to have with her. Was it too late to tell them she was his wife?

The wooden handle and glass door were heavier than she expected. Holding the door awkwardly as she stepped around it, Fiona moved into a pastel world, a world with a vanilla scent. Most of the pictures on the walls were large R. C. Gorman prints of Indians, which she had never liked. She was happy that he had found success as a Navajo artist. But why did he have to make his women so meek?

Looking at the triangular shape of a woman bent placidly over a basket of corn, she gave her head a shake.

"And they're originals too." A woman at a modular gray desk was grinning at her as if she shared Fiona's feeling. Though plump, she was wearing the white company shirt and a bright yellow jumper with wide straps. She had curly gray hair and small, very white dentures. Her half-glasses made Fiona think of Mrs. Santa Claus. "How can I help you?"

Get these paintings off the walls. "I'd like to speak to whoever's in charge. My name's Fiona Reina."

"Well, hi, Fiona. Is it about employment?"

"No. No, I'm not looking for a job. It's about something that happened. Something important."

The woman hesitated. "Why don't you just wait there a moment?" She motioned to a sectional sofa, a pale salmon and mint-green design. Fiona sank into its comfortable pillows and waited, noticing that the off-white walls were actually wallpaper with a diamond-shaped pattern.

It was not what she had expected. After the office in Taos, after the way the FAA rep complained about Day Star equipment, Fiona had assumed that they were a no-frills airline, operating out of storefronts and vacant hangars. If their equipment wasn't up to snuff, why this office? Why the original Gormans?

The woman behind the desk smiled at her again, but did not pick up the telephone to tell anyone she was there. Fiona imagined her pressing an unseen button for security. Had she given her name when she called yesterday?

A moment later she heard the wheeze of the heavy door and the staccato click of cowboy boots. A woman hurried past, almost bumping the corner of the reception desk. She looked to be in her late forties, dressed in white jeans and a coral Western-style blouse. Patting her leather shoulder bag, she called, "Wait till Will gets a load of these RPMs!" Her voice was emphatic, but Fiona could not tell if she was upset or jubilant. "And we're getting another Better Business award."

Something about the woman's twist of golden hair and her drawl were familiar. She knew that voice. As the woman started down the hall, Fiona cried, "Wait!" Her voice ballooned into the room like a loudspeaker announcement.

The woman whirled around. Her lovely features—wide blue eyes, a small, perfect nose, and sweet mouth with an ancillary dimple—looked affronted.

"You're Miss Ginger!"

It had been years since she'd watched *The Jesse Wilcox Show*, but when she was eleven, she had waited anxiously for Friday nights. At the ranch, Ginger Lee had acted as the Bar J-G's den mother. She would gather unhappy young cowboys around the kitchen table and declare, "Now you just tell Miss Ginger all about it." Then she would proceed to make things right, either by intervening with Jesse, or by giving them her own worldly-wise counsel. Fiona had daydreamed about having the rips and tears of her own life repaired by Miss Ginger.

And now, here she was! It was like being invited to meet the president.

"I loved you. I wanted you to be my mother!"

Ginger Lee laughed and moved back toward Fiona, raising her palms in the air. "Guilty as charged. Where did you grow up?"

"Oh, you never heard of it. Lamb's Tongue, Iowa?"

"No, but I know these small farm towns. I grew up in Nebraska. I left when I was very young, of course." Her look turned studiedly wistful. "Life disappears so quickly. Please don't tell me that I 'haven't changed a bit.'"

"But you haven't!" Should she ask for her autograph? No, she was an adult now. "I was devastated when the show ended."

"So were we." Ginger Lee gave her a warm smile, then turned and moved back down the hall.

"You have a good memory for faces," the receptionist complimented Fiona. "That show's been off the air for twenty years. And they weren't exactly Roy and Dale."

"No, they were better. But why is she here?"

The receptionist peered over her half-glasses, surprised. "You didn't know she and Jesse started Day Star? Will Dunlea, Ginger's son, is the CEO."

"I didn't know at all. Is Jesse here too?" She had not been as taken with Jesse Wilcox in the series. He had been generous and pleasure loving, but too strict about enforcing the rules.

"Oh, I haven't seen him for ages. So sad the way his mind has gone. He mostly stays at their ranch in Colorado now." She gave a sudden giggle. "Will and Ginger Lee look like twins. Plastic surgery is a wonderful thing."

Fiona didn't like that comment about her almost-mother. "Is she still acting?"

"Not for years. After the show ended, she tried, but she was typecast. Now she's busy accepting civic awards and being a presence in New Mexico."

"I thought you said she lived in Colorado."

The receptionist grinned. "This is an airline, honey. These people hop in their helicopter to go to the supermarket. There's an airfield at the Ranch, and Santa Fe has an airport too."

At Fiona's look of surprise, she added, "Small. Three runways. But Day Star's negotiating with a wilderness travel outfit to do charter flights from there."

"Huh. Did you tell anyone I was here?"

"Oh, Will's not in yet. Ginger's cooling her boots back there too." She didn't sound as if the prospect saddened her. "Most of us work from nine thirty to five thirty, except for two girls who take bookings in back until nine o'clock. But Will works Will-time."

"This is your main office?" It seemed important to learn everything she could about Day Star.

"Pretty much. We have an airfield in Denver to maintain our planes. There's always one or two there. But our flight attendants are trained by American in Dallas."

"What kind of—"

She stopped as the door wheezed open again and a man came in. He had smooth light hair worn close to his head and was very tan. Inherited dimples that showed as he smiled at them. Intelligent blue eyes the shade of washed denim. The only anomaly was the narrow nose that ended in a sweeping point. *Get him an Alpine hat and teach him to yodel!*

Still, he was impressive. His flashing teeth were perfect and he had the aura she was familiar with from interviewing celebrities for *Gusto!*

"Mom's waiting for you," the receptionist said, teasing.

"Haven't seen her in a bobcat's age."

They both laughed. "And so is Miss—"

"Reina. Fiona."

"Yes, Miss Reina. Pretty name, like a queen. She wants you too."

That smile again. "Now I'm flattered." He disappeared down the light gray hall. Fiona noticed that he did not carry a briefcase.

"Maybe you'd like to use the restroom first? It's right around that corner."

So the receptionist could speak to Will Dunlea about her? But she said, "Sure."

The bathroom was small, with wallpaper in a pale peach half-circle design. A white basket of artificial flowers decorated the toilet tank. The sweet floral scent made Fiona think of funeral homes.

She assumed she would have to wait to see Will Dunlea until he was finished with his mother, but when she came back into the lobby the receptionist pointed to the hallway. "Last door on the right. Just go in."

She found Will in there alone, arms spread over a huge burled walnut desk. Above his head, suspended by wire, was a paper model of what must have been the first Day Star plane. Jesse and Ginger Lee's private ride.

She sat down in the yellow leather chair he beckoned her toward.

"What can I do for you, Fiona?"

"I need some information, Will."

He continued to look pleasant, fingers drumming on one side of the desk. "What kind of information?"

She hesitated. *Shoot for the moon and land in the stars.* "It's about the flight out of Taos to Denver Sunday morning. I understand you had to make an emergency landing."

He stared at her, mouth turned down, genuinely puzzled. "Who told you that? We had to make a refueling stop; the pilots thought the flow seemed irregular, but it was no emergency. This is the way rumors start." A reproving look. "Changing the fuel out made us late, but we got everyone to Denver."

"Not everyone. Because several people who were supposed to go on to New York never got there."

"But we don't fly to New York."

"No, I know you don't. They were supposed to get the flight in Denver, but never did."

"And these people were on the Day Star shuttle?"

She lifted her hands, palms turned up. "That's the question."

He straightened up soberly. The collar on his blue-and-white-striped shirt was high in an oddly old-fashioned way, his navy tie thicker than normal. "And what's your interest in this?"

"The man I live with was on the plane. He never got to New York, and he hasn't called. But there are other people too. Nobody from other places has contacted you about missing passengers?"

"No." His eyes flicked to a far wall, then back at her.

You're lying.

Calm down. You're not interrogating a witness. "So I need to see a passenger list, to see who was on that plane."

His expression was a blend of amusement and incredulity, as if she had asked him to hand over his watch. "I'm sorry, but that's information I can't give out. It would be violating every rule of confidentiality. Airlines are hog-tied by regulations you couldn't begin to imagine, but that one's pretty clear. Before I could release anyone's name I'd have to contact them and get their permission." He looked stern, then added, "And I'd have to have a damn good reason for doing it. What I can do—though I probably shouldn't—is check and see whether your party was on the flight."

Why do you think I came? But she said, "How do I know you'll tell me the truth?"

Will Dunlea jerked back in his leather chair, the movement stirring the paper plane above his head. Tenting his fingers, elbows on his desk, he gave her a long look. "What have I said that would give you the feeling I would lie to you? You come in here without an appointment, I take the trouble to see you right away because my receptionist says you're upset, I try to address what's on your mind. Then because I can't give you everything you want, you accuse me of lying!"

"You know what? You look like Robert Redford in *The Sting*."

He gave a surprised bark of laughter. "And why should I believe *you*?"

"People must tell you that all the time."

"Look—Fiona. Will you at least let me look up the information about your friend for you?"

"Of course. Thanks."

He moved in his seat, angling the computer screen at the edge of his desk so she could not see it. "What's his name?"

"Lee Pienaar. It sounds like pine air, but it's spelled P-i-e-n-a-a-r."

After a moment of tapping in various commands, Will said, "We have him flying out of Islip MacArthur and into Taos on August 19."

"That's the date he left Long Island," she agreed.

Will Dunlea looked back to the screen, tapped another several keys, and then turned to her with sympathetic eyes. "I'm afraid that's it."

"What do you mean?" She felt as if he had reached out and shoved her against the chair back. "That's *it*? But he texted me from the airport when he was about to board! Why wouldn't he have gotten on the plane?"

"Maybe he gave up his seat to someone. I see by the roster that the plane was full. You're sure he was at the airport."

"He said he was."

"Plans do change."

"Can you at least check the name of *one* of the other people?"

When all else fails, negotiate.

"I told you, Fiona, I can't do that. The families would have to inquire themselves."

"But it would really clear things up."

"I'm sorry…"

She sighed theatrically. "I guess this has been a wasted trip then. I'll have to scrounge around and buy a ticket home."

Now he looked alert. "If money's a problem, I'm sure we can work something out. Like every airline, our flights aren't always full. If you're flexible, I know we can find a spot for you."

"Really?"

"When were you thinking of going?"

The question caught her off guard. "Well, if I wanted to do any sightseeing—Friday morning?"

"Good. Then you can have dinner with me tonight."

Was it a serious invitation?

"You don't know anyone else in town, do you?"

"No. But you don't have to do that."

"I want to. Where are you staying?"

"The Turquoise Trail Inn." Was it a mistake to tell him that?

"I'll pick you up about seven o'clock. Is that too early?"

"No, it's fine. I'm still on Eastern time."

"It's a plan." He got up from his desk and skillfully ushered her out.

Chapter Sixteen

Outside on the sidewalk, Fiona blinked and reached in her bag for her sunglasses. The light was harsh now, the leaves of the trees above her a blatant chartreuse. *I don't want to be here.* She should have asked Will Dunlea for a voucher to leave immediately. Of course, she could always pick up her things, drive down to Albuquerque, and get a flight from there.

Yet would being home be any better? Without Lee, without the future they had been planning, she would have to creep back to Sydney Beach and figure out how to live next. *How could you do this to me?*

She found a white ironwork bench in the next block and slumped down on it. These were the facts: Lee had never been on the Day Star flight. After a delay it had landed safely in Denver without him on it. Without the other people on it too, evidently, but she could not think about them now.

Seven months had not been a long time. She and Lee seemingly could not get enough of each other, but love had blinded her to what she did not want to see. Perhaps Lee had been secretly judging her all along, hiding any reservations he felt. When they were finally apart, objectivity had made him realize that the relationship would not work. Fiona had been a charming novelty, not a lifetime partner.

Always before she had kept some part of herself in reserve, enjoying the men she was with, but knowing she would survive if the relationship ended. As it always had, with some wistfulness but no devastation. This time she had held nothing back—and this is what happened. But why wouldn't Lee just tell her? Perhaps he could not face her shock, her entreaties, her tears.

Maybe he was back in New York right now, packing what he wanted to take to South Africa. Maybe he had begged the magazine to tell her he had not been in touch with them. She let herself think what she had been resisting until now: He had met someone else. She remembered how immediate their attraction had been, how they had gone back to his apartment that first night. Maybe that was the way it worked for him. He might have run into a former lover or planned to meet someone in New Mexico.

Sarah. They had lived together for eight years. Eight years! That was practically like being married. Ironically, she had finally left him because he didn't want to take the next step, had no desire for a settled life or children. Fiona suddenly heard Uncle Eimer's voice: He's a bounder! What was a bounder anyway? Maybe Lee had decided it *was* time to settle down, and Sarah was a known quantity. They had split up over a year ago, but eight years was a long time.

Fiona shifted her bag from her lap to the white metal. If a client had come to her and told her the story as a lawyer, she would have advised the client to forget him and just move on.

But then she thought of her Saturday-night FaceTime conversation with Lee. He had not been in a hurry to get off the phone with her. There hadn't seemed to be anyone else in the room with him, and they had ended with their usual love talk.

I won't believe it until he tells me himself.

SHE DECIDED TO call Rosa.

The phone was picked up on the first ring.

"Fiona?"

"Uh-huh."

"How *are* you? What have you found out?"

"Have you heard from Susan?"

"No."

"Day Star told me Lee was not on the flight." It was hard to say the words without choking up. "I don't know what to do."

"And you believe them?"

"Why would they lie about it? Anyway, the CEO, Will Dunlea, asked me out to dinner tonight."

"Really? Are you going?"

"Sure." She was used to being asked to strangers' homes around the world. She always brought a gift and had had many interesting meals.

"You'll charm him. Did you get a chance to stop by Susan's?"

"No, it was late when I got here." *And I fell asleep.*

"Hold off, then. I've got a couple of other ideas. What about Dominick's daughter?"

"The kid next door said her mother put her on the plane. He also said Dominick's wife went off to Mexico with her lover."

"Oh, Lord. What fools these mortals be."

"I guess I'll go to the library. The woman next to me on the shuttle said that Day Star had some trouble a while back. I want to find out about that."

"You never know. And good luck tonight."

THE MAIN BRANCH of the Santa Fe Library was an attractive tan building with a desert garden in front, and lacy latticework along the second-floor balcony. Fiona moved into the foyer and looked for the reference room. In a few minutes she was settled in front of a staff computer looking at the *New Mexican*. She caught sight of her face in the gray screen, hair carelessly tumbled around her shoulders, then jerked back as Lee's face appeared next to hers as if posing for a selfie with her.

She whirled around to get a better look. "Lee! Why didn't you call me?"

But there was only air.

I saw him, I know I did.

I'm going crazy.

She scanned the room, then sat with her hands covering her face, elbows on the table. Finally she felt a soft tap on her shoulder. *Lee?* Looking up, she saw it was the reference librarian, his pale face concerned. "Are you all right?"

"I'm okay. It must be the altitude."

"It's tricky when you're not used to it," he agreed.

She clicked back to 1993 and began to read.

In the beginning there was one small plane, which Jesse Wilcox and Ginger Lee bought to fly to their ranch just over the border in Colorado. They had an airfield constructed on their property so that their California friends could fly in as well. Soon those friends were buying property and building vacation homes nearby, so when a local airline went belly-up they all chipped in to buy it. As an investment. As a lark.

The local press had been skeptical, but eventually came to dote on them. Fiona read reports of Day Star's expansion, their acquisition of more and better aircraft, their strategy of taking over routes to secondary airports in large cities. Code sharing with larger airlines to bring Westerners to major hubs had been a smart move.

Caught up in Day Star's golden successes, Fiona was unprepared to come upon the next headline: "Commuter Plane Crashes in Eleven Mile Canyon." She glanced at the date. Nearly four years ago. It had happened a few miles south of Denver. Four years ago, she was based in Paris and would not have heard about it. Nineteen people aboard, a small crash in a small area. The world had blinked and then gone on to political upheaval in Russia.

The *New Mexican* covered the aftermath of the crash in great detail, each issue another sad requiem for the dead. Fiona skipped past their descriptions and searched for the cause of the crash. Because there had been no black box on board and no survivors, investigators decided on a phenomenon known as wind shear. The account explained that in mountainous areas, waves of air sometimes accelerated when passing over a peak, smashing downward in a welter of turbulence. Such downdrafts could take even a large plane and crash it against the mountain. Thunderstorms helped to foster a wind shear.

Day Star had been stunned by the accident, but they had done the right thing, voluntarily compensating the relatives of the victims and offering them bereavement counseling. Even so, there had been one lawsuit, brought by the husband of a woman in her thirties. It asked for four million dollars for wrongful death and loss of services and earnings. The suit had been settled last year for the usual "undisclosed amount."

It must have cost them plenty, Fiona decided. A working spouse was a valuable commodity in the eyes of the law. Day Star's net worth and its stock had dropped sharply after the accident, and there had been rumors of bankruptcy. According to one journalist, Jesse Wilcox and Ginger Lee put all their personal assets into keeping Day Star flying; over the years they had bought out everyone else. The loyal staff, from pilots to mechanics, took a voluntary pay cut.

Fiona read up to the present, then sat back in her chair, rubbing her eyes. Day Star had taken responsibility and acted honorably in that situation. No tricks, no rationalizations. There had been no cover-up. Instead of retreating into bankruptcy, they had sympathized with the victims and their families, settled their debts, and kept going.

She recast her contacts with Day Star in that light. They had answered her questions consistently and politely without violating any disclosure laws, something that as an attorney she could not fault them for. Maggie's father and the older cowboy had arrived safely on the shuttle from Taos. The FAA agreed that the plane had landed. There had been no sense of panic at the airline office this morning. According to their computer, Lee had not been on the flight.

Face facts.

Chapter Seventeen

WILL DUNLEA ARRIVED at seven o'clock in a small white car that Fiona identified as a Porsche. As she jumped up and descended the porch steps, he got out and came around to the passenger door. Fiona saw that he was wearing a red polo shirt, white pants, and boat shoes. No doubt he had correctly gauged the limitations of her wardrobe. At least she had borrowed an iron from the innkeeper and pressed her khaki pants and black, scooped-neck T-shirt, then brushed her hair until it shone. But that was ridiculous. Would Will confess that something had happened to Lee if her hair was pretty enough?

As they settled themselves in the car, she couldn't hide a smile. "Something funny?"

"No, I was just thinking about the movie where an English lawyer had a daughter named Portia. From Shakespeare? And his gangster client said to him, 'Wow. Imagine naming your kid after your car!'"

Will smiled tolerantly.

"I guess you had to be there." She glanced around at the red leather interior. "Do you have a Porsche for every outfit? Or just an outfit for every Porsche?"

"What?" The engine hummed as he switched on the ignition. "Oh. Nope, it's my only car. And they aren't even Day Star colors."

"Let me guess. Yellow and dark blue."

"Bingo." At the end of the street he signaled toward the plaza. "We could have walked. I think you'll like this restaurant."

La Cantina, new to Fiona, was off Palace Avenue and through a greenery-filled courtyard. It was Southwestern inside, decorated with oversized plants.

A blonde in a short black dress and tights seated them, handing them menus.

"I'll tell you what's good here," Will announced, without looking at his. "Black bean soup in a loaf of bread, the prickly pear salad, and red chile pasta. I like the salmon myself. What kind of wine do you drink?"

"Alcoholic."

He laughed and ordered a bottle of pinot grigio. But instead of heading to the bar to place their order, the waitress veered over to the piano. Several other servers were waiting for her, arranged in a semicircle. Throwing their arms open, they burst into "Oklahoma."

Fiona was enchanted. It was definitely a place to include if she ever wrote a sequel guidebook to Paris and New York. *Santa Fe's Hottest Chiles.* As soon as she'd thought it, she wished she hadn't. The book made her think of Lee and how happy she would have felt if he were there instead of Will. Still, she decided she would have a good time. If Lee had gone back to Sarah . . .

"They're really a musical troupe," Will said. "They only serve food between songs."

"It's charming."

"Santa Fe has many charms."

Including you.

As they sipped the chilled wine and broke off pieces of bread, Fiona tried to read him. What did he want from the evening? It fell into a crevice between a date and business entertainment. There was no emotional connection—how could there be—yet he touched her arm easily to get her attention or make a point.

"Are you really Ginger Lee's son?" At his quizzical glance, she added, "I mean, I always wanted her to be *my* mother. So I don't know whether to envy you, or what."

He drained his wine glass and grinned at her. His formality in the office was yielding to a fresh-faced warmth. "Stick with the 'or what,'" he advised.

"Why?"

"Why." He poured more golden liquid into both glasses. "Growing up, I probably saw less of her than you did on TV. She didn't raise me."

"You had governesses?"

"No, I had her mother. My grandma. Ginger was young when I was born, still in high school. So it was logical to give me to her parents and leave town. Things were different years ago." The furrows around his mouth indicated that they hadn't been for the better.

Fiona waited until the waitress set their salads in front of them and then said, "Your background sounds so much like mine. Where did you grow up?"

"Nebraska. On a farm."

"Wow! I'm from Iowa. So you didn't see Ginger much?"

He shook his head, the charming, rueful smile in place. "By the time she had established herself as an actress and lowered her age to fit, I was much too old." He laughed. "She would have had to have had me when she was seven. Besides, any cover story she made up for me would have been disputed by everyone in town."

Fiona retrieved the avocado from her salad, her favorite part. "The difference is, my mother died when I was two. I was raised by my aunt and uncle."

He winced. "That's tough. The thing about Ginger is, she never sent her parents anything, even when she and Jesse were pulling down millions. He was the one who finally brought me into the family. He was a generous guy. But by then, of course, I was grown."

"But—he's still alive, isn't he?" She was confused by the tense.

"Sure. I was talking about back then. His mind is pretty much gone now. He sits and watches reruns, poor guy. But enough of that. Tell me more about your family."

Fiona, already giddy from the wine, started to laugh. "It's worse than yours. My mother was the family black sheep. She hung out at a bar called the Cat's Paw. She drowned herself when I was two."

"That's terrible!" He reached out and put a hand on her wrist. "So you never really knew her. What about your father?"

Fiona put down her salad fork and looked at him. It was easier to tell someone who wouldn't feel sad for her. "I used to have this fantasy that he was a Mohawk Indian and would come and rescue me. But he didn't, and I finally stopped thinking about him."

"Did you ever try to contact him?"

"No." That wasn't exactly true. Periodically she looked on the Internet, but had found no one with that name who was the right age. Her guidance counselor found that Leonard Charley had left the Chippewa reservation as a teenager.

They stopped talking to listen to their waitress do a solo of "I'm Just a Gal Who Cain't Say No."

"Did you get along with your relatives?" Will asked.

"Well, put it this way." She had had enough wine to make her life an interesting story. "When I drove up to the farm after college graduation, there were all these plastic garbage bags on the porch. 'Hi, Mom, what are those?' I asked. 'Well, Fiona,' she said, 'they're your things. All your clothes, school papers, photographs, every last trace of you. If you don't get them out of my sight, I'm taking them to the dump.'"

"Jesus!" He moved his hand down to hers and squeezed it. He barely moved his arm as the waitress set down Fiona's dinner of chicken in a red-pepper cream sauce.

"Actually, it's a joke. She had all my stuff on the porch, but because she thought I might want it to take east with me. I think. They weren't bad people, really."

But he kept his eyes on her sympathetically. "You deserved better." His voice was soft.

"Yes, well—it's all in the past now. How did you get involved with Day Star?"

"Family business. Jesse wanted to retire, and his sons with Ginger are hooligans. Never worked a day in their lives."

"Were you there four years ago?"

He looked up sharply, fork in midair, as if she had said something rude. "Why?"

"There was that plane crash."

He sighed. "Our darkest hour."

"Something like that must get expensive."

"That's what insurance is for. But I can see you're still in denial about your friend."

"Maybe." She put down her fork, suddenly dizzy. They were on their second bottle of pinot grigio.

The staff regrouped to sing "People Will Say We're in Love."

Will Dunlea, all charm, smiled at her.

Some men needed to make the whole world fall in love with them, she decided. In his case, it wouldn't be hard. "Have you ever been married?" she asked.

"Nope. I'll do that when nothing else works."

She laughed.

"I fly and skydive. And I'm a big ski bum. But a classy bum." The wine was having its effect on him as well. "Not one of those stereotypes around here on Friday nights, in a van with a loaded gun rack, pulling a speedboat and an ATV."

"You don't have a Budweiser cap?" she asked, teasing.

"It's Coors out here."

"I need the restroom." She pressed both hands against the table and stood up unsteadily. Maybe in the calm of a stall she could figure out where all this was going.

"Go back past where we came in, then on down the hall a little farther," he said. "I'll settle up here. We can have coffee back at my place."

"Uh." Through her fog a bell began to clang. "I'm pretty wiped out. Maybe we'd better have coffee here."

"Okay." He looked only a little regretful. "Regular or cappuccino?"

"Cappuccino would be great."

"Shall we take a peek at the dessert tray?"

"Will it get upset if we don't?"

"They make a great Death by Chocolate here."

"Split it?"

"Why not?"

In the ladies room, Fiona patted cold water all over her face and then smoothed down her hair with wet hands. Had she learned anything from him? What had he learned from her? Maybe that you can overcome one hard-luck story until life flattens you again. She had not told him everything, of course.

Over coffee, Will blinked and said casually, "So, tell me about these other New York people. Who are they exactly?"

"Just people I met at the airport. They don't know if their relatives were on the flight, and you won't tell me."

"Because I can't. But you know what I think?" He relaxed against the bentwood chair, hands clasped behind his head. "Given what you've told me about yourself, you don't trust people easily. Why should you? When you finally do, it's impossible to believe someone you love would treat you this way. So you're looking for people in the same situation, even though they may not be." He tilted his golden head. "Could that be true?"

"Could be."

"This Lee is making a big mistake. Maybe he's like a friend of mine. He couldn't bear to ask his wife for a divorce and hurt her that way. So he killed her."

Fiona's coffee cup clattered against the saucer. "A *friend* of yours?"

Will gave her a sheepish grin. "Okay, I read it online. But I can understand the logic behind it, the thing that would make someone want to disappear without a confrontation."

He leaned forward and pressed his fingers around her forearm, suddenly commanding. "I want you to stop by my office tomorrow morning and pick up that voucher. It'll be standby and it's a

Friday, but if you get to the airport early in the day, there shouldn't be a problem. I'd feel very badly if you had to pay to fly home when it's in my power to do something for you."

"Both flights?"

"Both flights."

"Thanks!" She hoped she could retrieve her frequent-flyer miles. "Do you travel much yourself?"

He shook his head. "Not as much as I'd like. But I could be persuaded to come to New York once in a while."

And do what?

"By the way," he added, his voice soft, "I never even asked what you do there."

She knew she would enjoy this. "Well, Will, I'm a lawyer. I always wanted to travel, though, so right now I'm doing that and writing about it instead of practicing law."

He laughed as if she had made a joke.

She knew the part he found amusing. "I'll never go back to the law. Unless I get desperate for money again."

"You're telling me you're a lawyer. Like going to law school and passing the bar."

"That's how they do it in New York."

"Wow." The aw-shucks grin reappeared, a little forced. "It's just—you don't *act* like a lawyer. Or dress like one. But congratulations; that's wonderful."

I get more information from people when they don't think I'm going to sue them.

She smiled and watched him sign the credit-card slip the waitress had brought with the coffee.

Out on the street a breeze had kicked up, tumbling daytime refuse through the empty plaza.

When they were back in the Porsche, Will said, "You're sure you won't come up for a liqueur? I've got a great view of Santa Fe. We could go in the sauna and I could take advantage of you."

With that, he let her know he was rescinding the invitation. Whatever activities he had been planning had been with a wide-eyed girl from Iowa, not a New York attorney.

Chapter Eighteen

A FEW MINUTES after Fiona climbed into bed and started to fall asleep, her phone dinged with a text. Groping around the night table, she picked it up and stared at the lighted screen:

Don't worry about me. Go home, and I'll explain everything later.

My God. She pressed in Lee's number immediately and listened to the phone ring six times, and then his warm voice telling her to please leave a message.

"Lee, where *are* you? Just talk to me. Pick up! I know you're there."

She ended the call and waited. *Why are you doing this to me?*

Her phone stayed silent.

Finally she sat back up and sent him a text: *Lee, I have to hear from you. It doesn't matter; I'll go home, I just have to know you're okay.*

Even if you don't love me or you think moving in is a mistake.

There was nothing more.

Sleep was impossible after that.

WHEN FIONA CAME back to her room from the shower, she saw that the message light on her phone was blinking. Lee was calling back! They would finally talk; everything would be revealed, as devastating as it might be for her to hear. She snatched the phone from the nightstand. *Thank God, thank God.*

The message was from Rosa Cooper. They were at Kennedy Airport, about to board a flight to Albuquerque, changing in Dallas. They would drive up and meet her around four o'clock, as soon as they knew where she was staying.

No. Fiona stared at her phone. Why were they coming out now? *This party has been canceled.* There was nothing to find out, at least as far as Day Star was concerned. Rosa could still solve the mystery of Susan, and Dominick could try to wrest his daughter back from his wife, but any answers lay elsewhere.

She punched the redial button immediately. If they were still at the airport, it would be okay. But her call went right to voice mail and Fiona pictured Rosa in an airplane seat, her phone compliantly switched off. She left a message anyway. "Hi, Rosa. I'm not sure there's anything to find. But if you're on your way, I'm at the Turquoise Trail Inn on Merriwether Avenue in Santa Fe."

A few minutes before ten, Fiona walked over to the Day Star office to pick up the voucher. She hoped she would see Will Dunlea. Somehow seeing him, hearing his sincere reassurances, would make her feel better.

But when she got to the office, Will was not in yet. The same receptionist as yesterday, the stout woman in the yellow pinafore, eyes still twinkling, told her he had phoned in and made the arrangements for her voucher with his assistant.

"I know he can decide who'll fly on Day Star," Fiona said, "but what about Voyager? What if all their flights are filled?"

"Oh, they always hold a few seats back. Bereavement flights, professional courtesy. There's always one or two no-shows." She cocked her head at Fiona. "So you're leaving us already?"

"Looks that way. I think I've been left at the altar." And then she was telling the sympathetic receptionist the whole story: Lee's never arriving in New York, her waiting frantically at home for him to call, finally coming out here to see what had happened to him. "I guess he didn't love me. And I don't have any family I'm close to."

She told the woman about growing up scorned in Lamb's Tongue, her mother's suicide, her unknown father, embroidering only a little for effect. *My life as romance novel.*

The woman's eyes glistened. "Oh, you poor thing. On top of everything, to feel that this man abandoned you..."

Fiona gave her a wan smile. "Thanks for listening to my sad story. I guess I'll just go home and stick my head in the oven."

"Don't do that! I have a daughter, she's had some hard luck too..." The woman hesitated, biting at her lower lip, but only gestured toward the hall. "You know your way. It's the office just before Will's."

The young woman who handed her the envelope was friendly enough. "You do know it's technically standby."

"I've flown standby before. Thank Mr. Dunlea for me."

As she left the office, she found herself assessing the assistant, her blonde curls and wide smile, and wondered if Will was attracted to her. She gave her head a shake. And that mattered because?

Back into the lobby she glanced again at the R. C. Gorman prints, at the long-suffering Indian women eternally grinding their cornmeal. The receptionist was a blur at the corner of her eye.

"Oh, you've got a leaf caught in your hair!" the woman called to her. "Come here and I'll get it out."

A leaf sounded picturesque, but Fiona turned and went toward her obediently. As the receptionist moved behind her, Fiona felt something stiff being pushed against her hand. Belatedly she closed her fingers around it.

"There! Now you're decent again."

"I'm never decent. But thanks." She turned to smile at the receptionist, but the woman, half-glasses at the tip of her nose, had gone back to whatever she had been reading.

Fiona waited until she was across Paseo de Peralta, around the corner and out of view of Day Star, before she opened her hand. She saw that she was holding a small Post-it note with the Day Star logo. Handwritten in blue ink were the words, "It happened between Taos and Denver."

Chapter Nineteen

SHE HAD TO go back. She didn't want to get anyone in trouble, but she *had* to know what had happened. She would be discreet, she would get the receptionist off to the side and talk privately. She would promise not to tell anyone where she had gotten her information. It had been brave of the woman to give her the note at all.

But I have to know.

It took less than five minutes to walk back around the corner and up the path to the heavy glass door. Fiona kept herself from running. But when she pulled the door open and stepped inside, the receptionist's desk was empty. *She's only in the bathroom*, Fiona pleaded. *She's just getting a cup of coffee.* Instead of hovering beside the modular desk, she went over to the couch and sat down.

But the receptionist did not return. Finally Fiona went down the hall to the next-to-last office and stepped inside.

The young woman looked up, startled.

"Is the receptionist around? I promised to give her something—a book."

"She and those novels of hers! No, you just missed her. She said her husband had called; he had been in a fender bender. She was pretty shaken up when she left."

"Do you know when she'll be back?"

Her pretty face grimaced. "Not today, I'm sure."

"Can you tell me where she lives? I'll deliver the book myself."

"Oh, you don't have to do that! Just leave it on her desk."

"Okay, fine. What's her name, anyway?"

"Priss." But her light eyes were appraising Fiona as if she found the question odd.

Fiona stepped back out the door and stood beside it. In every TV mystery she remembered watching, the person who had been questioned called someone to report it.

This one didn't. There was only the click of computer keys.

Finally, Fiona left.

BACK IN HER room, she did something she should have done immediately: Google Will Dunlea. A number of listings having to do with Day Star came up, but there was also a short Wikipedia article about him.

Fiona read it and then sat on the edge of her bed, staring at her laptop.

Will Dunlea had not grown up in the wilds of Nebraska. He had lived in Bel Air, attended an exclusive Southern California prep school, Chadwick, and then gone on to UCLA. He married his high-school sweetheart and had three children. Jesse and Ginger and their careers were mentioned, of course, in the context of their founding Day Star. In 2001 Will started working for the airline.

He sure had me fooled.

But how had he known to mirror her background? She tried to remember if she had talked about growing up on a farm in any of her online travel blogs. No doubt she had. And she had told Ginger Lee where she was from. The only thing she had never written about was being a lawyer.

THE OTHERS ARRIVED at five. Fiona was sitting on the front porch, half-heartedly scribbling notes about the city's attractions—the cafeteria on Museum Hill, in particular—when a white Explorer with Dominick driving stopped, hesitated, and then pulled into the parking area. Fiona jumped down and ran back to meet them. Odd how glad she was to see them when a week ago they hadn't known each other. Thank God she'd been too late to stop them from coming!

Dominick opened the door from behind the wheel, but Rosa was the first one out, beaming at Fiona. She was wearing an expensive-looking black sweat suit with "Courtesy of the Brain Trust" in red letters on the front pocket. Greg, right behind her, gave Fiona a salute.

"I didn't expect to see *you*," she said.

"Yeah well, I got a free ticket. To make up for the flight I missed to Portland. I've brought my climbing gear."

"He wanted to stay in this forty-nine-dollar motel on the highway," Rosa announced, rolling her eyes. "Can you imagine?"

"Hey, it had a pool. I don't see any pools around here."

"Pools are for *children*."

"You can't swim?"

"We don't have a pool," Fiona said. "But we're right in town."

"Next time find a pool. It's August, for Christ's sake!"

Dominick moved around the hood of the truck, smiling, and gave Fiona a bear hug. "This looks like a nice place."

"The problem is, they only have one vacancy. With twin beds."

"Thank God," Rosa said. "I hate B-and-Bs." She squinted at the Territorial-style building and gave her dark wiry hair a shake. "The furniture is uncomfortable, you have to smoke outside like a felon, and they always have pets who want to sniff your crotch."

Greg rationalized that if he shared the room with Dominick, it would only cost half as much. "That is, if they don't want me to stay at the farm. They probably will, but they'd better not expect me to work."

"What farm?" Fiona asked.

"Dimitri's father's. I want to know if *he* knows what the hell's going on."

Dominick grinned at Fiona.

"Do you want a roommate?" Fiona asked him.

"Oh, I don't mind. I'm used to bunking with my boys when we travel. And frankly, I can't afford to be away more than a night or two. Is the airline office around here?"

Fiona hesitated. "Why don't you check in? They're still serving tea in the garden, and we can talk." As they climbed the porch stairs, she said to Dominick in a low voice, "Did Rosa give you the message?"

"That you didn't find Coral in Taos? Yeah, she told me."

"And that your wife has—uh, gone to Mexico?"

"So I heard." He made no reference to the "power mower." "But I want to talk to the neighbors."

As soon as the men had taken their bags to their room and Rosa had called the most expensive accommodation in Santa Fe, the Inn of the Kachinas, they sat down at a black metal table surrounded by pots of hibiscus and wild roses. Fiona waited until they had been brought tea and a plate of churros, then unfolded the note and laid it in the middle of the table, centering it on a black iron rose. Each of them leaned over and read it in turn, then looked back at Fiona. No one touched the paper.

"Is this like Clue?" Greg asked finally.

"It was smuggled to me when I left the Day Star offices this morning." Fiona told them about the receptionist, how she'd gone back as soon as she'd read the note, and found the woman had already left. "All I know is that her first name's Priss. I looked on the Day Star website—sometimes they introduce their personnel with their photos—but nothing. It was just about making reservations for the airline."

"She'll probably be there tomorrow," Rosa said. "How did you make out last night?"

"Oh, right." She told them about dinner with Will Dunlea. "I tried pushing him a little—and he offered me a free flight home! I should have known you don't try to buy people off if you've got nothing to hide. I thought he was just being nice."

"You got a free trip too?" Greg looked put out.

Fiona reached for her cup but didn't pick it up. The air around them was so fragrant, the dappled sunlight so glorious, that for a moment she forgot Lee and why they were here. Then it came crashing back. But why would he send her a text telling her to go home, and nothing else? There was probably a way to find out where the message was sent from. She turned to Greg. "You know computers. How can I find out where somebody sent me a text from?"

"You mean what transmitting tower the phone used?" He shook his head. "If that's what you want, you're shit out of luck, honey. Only the cell company knows and you'd need a subpoena to find out."

"Damn." Then she noticed that Dominick was sitting with his face in his hands, fingers over his eyes. "Hey, are you okay?"

He straightened up and gave her a bleak look. "That note makes it sound like something did happen. Why do you think someone who works for the airline would give it to you?"

"I think she felt sorry for me. I told her about Lee and being an orphan, and it made her tear up. Maybe she secretly hates working there."

"But if something happened to the plane, they couldn't keep it a secret."

"Why not?"

Dominick looked as if she had suggested robbing the mint. "Because people have to obey the law in this country! There are rules for airlines."

"You have a lot of faith in the system."

He pushed back in his chair, scraping metal on slate as if to reiterate his position. "You don't?"

"Not that much. Remember Enron?"

They smiled at each other uneasily.

" 'It happened between Taos and Denver,' " Rosa said somberly. "We'll talk to her first thing tomorrow morning."

"But why aren't people from other places out here looking for missing passengers?"

"Who says they're not?" Greg took a churro from the plate and stuffed it in his mouth, staining his lips with powdered sugar. Fiona looked away. "Say you have thirty people on the Taos shuttle going to Denver. Of those, five are flying on to San Diego, maybe two more to Seattle. Three to St. Louis, four to Long Island. And so on."

"Five to Long Island. That's what I'm talking about. I want to know where the people from Seattle are."

"Maybe you just haven't seen them," said Rosa. She had a black cigarette holder out and was about to light up. "The airline is hardly going to tell *you*."

"When I asked Will Dunlea, he said no."

"I rest my case."

"Yeah, why do you believe everything this guy tells you?" Greg asked in a demanding tone. "He's the enemy."

"But we know the problem isn't with the plane," said Dominick, spreading his darkly tanned hands on the edge of the table. His normal optimism was back. "It landed safely in Denver. People like Maggie's father arrived okay."

"So what could happen to some people on a plane but not others?" Fiona asked. "Wasn't there that case where a couple from Australia got sucked out of a window? If an outside piece ruptured, and some of the people were pulled out..."

Rosa put her hand to her face in horror. Then she laughed. "And no one in Denver would have noticed a hole in the side of the plane when it landed? Passengers would have been on their phones before the wheels hit the ground."

"That's true. But sometimes there are fires on board. That Canadian songwriter died in one."

"It's the same thing, Fiona," Dominick said. "You can't keep something like that quiet."

"So what could it be? Anyway, we should call Maggie and see if her father's gotten there or if she's heard anything else. He's the one who can tell us what really happened." She reached down into her bag, her fingers closing over her phone.

She scanned her own texts first. There was only one from the magazine editor, wondering when her column on the dangers of beauty would be submitted. *Damn.* Today was the day she was supposed to have it in.

She pushed the number that she had stored for Maggie. It was her landline, given to Fiona by Derek's school.

The phone rang five times before it was picked up. "Sorry," Maggie gasped, "I was saying good-bye to the patterning therapist. Do you want to come over?"

"No, I'm in New Mexico. Did your father get there?"

A hesitation. "Yes. Yes, he did. This afternoon. I'm so glad he's here!"

Fiona covered her phone. "Her father got there." Then she removed her palm and said, "How's he feeling?"

"Oh, you know. The airline even sent an attendant with him, and they arranged for a medi-van from the airport."

"That's great. Did they say what happened exactly?"

"Well, just that he had—what did they call it? 'A minor cerebral accident.'"

Fiona held her breath. "Did he talk about what happened on the plane from Taos?"

There was a long silence across the miles. Then Maggie whispered, "He doesn't remember anything at all. I asked him when he came."

How can that be? "He doesn't even remember being on the plane?"

"Not really. But he's...old, Fiona. I told you how confused he gets. The stroke or whatever it was put everything out of his head."

It wasn't anybody's fault, but Fiona wanted to scream. "Could you ask him again?"

"I'll try in the morning. He'll be fresher then."

"In the morning, okay. We'll call you." Could she suggest that Maggie take her father to a hypnotist? Would Maggie agree? Fiona decided to wait until tomorrow and see what he remembered on his own. She knew she should tell Maggie again how happy she was for her, but she was too upset. "Okay, we'll talk to you tomorrow," she said and ended the call.

Fiona looked into Dominick's expectant brown eyes, then at Rosa, who was moving a gold herringbone chain to the outside of her sweatshirt. "Her father doesn't remember the flight. Our only hope, and he doesn't remember a damn thing!"

She heard Dominick exhale. "But he was on that flight? He was on that flight and he's okay?"

"It looks that way."

He shook his shaggy head. "Then I'm sure Coral wasn't. It's my wife playing games."

Greg pushed back from the table, tipping it slightly. The others reached out to save the china. "Whoops. I'm going up to find Dimitri."

"Wait!" Fiona said, as an idea she had had earlier took shape. "What time will you be back?"

He shrugged, surprised. "I kind of thought we'd go our separate ways when we got out here."

"I just thought you might want to go somewhere."

His expression morphed into pleasure. "You have anything special in mind?"

She smiled at him. "Maybe. About seven thirty?"

"Seven thirty? Why so early?"

"We're still on Eastern time. I'll meet you on the porch."

"You've got it." Greg gave Dominick a wink that any of them could read as *Don't wait up for me.*

But when he demanded the keys to the Explorer, Dominick shook his head. "I have to go up to Taos tonight."

"You can use my rental car," Fiona told Dominick. She was not sure of the legality of that, but he was probably a careful driver. She would not have offered it to Greg.

"You're sure?"

"I'm not going anywhere. There's even a street map of Taos. I'll show you where the house is."

"Stop in front so you can drop me at the Inn," Rosa ordered Greg. "My bags are still in the back."

Fiona smiled at her. "I'm so glad you're here."

"Well, I have my own selfish motives." She smiled back but looked weary, older than Fiona had first thought. "Publishing is a different world these days. They make me feel like a relic. If I can show them with Susan that I'm still in the game…" Then she added briskly, "Besides, I haven't been anywhere interesting since my husband died. I can't stand those tours that cater to old people. Anyway, this will make a fascinating story—however it turns out."

Fiona wasn't ready to admit she was in the middle of a story. She told them what she had planned for that evening with Greg.

Chapter Twenty

ALTHOUGH IT HAD been three years since he had been to the farm, Greg found Trucas easily. That movie, *The Milagro Beanfield War*, had been shot there, and the town still looked better thirty years later. Mr. Alvarez had refused to cooperate with the film guys. Stubborn old bastard, yelling at people to stay off his land when they were offering him cold hard cash.

Greg still smarted when he thought of his conversation with Mr. Alvarez on Sunday night after he left the airport. Dimitri had not answered any of his texts, and the farm was the only other phone number he had.

"Hello, Mr. Alvarez? This is Greg Sanderson."

"Sí."

See what? "Remember me, from New York? Dimitri and I were going climbing in Maine; he was flying here to meet me. But he didn't come."

Silence.

"So I wondered what the story was. Is he there?"

"Here? He don't live here."

"I know that. But you must have heard from him." *Keep it cool. Why were these people so stupid?*

"His mother see him last Thursday." The voice sounded unwilling to tell him even that. "He come by to pick up his gunnysack."

Backpack, Greg translated. Mr. Alvarez had been over the border for thirty years but had never bothered to learn his verb tenses or the American names for things. He tried to play dumb, a simple peasant, but Greg was sure it was an act. Dimitri's mother, emigrated from Russia as a young adult, spoke perfect, careful English.

"Did he say anything to her about his plans?"

"That boy don't make plans. He say yes, yes, I go, then he decide to do something different."

"What kind of something different?" It was Greg's worst fear, that Dimitri would steal the program and cut him out. "You think he got a better offer?"

"Bitter offer?"

Bitter would be exactly right if Dimi did that. And what proof did Greg have, other than the money he had sent him every month? Dimitri promised him that they were nearly there, but refused to let Greg see the program.

"That boy, he don't know what he wants."

"He didn't, like, say anything about going out to California?" Greg had felt the drops of perspiration on his forehead swell and join forces; it was the effort of trying to be civil.

"To California? To maybe be a movie star?" The old man thought that was funny.

"Look, if he stops by, tell him to call me immediately. Greg Sanderson. I'm at my apartment."

"*Si, señor.*" It was definitely mocking.

Sí. GREG REASSURED himself again that if Dimitri stopped by for his backpack, it meant he was headed for Maine, not Silicon Valley. He drove past fields of rolled hay bales basking in the late-day sun and thought again how amazing it was, living in a town where the library hours were painted on the building (Tuesday and Thursday 1:00 p.m.–5:00 p.m.), Dimitri had heard of MIT, applied after some prodding from his math teacher, and ended up with a full scholarship. A perfect score on his math SATs and about 250 on the verbal, but someone in Massachusetts had been tickled at the idea of a Russian-Hispanic chili pepper on campus.

Greg picked out the tin roofs of the ranch buildings ahead, the pens that housed a few chickens and goats, and then brought the SUV to a surprised screech along the gravel. Fifty yards ahead of him, loading bricks into the back of a pickup, was the unmistakable dark head of Dimitri. Shit! This guy was becoming a world-class loser. Not even to have the fucking courtesy to call.

He slipped the truck into first gear and let it crawl along the side of the road, narrowly missing a ditch. Dimitri's back was still to him. At least he wasn't in Silicon Valley, spilling his guts. Probably something had gone wrong with the program and he couldn't face Greg.

When he got close, he stopped the Explorer and gave a long, rude beep. Dimitri spun around, dark face stormy, then walked deliberately toward him and around to the driver's side. Greg was forming the words "I want my money back, asshole" when he realized who it was. What was the kid brother's name anyway? Ivor? Ivan.

Greg rolled down his window, jerking back to avoid the dust in the air. "Hey. Remember me?"

Ivan grinned at him. "Sure, man. From three years ago? From New York?"

"You've got a memory like your brother. You working here now?"

"Yeah. I don't got the smarts Dimi had." He wiped at his forehead with a muddy palm, streaking it sienna. "Maybe I'll come out better though."

"How's that?"

"*You* know."

After a brilliant career at MIT, Dimitri had been accepted to every graduate program to which he applied. Shockingly, he had washed out of all of them, drifting back to the farm between acts. It wasn't his fault, he protested; he was put in bogus courses and given advisors who hated his dark skin. As a TA, he was given all the shit work. Dimitri could talk all night about what had gone wrong in his life, and he was pretty damn convincing.

"Is he around?"

Ivan shook his head. "Haven't seen him in a couple weeks. He'll turn up though; he crawls home like a wounded coyote. That's what my father always says."

"So, where is he? I came all the way from New York. He's not around?"

Ivan squinted. "He, like, knew you were coming?"

"No. He was supposed to fly out Sunday and meet me to go climbing in Maine." *And bring me the data-compression program he was writing, a program that didn't eat memory and would make us millions.* He believed in Dimitri so much that in the past few months he had sent him over sixteen hundred dollars so he could keep at it. "But he never showed."

"No? And you came all the way out here to find him?"

"Not exactly." He didn't like the way that sounded, as if he cared too much. But would Dimitri have told this kid what he had discovered? "So where's your brother living? Where does he keep his computer?"

Ivan pushed at his lip with a grimy finger and shook his head. "I don't know, man."

Give me a break. "You don't know where your brother lives? For real?"

"Naw. We just see him when he stops by."

"You don't know where he keeps his stuff?"

"Wherever he's living, I guess."

This was going nowhere. Of course he knew his brother's address. Had he told Ivan not to give it out to anyone? It was ridiculous that Greg himself didn't know it. On the rare occasions when he had to use snail mail, he had sent it to a Santa Fe post-office box. "Maybe I'll go say hi to your folks." They had to know where their son lived.

But Ivan frowned, giving his dark head an animal shake. "You don't want to do that, man."

"No?"

"My old man's kinda pissed at Dimi right now. Dimi won't work regular, he won't get married, he just drifts around taking people rock climbing and doing computer stuff. My father thinks you gave him bad ideas." He licked the sweat from his upper lip. "Not just you, man, all those guys."

"How about a girlfriend? Or his friends. He got friends in Santa Fe?" Surely the guys he hung out with knew where he lived. And once he had the address, even if Dimitri wasn't there, there wasn't a computer he couldn't get into. And there had to be a backup. Even if Dimitri didn't trust the Cloud, he would have kept it on an external drive and in his own machine. Tomorrow he would go to the post office and get his street address. Or why not go to the phone company? Even if they billed him over the Internet, they had to have his address.

Hell, it might even be better if Dimitri was no longer around.

He quashed that thought. They would need each other to get it up and running, to market it right. Besides, Dimi was his friend.

"My brother don't tell me nothing." But Ivan's face brightened. "But he's gonna buy me a truck, a Ram Big Horn. *Loaded*. And send my mother back home for a visit. My father won't go."

That was good news. "Look, as soon as he shows up, tell him to call me. Greg Sanderson?"

And don't forget to make something of yourself.

Chapter Twenty-One

SANTA FE WAS approaching the magical hour when its buildings glowed like a storybook village, the rose-orange light splashing them with gold. Sitting on the porch, Fiona forced herself to enjoy it. Lee would have made it something extraordinary. Was he somewhere right now, taking beautiful photographs? But that thought was horrible. It made her think of those condolence cards for dead pets showing them peacefully on the other far side of the "Rainbow Bridge."

She wished Greg would get here.

Finally, a little after eight, the Explorer pulled into the parking area, and Fiona jumped up. She debated leaving her leather bag in her room. It might be a hindrance to what she planned to do. Yet having it with her made her feel secure, so she adjusted the strap over her shoulder and went to meet Greg.

As they passed The Old West restaurant, a scent of grilling beef wafted out and grabbed at her stomach. After the tea and pastries she hadn't felt hungry, but now she wished she had eaten for energy. Street food...but the stands they passed were shuttered.

Even the one that sold the frozen mocha drink known as Adobe Mud had its striped canvas covers lashed down.

They crossed to Paseo de Peralta, and Greg turned on her. "We're getting out of town! There's nothing going down around here." Before leaving, he had insisted on going back to his room and changing into a blue-and-white-striped polo shirt and a pair of white duck pants that she would not have imagined him owning. He was darkly handsome, his ponytail pulled back, but she preferred Lee's soft light hair.

"It's a quiet place. But special," Fiona said.

"Good. I'm parched."

As they came into the block where the Day Star offices were located, Fiona paused.

Greg looked across the street to where she was looking. "You brought me here? But it's closed."

"That's the point."

"Aww, *no*." He put his hand on her shoulder as if to force her to keep moving. "You said we were going for brewskis."

"We will. This won't take long. But Will Dunlea has the passenger list on his computer! Once we have that, we can check on the other passengers and go to the police."

"Help me with this. You think he's going to save something that incriminates his airline?"

"He doesn't expect anyone else to see it." She started to cross the street to the front of the building. "The receptionist said something about agents working late in the back of the building. Let's go around."

But Greg wasn't moving. "Wait a minute. You plan to break into his computer?"

"If we can."

"How?"

"You know about computers, don't you?"

"I meant how are we going to get to it?"

"I have a plan, sort of." She started across the street and he followed her, shaking his head. As they passed the front window, Fiona saw the receptionist's desk standing empty in the dim lobby. The whole building seemed dark, but in the back parking lot were two cars, both compacts, one crimson and one white. *Snow White and Rose Red.*

Two cars, but there could be other people who had walked there. The solar path lights that were set around the back door had not yet turned on. Their metal gleamed dully from beds of miniature evergreens.

Fiona hesitated. If the door was unlocked and opened onto a hallway, they might be able to sneak past. If the door opened right into the room where the agents were working, she would bring out the voucher from Will and say she had a question about it. And that would be that.

She could feel Greg pressing close to her as she tried the knob. It turned easily, and the carved wooden door swung away from them. Moving around it, Fiona saw that the first room on the left was lit up, but the door was only slightly ajar; there was no way to avoid walking past that room, but there was a chance they could do it. A phone chimed inside and stopped after the first ring.

Clutching Greg's wrist, she moved silently past the room without looking inside.

Nothing happened. Perhaps they were assumed to be security staff or cleaners or had not been noticed at all. But every moment, Fiona expected lights to flash on and someone to come running after them. Weren't there things called silent alarms? Maybe even now a switchboard somewhere was coming alive.

When they reached Will's office, she had the irrational idea that he would be seated behind his beautiful walnut desk, blood oozing from a bullet to his chest, blond head looking down at nothing. All those years of watching *NYPD Blue* . . .

Her heart thwacking hard, she stepped into the office. Although it was not dark outside yet, the narrow blinds had been pulled down over the windows, turning the furniture into dim shapes.

"Don't turn on the light," Greg said hotly against her neck. She heard the click as he closed the door completely.

"But to turn on the computer…" she whispered back.

"Businesses don't shut their mainframes off when people are still working on them. There'll be enough light from the screen when we activate it." Grasping her shoulders, he moved her around to the dark bulk of the desk. As her eyes adjusted, Fiona saw a small line of light glowing at the bottom of the blinds.

Greg settled himself in Will Dunlea's chair, leaving Fiona no choice but to kneel on the carpet by his feet. She watched as he clicked in commands. He was frowning, trying various keys, completely intent on what he was doing. There was a beauty in seeing someone so rapt, so given over to the moment, but she was too anxious to appreciate it. The closed door would give them a minute to crouch behind the desk if someone started to open it, but it meant that she could not hear anyone coming on the soft carpet outside.

After ten minutes Greg slumped back in the leather chair and shook his head. "I'm not coming up with any passenger lists."

Her heart dropped. It *had* to be on there. "Isn't there anything about the flight? Try rosters. I think they call them rosters."

"Yeah?"

"No, maybe manifests. Try manifests!"

He went back to the machine. With the air conditioning on, the room felt cold. Fiona pressed her palm against a yawn. It was exhausting keeping alert, straining to hear the whisper of a sound. If Will came by to pick something up, they would have no excuse at all. She turned her wrist to stare at her watch by computer light. Already 8:35 p.m.! A black fear seized her that the agents would switch the system off for the night any minute now and get ready to leave. Perhaps she and Greg would be locked in. Passenger list or not, they had to be out of the building before nine.

"Do you need a password?" Fiona whispered.

"Naw, it's a matter of knowing what file name they use. I've gotten this far and that's it."

"Try Lee! Lee Pienaar." Frantically she spelled the name for Greg.

"What kind of a name is that?" But he was already at work. "Okay. Got him. But this one lives in Brooklyn."

"That's him! Was he on the Sunday morning flight?"

He turned to her. "Says so here. In Wednesday and out Sunday."

"Really? That bastard! Will Dunlea. He sat right in that chair and said there was nothing about Sunday. He made me think Lee was just trying to avoid me." She wanted to reach up and rip the model plane from over Will's desk. Good news and bad news. Lee had not disappeared somewhere with Sarah instead of flying home, but he was still missing. And what did that text message with no follow-up mean?

"If I can get this to sort, I can pick out the other people on the flight. I *do* know this program." He returned to pressing keys.

Fiona chewed on her lip. Why did everything take so long?

"Okay. Got it." He raised one fist in triumph and turned the screen toward her. She stood up and crowded in over his shoulder to see.

The search bar read "Select Flight 101 August 23."

She fumbled frantically in her bag. "I have to start copying down names!"

"No, just give me a flash drive."

Damn. She did have one with her, two in fact, but they were back in her room with her laptop. She had not thought beyond looking at the list and seeing if their passengers' names were on it, but now it seemed important to have a copy. "I didn't bring one."

"Oh, God. Okay, open that slatted closet door and switch on the printer inside."

"Oh." She didn't ask how he knew the machine was in there.

Relying on touch, she pressed a button in the upper left. The printer started up with a hum, and she shoved the door shut, terrified that it would make too much noise. But except for a rising whir, oddly like the sound of a jet accelerating, the laser printer ran quietly and fast.

"Grab it, and let's get the fuck out of here," Greg whispered. "Breaking into someone's database could screw up my whole career!"

Fiona snatched the paper from the tray as Greg did some last thing to the computer. Then she opened the door very slowly.

The sound of voices made her lurch back. "Hide!" She pressed herself against the wall behind the door. Greg disappeared behind the desk.

The door was ajar now, and she could hear a man's voice, though not what he was saying. Then the door was pushed back, the doorknob pressing into her stomach, and a higher voice protested audibly, "But I didn't see anyone come in."

"They must have. I saw them go around to the back."

"Who are they, anyway?"

Instead of answering, he yanked the door shut.

Fiona couldn't get her breath. Either someone had been in a front office after all, or they were being followed. But why wouldn't they be? Will knew where she was staying; they had her car information from the rental company. While she wasn't paying attention, a net had dropped down over her.

"Give them a minute. What time is it?" Greg said very low.

"I can't—" She twisted her watch around to try to see the dial. "Almost nine!"

"Okay. Two more minutes and then we *run*."

Fiona folded the paper in quarters and stuck it firmly in the top of her purse.

"Come on." Greg stood up from behind the desk and moved silently to the door. She followed him into the hall, noticing that it was lit by a series of round lights at ankle height. She hadn't seen them before.

They reached the bend to the left that led straight to the back door.

"Now," Greg said, and they raced past ghostly photographs of the airline's history, past the lighted room, and into the parking lot. They stopped outside only to take a breath, then ran again along the path, stopping finally on Paseo de Peralta.

Fiona barely glanced at the car sitting opposite the Day Star entrance.

Chapter Twenty-Two

THEY STOPPED FOR fajitas and beer in a bar on Guadeloupe Street, Cactus Joe's. The long narrow room was packed with a summer crowd, but they managed to find a table against a mural of cowboy rabbits and pink coyotes wearing bandanas. It was also across from the kitchen.

"Jesus, it's brutal in here," Greg complained, pulling his striped shirt collar away from his neck.

"I know. That's why there were no tables outside."

Jammed against the wall, Fiona wondered how two large plates would fit on the tiny circle of tile. She was finally hungry and gratefully gulped the beer from a clear plastic cup. Then she looked back down at the list that was taking up the table space. The names had a terrible finality.

Greg stared at the page along with her:

(Allmayer, Susan)   454 Margarita Way, Santa Fe, NM
Alvarez, Dimitri   RR 3, Truchas, NM

Basilea, Coral, 12	15-02 Valverde, Taos, NM
Bellows, Kirsten Anne, 10	14 Albion Way, Santa Fe, NM
Black Hook, Clayton	Taos Pueblo, NM
Boehngarm, Dieter, 7	Venterstrausse 17, Bad Kreuznach, GER
Boehngarm, Gretchen	Venterstrausse 17, Bad Kreuznach, GER
Boehngarm, Petra, 3	Venterstrausse 17, Bad Kreuznach, GER
Boehngarm, Thomas	Venterstrausse 17, Bad Kreuznach, GER
Circanis, George	11 Bluebell Drive, Denver, CO
Curley, Johanna	1603 High Street, Newton, MA
Fuller, George (F.O.)	Mountain Trail, Taos, NM
Jones, Karleen (F.A.)	P.O. Box AB 121, Aspen, CO
Madden, Ralph (F.O.)	15 Old Santa Fe Trail, Albuquerque, NM
Marshall, Eleanor P.	3 Magnolia Street, Seattle, WA
Marshall, Ralph K.	3 Magnolia Street, Seattle, WA
Martinez, Victor	RR 1, Chimayo, NM
O'Malley, Francis J.	Leisure Village Way, Santa Fe, NM
Pienaar, Lee	137 Joralemon Street, Brooklyn, NY
Pittare, Alfonzo	57-13 17th Avenue, Apt. 3, Newark, NJ
Redhawk, Jackson (F.A.)	Taos Pueblo, NM
Seelander, Martin	University of Cincinnati, Cincinnati, OH
Washington, Kwani	RFD #2, Trussville, AL

"It's like—" But she could not say it aloud. "All those people who had never met before, who had different reasons for being on the plane. Now they're linked together forever."

"Hold your horses, Pedro. It's not like they're *dead*." Greg finished his beer, glanced at Fiona's cup, and waved two fingers at a passing waitress.

"We don't know that. Which one's your friend?"

Greg pointed to the second name. *Alvarez, Dimitri.*

"Francis J. O'Malley is probably Maggie's father. I know he's from Santa Fe. It's true, he didn't die…"

Then, amazingly, the reason why presented itself to her. She reached out and grabbed Greg's wrist. "You know what? Maybe the thing that 'happened' in the note was that terrorists took the plane hostage and no one is supposed to know!" Everything fell into place. "That would explain why Maggie's father was released. He's old and ill. The government is probably negotiating with the terrorists right now! They forced the plane to land somewhere, took some hostages off, then let the plane fly on to Denver. That's why they were late." She sat back, stunned.

"Terrorists?"

"Day Star can't let anyone know; it's the same as in a kidnapping when they warn people not to call the police." She looked into his dark brown eyes, willing him to believe.

But he pulled at an eyebrow skeptically. "What do these terrorists want?"

"I don't know—money, safe passage somewhere, the release of political prisoners from jail. What do terrorists usually want?"

"Publicity." He took a sip of the beer that had appeared on their table and wiped at his mouth, satisfied. "Groups like that always claim responsibility."

"This one didn't." She clung to the idea of the passengers being safe somewhere, being released gradually with a cover story. Why hadn't she thought of this in New York? "You know the government does all kinds of covert things."

"Then we're better off not interfering with negotiations."

Was he serious? "But everything fits!"

Greg handed her the list as plates of fajitas and sides of guaca-mole, black beans, and sour cream were crowded onto the table. Fiona refolded the paper in quarters and put it in her bag.

He tore into a fajita without speaking and then said, "Okay. So we give them fifteen billion dollars and the Empire State Building and people will come tumbling back. Not to burst your bubble or anything, but why would terrorists pick a no-name airline that flies in the middle of nowhere and expect to get anything out of it? And pledge them to secrecy instead of just making the federal government pay up?"

She dipped a chunk of chicken in the sour cream. "But that's just it. You couldn't keep it a secret if a 747 disappeared. But these are still American citizens, and the government will quietly save them."

"I thought we didn't negotiate with terrorists."

"That's why it has to be a secret." Fiona's hand brushed her cup and she righted it quickly. "I've got to tell the others!"

"Finish your food."

"I'm done."

She stood up, feeling in her bag for her wallet to pay.

Greg stood up too. "Hey, wait a minute. I'm still eating. " He put his arm around her, squeezing her shoulder blade painfully. "Besides, I thought we were going to howl!"

You think we're coyotes? But his mouth was already on hers, beery and warm, his hand massaging her back through her T-shirt.

She pulled back. "Greg, stop!"

"This is the reward for all my hard work?" But he moved away from her so quickly that she realized he had been doing what he thought a man in his position would. It was a persona he had adapted, a shorthand for dealing with the world.

She knew about personas.

"I've got to tell Rosa," she said urgently. "You can keep eating; I'll be back in a minute."

He sat down, eyeing her half-eaten food.

"You can finish it. I'm done."

Chapter Twenty-Three

THE INN OF the Kachinas was impressive. Just inside the carved wooden doors stood a cactus taller than Fiona. The largest copper pot she had ever seen was crammed with dried flowers and placed on a coffee table. The kiva fireplace was also oversized, large enough for a couple to dance in. The inn reminded her of a resort she once visited in Brazil.

Fiona moved to the reception desk. "I'm looking for a guest who's staying here. Rosa Cooper?"

"In there, I believe." The clerk smiled and pointed to the lounge.

"Really? Thanks."

Rosa was sitting at a tall table, a book open in front of her on the ruby cloth. She was wearing a deep blue dress smocked with an Indian design, a beaded sweatband pinning down her mottled hair. "Hi, there!" She seemed delighted to see Fiona. "Date over already?"

"We've got the list of passengers!" She found herself suddenly as breathless as if she'd run all the way.

"You're a wonder." She returned Alice Munro to her Guatemalan bag. "They've got piña coladas here to die for. Let me order you one." She waved to the waiter.

Fiona sat down on the stool across from Rosa. "Lee was on the plane. So were Susan and Dominick's daughter. Everybody who's missing!"

"Imagine that." She gave the waiter the order for two more drinks. "And they've got a fabulous piano player. He just went on break."

"Rosa, are you listening?"

"Of course I'm listening." She gave Fiona an irritated look. "But how is that different from what we knew?"

"It's tangible proof! We can take it to the police. And it shows that Day Star was lying to me. Why would they lie if nothing happened?" Reaching into her shoulder bag, she pulled out the paper and held it out to Rosa.

Rosa took it and held it far away from her. Then she laid it back on the table. "Why is Susan's name in parenthesis?"

"I don't know. Maybe she was flying standby?"

"Is Maggie's father on this list?"

"He's Francis O'Malley."

Rosa gave an emphatic and slightly tipsy nod. "We'll see what the police have to say about this."

"I think I know what happened." Quickly Fiona explained her theory about the terrorists. "The local police may have been told not to interfere."

"Terrorists!" Rosa reached over and clasped Fiona's arm. "I like it. That's why none of them could communicate with us."

She paused as the waiter set down two drinks on the table. Fiona stared at them. Like everything else in the hotel, they were huge.

"But I was thinking that we could call the people on the list—their homes—to see if they'd been released yet. If they were, they could tell us what really happened, what the government is doing."

"If they haven't been sworn to secrecy." Rosa was slurring her words.

"Good evening, ladies." A darkly tanned man in a pale yellow dinner jacket smiled as he passed their table.

"That's him," Rosa whispered and followed the man greedily with her eyes.

Fiona watched him approach a grand piano on a platform, surrounded by tall, rush-seated stools. Before he was fully on the piano bench, he had launched into "Someone to Watch Over Me."

Fiona did not recognize the next song, but Rosa closed her eyes and began to sing along, first softly, then gaining volume. To Fiona's surprise she had a beautiful, plaintive voice. "My buddy," she sang, "my buddy, your buddy misses you."

Was she thinking about her husband?

It was too much. It struck a match, illuminating all the sad relationships of Fiona's life that no longer existed. She thought of the best moments she and Lee had had together—sharing Chinese food in his apartment, parodying a silly movie, lying curled up in bed doing nothing at all. Would she ever see him again? Pushing up from the table, she fled to the restroom, feeling sick to her stomach. She sat in a stall, hands over her face, and tried to calm herself.

Remember that the terrorists are keeping Lee incommunicado, but safe. Don't think of the way those situations too often end.

ROSA WAS NO longer at the table. Fiona wondered if she been more upset than she had shown, or simply gotten tired and gone to bed without saying good night. Then, turning in the direction of the piano, she saw Rosa sitting to the pianist's right. A few other people had joined them, taking the empty stools and balancing their drinks on the piano top. They were singing "On the Sunny Side of the Street."

Fiona sat back down at the table. She wasn't a singer. She would finish her piña colada and go. Twisting around, she smiled reassuringly at Rosa, though her friend hardly seemed to need cheering up. How many of those coconut confections had she consumed? Fiona turned back to the empty red tablecloth. The list! Where was the list? She had left it in the middle of the table between them and now it was gone. Had the waiter taken it away by mistake? She had run off, Rosa had abandoned the table to wax nostalgic, and perhaps the waiter thought they were finished.

But no. He had left her own half-finished drink; Rosa's woven purse was leaning against one chair leg. Slipping off her stool, Fiona peered down into Rosa's bag. With great relief, she saw a white paper folded in quarters. Thank God!

Her pulsing heart slowed. She picked up the paper and, without unfolding it, stuffed it into her own bag. Then she sat back down, wondering at her flash of panic. Sneaking around Day Star and the shock of seeing the names on the list had pushed her close to the edge. That and the man's voice from the hall confirming that they had been seen.

It was past time to go. She went over to the piano and said good night to Rosa, thanking her for the drink, and made her way dizzily back through the lobby. What she needed was a copy machine, though she could photograph the list with her phone back in her room.

Halfway to her inn she remembered Greg, sitting at the table waiting for her. She had promised to come back. But it was so late already....All she wanted to do was collapse on her bed and sleep.

The bed and breakfast was still floodlit when she made her way unsteadily up the steps. She never drank this much when she was with Lee or traveling by herself, but people had kept buying her drinks. *Poor baby.* Moving down the long hall, Fiona let herself into her room and tossed her bag on her bed. The evening had cooled down nicely, and she unlocked the patio doors, opening them wide for some fresh air. She was too well trained not to wash her face and brush her teeth, so she picked up her travel kit from the dresser and headed for the shared bathroom across the hall.

When she came back, she locked the patio doors firmly and fell into bed.

Chapter Twenty-Four

FIONA WOKE THE next morning with an insistent throbbing at the back of her neck. Her first thoughts were of the German couple on the flight list and their two young children. Innocent tourists visiting America, caught up in a terrorist web. Lying under her sheet in the cool mountain air, she thought about the family. Where were they now?

Wondering if the parents were already back at work was an unwelcome reminder that she had to get to her dangerous beauty piece finished. It had been due yesterday. Could she push the deadline up to Monday? That left only today to find out as much as she could here, fly home Saturday, and pull it together Sunday. At least with the list, they could contact the other passengers. And surely Maggie's father would remember more this morning.

Glancing at the digital clock that came with the room, Fiona saw that she had only fifteen minutes before meeting the others for breakfast. If she showered quickly she could make it. Rummaging through her travel bag, she pulled out her jeans and a gold

T-shirt. Then, armed with the courtesy bar of soap and a rather threadbare towel, she opened the door.

She could immediately see that the shower was in use, and even the door to the toilet was closed. Rosa was right. The downside of authentic accommodations was their inconvenience. Deciding to give it another five minutes, she moved back into the room. Time to photograph the list. Her purse was still perched on the side of the bed she had not slept in, near the French doors.

Reaching into its leather depths, she came up with her sunglasses. They were smudged and needing a good cleaning, so she left them on the bed. She dipped into the bag again, and this time brought out a crisp square of paper. As she unfolded it, she saw that it was the travel voucher that she had picked up at Day Star. Well, she wouldn't be needing that this morning.

Another dip and she came up with the paper she had taken from Rosa's bag. She unfolded it then stared at it, uncomprehending. Instead of the list, it was Rosa's flight information, which she must have printed out from her computer after making the reservations. Chilled, Fiona dumped the rest of her purse's contents across the white bedspread. Her notebook, a cosmetic bag, wallet, rental car key, phone, five or six pens, tampons, her used boarding pass—and nothing else. Panicked, she put her hand inside her purse and flailed around.

No other papers.

Where was the list? It had to be here. Dropping to her knees, she raised the corner of the spread and looked under the bed, then jumped up and went to her dresser. Except for her deodorant, toothpaste, and a silver hair clip, the polished oak top was bare. She had been groggy last night, but she remembered walking down the hallway of the inn and reaching into her purse to touch the paper again for reassurance.

Except…she had been touching the wrong piece of paper.

Don't panic. Knowing how important it was, Rosa had probably stuffed it down further inside her bag or even taken it with her to the piano.

But Fiona knew she would not be able to eat anything, would not be able to think about anything, until she knew for sure.

Reaching for her phone on the bed, she found Rosa's cell number and punched it in.

"Fiona? Good morning! Want to have breakfast?"

"Thanks, but I'm meeting the guys. Do you have the list of passengers?" She closed her eyes. *Please, please, please.*

Rosa seemed to be thinking. "I overdid it a little last night, I was just so happy to be somewhere congenial. But let's see. The last I noticed, it was on the table where you showed it to me. When I didn't see it later, I thought you had taken it with you."

"No."

"But it has to be around. Why would anyone take it? I left my purse at the table, and it was fine."

Fiona could not think of anything to say that didn't sound paranoid. "Could the waiter have picked it up? Can you ask him?"

"I can try. I haven't seen him this morning, but I don't know if I'd know him if I did. I'll ask around, though. I'm coming over; I want to take the Explorer to Susan's."

"If you find the list, call me!"

Fiona was too upset to shower now. Dressing rapidly, she created another scenario. She had had more to drink than usual; she must have picked up the list from the table automatically and stuffed it in her bag. Perhaps Greg had come into her room last night when she was in the bathroom and taken it to show Dominick. He was like that: personal boundaries meant little. She remembered how he had simply announced that he would share Dominick's room.

It could not have simply disappeared.

When she came into the breakfast room, Greg and Dominick were already at a table, bending over compotes of bananas and vanilla yogurt. A pile of orange-blossom muffins waited in a basket between them.

Fiona pulled out the chair on Greg's right, breathless. "Did you take the list last night?"

"The list? The passenger list? You took it to show Rosa, remember?"

"No, I mean after that. You didn't come in my room last night and take it?"

He looked at her. "You think I'd just barge into your room and take something?"

Dominick chuckled.

"You never came back to the bar either. I was waiting for you!"

She slumped against the yellow ladder-back chair. "I can't find the list anywhere. Rosa doesn't have it, you don't have it." She recognized the panic in her voice.

"Well, someone has to." Dominick was using that voice meant to calm a child again. "We'll look for it after breakfast."

"Where? I've looked everywhere it could be. I'm sure it was in my purse when I went to bed."

"Do you sleepwalk or anything?" Greg asked.

"What?"

"Maybe you ate it in a dream by mistake."

She stared at him until he shrugged.

"Good morning!" A young woman Fiona had never seen before set the banana-yogurt cup in front of her with a flourish. "Care for a Mexican omelet this morning?"

"*No.*"

"Get this girl some black coffee," Greg said genially. "Set it down on the table and back away slowly."

"She's upset about something," Dominick said apologetically. *Stop being my father.*

Why weren't they as upset as she was? "You don't understand," she said slowly. "I either left the list on the table last night when I was with Rosa, or I took it from her purse and brought it to my room, where someone took it. Either way, it's gone. And Will Dunlea knew I was staying here." She had a sudden memory of leaving the French doors open when she went to wash.

Dominick was shaking his head good-humoredly. "I don't know, Fiona. From a plane disaster the authorities say never happened to people following you and breaking into your room, you've got some imagination. Greg was telling me that you think it could be a hostage situation."

"I think it could. It's the only thing that fits. Homeland Security could be the ones watching us." She didn't know if that would make her feel better or worse.

The young blonde woman cautiously set a cup of coffee near her elbow. Fiona muttered, "Thanks."

Then she thought of something else. Frantically she reached into her purse and brought out a pen and her used boarding pass. "We've got to write down the names and addresses of everyone we can remember!"

"I know Dimitri's."

God save me from idiots. "Not the addresses of people we know, the names of people we don't know. There was that professor from the University of Cincinnati, Sealand, or something like that." She turned the pass over and scribbled the name down.

Greg finally understood. "There was some dude with an African name from Alabama."

"You don't remember his name?"

"Why should I?"

"That family from Germany, I couldn't even pronounce their name."

"A couple of guys from the rez."

"Right!" She gave him an approving look. "I wondered about that. One last name was Black Arrow or something like that." She wrote it down. "And one of them was a flight attendant; there was an F. A. after his name. The pilot and the copilot had F. O."

Dominick, who was rubbing his chin as he listened to them, said, "Can't we just get another list?"

Greg pantomimed choking on his muffin.

"Not in this lifetime," Fiona said. "They'll really be on guard now."

"Assuming they even know you took it." Dominick didn't hide his skepticism.

"Oh, they know. They know exactly why we're here. Who else would be following us? They even sent me a text Wednesday night that was supposed to be from Lee. That means they have his phone."

Both men stared at her.

"Didn't I tell you? After I had dinner with Will Dunlea, I came back and my phone dinged with a text. It said something like, 'Don't worry about me. Go home and I'll explain everything later.' But I know it wasn't from him."

"Wait a minute." Dominick looked ready to shake her. "He sent you a text Wednesday night? From his phone?"

"It was from his phone, but it wasn't from him. I'm sure of that. When I called right back, he didn't pick up and talk to me. And it wasn't…personal. He always writes something at the end like 'Love ya' or some joke that only we would get. Okay, maybe he wouldn't make a joke now. Except"—she thought of something else—"if he was being held hostage, maybe that's all they'd let him write!"

One more piece that fit. "And to think, I was about to go home. Thank God the receptionist gave me that note!"

Dominick shook his head. "You're pinning too much on that note."

"No, I'm not. As soon as the office opens, I'm going to talk to her."

"I'll go with you. I want to see if Coral really was on the plane— which I doubt. Then I have to go to Taos and find a way to get in touch with Eve. We'll search your room after breakfast for that list," he said. "If it's that important, we'll find it."

Fiona reached for her coffee cup, not bothering to challenge his logic.

The Mexican omelet was filled with ham, jack cheese, onions, and jalapeño peppers. She watched silently as the others ate.

"You ought to get one," Greg told her. "It's free."

He was right. Why starve herself to death for being careless? If she ate a big breakfast, she wouldn't have to take time for lunch. She raised her hand and the young woman was there immediately, happy to bring her breakfast after all.

"When you went to the Day Star offices Wednesday, did the people seem upset?" Dominick asked. "Like they were in the middle of a hostage situation?"

Fiona thought about Ginger Lee bursting in with revenue reports and the receptionist joking with Will. "Not really."

"Don't you think if they were in the middle of an emergency, you'd know it? There'd be officials checking you before you even went into the door."

"Maybe. We'll see how they act today. I'm going to make some calls now. To Maggie, of course, and this professor, Sealand. I want to go to Taos too, to find the ones from the reservation."

"I've got things to do in Santa Fe," Greg said mysteriously, mopping up the last of his omelet with a corner of toast. "I'll see you when I see you."

Chapter Twenty-Five

FIONA TRIED MAGGIE several times and let the phone keep ringing in case she was busy with Derek. Maybe she was driving him to one of his programs. But there was never any answer and no machine picked up.

As soon as she hung up, "La Marseillaise" began and she answered quickly without looking. It could be Maggie just reaching the phone, it could be Rosa saying she had found the list. It could be...But it was Will Dunlea.

"Good morning, Fiona," he said cheerfully. "Good day sightseeing yesterday?"

"Yes." Was it time to confront him? "I went to two of the museums. Very interesting."

"Well, good. The Folk Art Museum is spectacular. I just wanted to wish you a safe trip this morning." His voice was warm and she felt herself responding just a little.

"Well, I'm not going back quite yet. My friends came in last night. We thought we'd drive up and take a look at the Pueblo."

"Los Alamos is interesting too. I'm afraid I can't offer you another voucher, though, until we open again on Monday."

"You're closed today?"

"We close on Fridays in the summer. A lot of businesses around here do."

"Even in tourist season?"

"Well, not restaurants or hotels. And we still take reservations and handle cancellations by phone or on the website. So we don't shut down completely. But it's summer vacation for our employees too."

Fiona cast around frantically for a way to ask him Priss's last name. "Listen, I really liked your—"

But he cut her off. "I'm leaving for the mountains in a minute myself. But I'll keep in touch, in case you have any free time…" He clicked off.

She sat there stunned on the side of her unmade bed. *Concentrate. Focus.*

Picking up her laptop, she went to the University of Cincinnati website. There was no one named Sealand on the faculty, but she found a Dr. Martin Seelander in the anthropology department. Close enough? Several more clicks and she had his home phone from whitepages.com.

What had people done before the Internet?

She pressed in the number quickly, and a woman answered.

"Mrs. Seelander?" *Why aren't you out in New Mexico searching for your husband?*

"Speaking." She sounded older than Fiona had expected, cheerful and self-possessed.

"I'm—uh, calling from Santa Fe. Is Dr. Seelander available?"

"Is this a work call? It doesn't matter, I'll put him on."

"He's *there*?"

"The dig ended last weekend." She laughed at Fiona's surprise. "He's working from home, getting over a fall. I'll get him to pick up."

A pause, then, "Hello?" The voice was open, Midwestern, the kind of voice Fiona had heard all her life.

"Dr. Sealand—Seelander, my name is Fiona Reina. I'm looking for people who were on the Day Star shuttle last Sunday."

He chuckled. "Well, I started out Sunday. A month of scrambling around the rocks with no trouble, then I go and tumble down a flight of boarding steps. Or so they tell me."

The phone was wet under her fingers. "What do you mean?"

"Evidently I lost consciousness for a while and banged up my ankle real good. They kept me overnight to check me out, then sent me on home. I'm fine if I keep my ankle elevated."

She made herself breathe out. "But you remember the shuttle flight from Taos?"

"Remember it? What about it?"

"Nothing about any—complications?"

He laughed again. "Well, there was a rather vivid movie about a crash. I was surprised, I thought airlines kept away from movies like that. On the other hand, on a transatlantic flight once I saw one about a computer hack threatening to blow up the world. So I guess you're no longer so sensitive, am I right? Although—"

"But you don't think you were *in* a crash?" she asked, interrupting. Didn't he know they never showed movies on short hops?

"In a crash? How could I be? Didn't you say you were from the airline? Don't worry, I won't sue."

"No, I didn't say. But thanks." She hung up.

Did that mean there hadn't been a terrorist takeover? Or had they just released him after swearing him to secrecy? More troubling, why was he associating a crash with the flight?

She couldn't make sense of any of it. But there was an answer here somewhere—there had to be.

Chapter Twenty-Six

SHE FOUND DOMINICK waiting for her in a wicker rocker on the front porch.

"They're closed. Day Star offices are closed. Will Dunlea just called me; he thought I was leaving today. But then he said they closed Fridays in the summer. Don't you think that's suspicious?"

Dominick tilted his head. "No."

"*No?*"

"Lots of businesses at home do that. I can't, of course; I'm on call twenty-four-seven in the summer. Which reminds me, I have to get home by Sunday."

"It's already Friday."

"I know. But once Eve confirms that she has Coral…"

"Coral's name was on the flight roster," Fiona said gently.

"That just means she was supposed to be flying. Not that she actually did."

The air had a crisp, unspoiled smell. "Okay, but let me tell you about Dr. Seelander." She detailed the conversation as exactly as she could remember it. "But don't you think it's funny about Dr. Seelander thinking he was watching a movie?"

"Maybe he was."

Keep calm. "It couldn't be. They don't show movies on short flights like that."

"Fiona." He looked up at her as if gauging how upset she was getting. "I'm no Einstein, but so far all you've done is find people who were on the flight and are okay."

"With injuries," she said stubbornly.

"You don't know that. Not that man at MacArthur Airport."

"Him? I think he was a plant. I think he was sent by Day Star to tell me that."

Dominick shook his head. Now he was openly laughing at her. "And how did he know to tell *you*?"

"Because I was asking! It's not rocket science. I was obviously waiting for someone who hadn't come. Anyway," she said, smiling back at him unwillingly, "let's go to Taos. I need to see about those guys from the Pueblo."

"And what about that text from your boyfriend?"

"The one Wednesday night? I think it was a fake."

"Fiona." He stood up then and put his hand on her upper arm. "You're—what does my wife call it?—you're in denial."

She pulled away. "I'm in denial? *You're* in denial." What an aggravating man.

"Okay, but just tell me one thing. How many survivors will it take to convince you?"

"All of them."

"Good luck with that."

And then, inexplicably, they started to laugh. He reached out and put his arm around her shoulder.

Chapter Twenty-Seven

As she stood beside the Explorer, Rosa hesitated. She was registered as one of the drivers, but she didn't like trying to maneuver anything this large, especially on unfamiliar roads. No, she would take a cab. Susan lived in a gated community overlooking the hills, so the house wouldn't be hard for a driver to find.

Since she had not seen any taxis prowling the streets, Rosa walked around to the Turquoise Trail Inn reception desk. "I'd like a cab," she told the young woman, a Mia Farrow waif with blonde bangs and a wistful face. "I need one that will wait for me and bring me back."

The girl's green eyes danced. "Good luck with *that*. We only have one taxi company, and people make a lot of complaints about them online. They don't show up on time, they don't know where they're going, and they charge too much."

Rosa sighed. "That bad?"

"That bad."

"I guess I'll just have to drive."

"You have a car?"

"A rental car. But I don't really know the area."

"You have a GPS?"

"Yes."

"There you go." The young woman turned away and picked up a ringing phone.

There had been a time when this would not have been a concern. When had she gotten so cautious? It must be this situation that was putting her on edge: last-minute flights and the drive up from Albuquerque. Fiona's hysterical phone call about the missing passenger list. Rosa supposed Fiona and Dominick had gone to the Day Star offices, but she didn't want to wait to find out what they'd learned.

She went back to the parking lot and unlocked the Explorer. Fastening her seatbelt and looking over the controls, Rosa programmed 454 Margarita Way into the GPS. As soon as she turned onto Washington Avenue, her confidence flooded back. The cheerful English butler's voice that had guided them to Santa Fe—Greg had called him "Jeeves" and enjoyed mimicking him—took over. Rosa was soon above the city.

As she drove, she thought about what could have happened to Susan. She lived by herself; what if early Sunday morning, showering and getting ready, she had slipped and fallen? She could be lying unconscious on her bathroom floor! Or she could have locked herself in the bathroom by accident.

Rosa had heard stories about people who had done that, people who had been unable to break down a jammed bathroom door. The worst story had been about a woman who had been scheduled to leave for Europe the day she locked herself in. She missed her flight and was found starved to death three weeks later.

After hearing that, Rosa never closed her bathroom door all the way. It was something Susan might not have known about.

What if Susan had been in her house all this time? People could survive for a while, but it had been nearly a week.

The drive only took twenty minutes. There was no one in the wooden gatehouse and no impediment to driving in, so Rosa followed Jeeves's instructions to turn right. She parked the Explorer and moved up the path, past a monkey-puzzle tree set in white stone chunks. A black enameled door was firmly closed and did not yield when Rosa twisted the knob. She tried to look in the metal casement windows, but the glare of the sun was too strong.

She banged on the door more loudly. *Susan, can you hear me? Give a sign!* But if she were trapped or unconscious . . .

Did people leave keys with their neighbors out here? Edging across the grit, she approached an identical stucco house next door. As she moved closer, she thought she heard the smooth voice of a radio commentator coming from the backyard.

"Hello?" she called, moving to the side with the metal gate. "Hello?"

After a moment, a woman close to her own age came around the side of the house. Rosa was glad to see her white hair and the expensive, unfashionable light blue Bermuda shorts. *My kind of people*, Rosa thought.

The woman smiled graciously.

"Hello, I'm Rosa Cooper, Susan Allmayer's editor." She gave a quick nod toward the house.

"But what are you doing here? She told me she was going to stay with you in New York. I *think* I got the name right."

"Yes, you did. But she never got there."

"She never got to New York?" The woman unlatched the gate quickly and brought Rosa to a small patio with a white iron table and chairs. A man, also in his seventies, was sitting with a cup in one hand, reading the newspaper.

"Frank, this is Rosa Cooper, Susan's editor. Susan never got there!" She turned to Rosa. "I bet you'd like some coffee."

"I'd kill for coffee."

Frank laughed and pulled out a seat at the table for her. "What did Alice mean about Susan?"

Rosa waited until Alice was back. "I went to the airport to meet her plane Sunday, but she wasn't on it. I haven't heard a word since, and I'm really worried!"

"Of course you are," Alice said warmly. "She's such a wonderful person. But we haven't seen her since Sunday either."

Rosa took a long sip of coffee. It was strong and black.

"I know she never would have missed *Good Morning America*. We watched, but she wasn't on," Alice said.

"Could it have something to do with her book?" Frank asked. "Someone she may have antagonized?"

"I never thought of anything like that," Rosa admitted. "She's interviewed a lot of criminals, but most of them are already in jail."

"Maybe she had a relapse," Alice said. "She got to the airport and didn't feel well enough to fly after all."

"A relapse of what?" Susan hadn't mentioned having the flu.

"You know. Her health issues." Alice gave her an urgent, appealing look, as if she did not want to have to talk about them.

"What health issues do you mean?"

Alice sighed. "Sue has stage-four liver cancer. She's fighting it, but I know it's spread. She's in so much pain, I don't know how she stands it. Some mornings she can't even get out of bed."

"Are you kidding? She never told me! Why didn't she tell me?" Was she the kind of person people didn't confide in?

"She said she didn't want it to interfere with publicizing her book."

Now it was more important than ever to get in the house. "Do you have a key?"

"Of course. We water the plants and check if there's anything suspicious. Not that there ever is." She pushed up from the table and disappeared, but was back immediately.

She held out a key threaded with a blue ribbon. "Do you want Frank to come with you?"

"Yes, please." Now besides locked bathroom doors, there was the real worry that Susan might have collapsed.

They passed between the two yards, and Frank unlocked the door for Rosa.

When Susan had turned fifty four years ago and mentioned moving into this community, Rosa was skeptical. "Why would you want to shut yourself off with a lot of old people?"

"It's not that way. You wouldn't understand, but I'm a woman by myself. I need good neighbors and my mod cons."

And if everyone was as nice as Alice and Frank, Rosa could understand the appeal.

The living room was dim and quiet, with nothing out of place. It might have been in a model home.

Susan's kitchen was bright from the skylights set into the roof. Strings of chiles, garlic, and dried flowers were everywhere. A bay-leaf wreath hung above the sink, and invitations and *New Yorker* cartoons were magnetized to the refrigerator. Rosa guessed that the shelves inside would be tidy and nearly bare except perhaps for jars of imported mustard and a bottle of white wine. She thought of her own refrigerator crammed with odd condiments and restaurant meal leftovers that didn't seem as appealing the next day.

The only room in any disarray was the office off the master bedroom, and that was because it was piled with books and file folders. On the desk was a state-of-the-art computer system and a laser printer. Next to it was the one-volume edition of the *Oxford English Dictionary* with its magnifying glass dome sitting on top. Susan claimed that the online dictionaries were for the verbally challenged.

Rosa was suddenly anxious to check the bathroom. She looked for it and saw that the door was ominously shut. Her heart beating fast, Rosa twisted the knob and pushed the white-painted door back, then stared into the room. There was no one inside. She gave a quick glance at the fluffy white towels and plants grouped under the skylight, feeling her heart drop as she understood how badly she had wanted to find Susan here, weak but alive.

Returning her attention to the bedroom, she found it model-home neat as well, except for a carry-on suitcase sitting open in the center of the bed. Rosa moved toward it and looked inside. Piles of neatly folded clothes, and on top a black Chanel jacket and ecru blouse.

Rosa knew it was Chanel because Susan was planning to wear it on *Good Morning America*.

She turned to Frank suddenly. "How was Susan planning to get to the airport?"

He chuckled. "That was a bone of contention. We thought she should take a limo to Taos, but she was determined to drive. She said it would cost a fortune to hire a cab, and they weren't that reliable."

"So I've heard. We could see whether her car's here or not."

"Good idea! She always keeps it in the garage. I don't have the opener, but I doubt it's locked."

The garage was not locked. Frank pulled the door up, and they stared at the silver Toyota Camry centered in its space. Rosa was the one who noticed the black plastic bag stuffed in the exhaust pipe.

She rushed to the passenger side. Susan was slumped against the steering wheel, her dark curly hair hiding her face. Rosa didn't try to separate and identify the terrible odors coming through the window. *I'm not seeing this. This is not real.*

"It's locked," Frank said from the driver's side.

But Rosa was looking down at a note on the passenger seat, printed large and angled so it could be easily read: "I can't pretend anymore. This is getting worse."

Chapter Twenty-Eight

THE CAMPBELL FAMILY vacation was progressing as their vacations always did—a fact Ed never seemed to remember when he was ensconced in his study in the deep Minnesota winter, making plans.

"Come on, Dad. Not another ghost town!"

"Yeah. We're never gonna get to the Grand Canyon."

Ed pushed up his glasses and stared in wonder at the abandoned buildings. "Sure we are. That's on next week's schedule. This will be the last one for today. And then we'll find a nice motel with a pool."

He hadn't plotted out this trip to have the best parts over in five minutes. Marysville was supposed to be exceptional. "Amy, you tell us about this one."

His daughter rolled her eyes as her mother handed over the copy of *Lost Mines of Colorado*. "I don't even know where we are!"

Ed flipped up the hinged sunglass lenses on his bifocals and peered over the seat to look at the guide. "It should be under Marysville. Or Baldy Mountain. *There.*"

The two younger boys ghost-punched each other as their sister skimmed the text.

"Gold was discovered here in 1866," Amy announced. "Something new and different. They had a newspaper, a drugstore, one church, and three dance halls."

"No feed store?" Ed asked genially, ignoring her tone.

"It doesn't say."

"With a population of over five thousand? They most likely did."

"Oh, this is interesting." She began to read aloud. " 'After a while, Marysville residents began to whisper about travelers who stopped overnight at Kearney's Log Inn and were never seen again. Travelers who arrived at Questa raved about the meat they had been served. But it wasn't until Mrs. Kearney—' "

"Amy, I don't think this is something we need to hear." The legend of cannibalism was coming back to him now. "What does it say about total mining wealth produced?"

She was ready for him. "Over four million dollars. 'But it wasn't until Mrs. Kearney arrived in M-ville claiming that her husband had robbed and killed sixteen travelers, and eaten two of her children who annoyed him' "—Amy turned a significant gaze on her brothers—" 'that authorities were persuaded to—' "

"You're making that part up," Timmy cried.

"Am not. Anyway," she started to skim the text before her father could snatch back the book. "They put him on trial, but people were too scared to convict him, so a posse dragged him out of jail and hanged him at night. And you know what?"

Ed sighed. "What?"

"They sent his skeleton to the Smithsonian."

Ed's wife laughed. "They must have wanted to analyze the protein content."

"Give me the book!" Ed held out his hand to Amy.

"Why can't we get out?" the younger boy whined. "You never let us get out."

"Don't you want to learn something about what you're seeing first?"

"No!" Both back car doors opened, and the children pushed free.

"A lot of the wood from these buildings was burned by residents during harsh winters," Ed told his wife sadly.

"There's still a lot of the town left."

"I know, but it's not what it was. In 1936, they tunneled right through Baldy Mountain looking for the mother lode. They never found it."

"You're sure it's safe for them to be poking around in there?"

"They know better than to touch anything." But it gave him the excuse not to delay his pleasure any longer. Picking up his camera, Ed visually restored windows, chimneys, and hitching posts, and peopled the streets with miners and farmers. He imagined an earlier version of himself as a parson in a string tie. Here was history in the raw, a town untouched by archeologists.

At the end of the main street, he turned the corner and saw the remains of a tall brick building with an ornamental plaster facade of ears of corn. Beyond it was the white church he was interested in. He was surprised to see wooden sawhorses like police barriers arranged across the dusty road in front of both buildings. What was going on?

As he hesitated, his younger son came running to meet him. "Daddy, that church made Tim *sick*."

"I thought I told you never to go inside!" It was the structures that needed protection, not his children.

"We didn't. We just snuck around to the back."

Ed moved closer as Amy came out of a side alley and joined them. A sweet, putrid smell drifted toward them on the dry air.

"Mr. Kearney's been at it again," Amy said. "And Tim upchucked."

"He threw up? Where *is* he?"

"I'm here." Tim appeared suddenly, looking greenish. "Dad, there are *people* in that church."

"Are you okay?" He put his hand on Tim's shoulder. "Go back to the car and take it easy. All of you."

Ed had come across these New Age gatherings before. The white wooden church was almost intact, after all. That explained the sawhorses and the two vehicles parked outside, a large black truck with a design on the door and a vintage pink-and-white Cadillac. Probably they were burning some kind of horrible incense that upset Tim's stomach. Ed hoped it wasn't meant to cover the stench of animals being sacrificed.

Before the children could leave, the door of the truck pushed open and a young man stepped out. He had a bland, open face and was dressed neatly in jeans, but his holster and gun made Ed feel uneasy.

Still, his voice was good-natured. "Can I help y'all with something?"

"Oh, no. We're just poking around."

"You have permission?"

"Permission? No…"

"This is private property." The blue eyes were a little chalky now. "The owners don't want people on the property. Liability and all that. You break a leg, y'know?"

"Oh, but we wouldn't sue anyone. Can't I just take a few pictures?"

But the man was slowly shaking his head no, pendulum style. The way he seemed to be enjoying the situation made Ed more uncomfortable. Why hadn't the guidebook said anything about needing permission?

"Are you having some kind of meeting inside?"

"Something like that."

"Where do I get permission?"

"Not sure."

"Okay, we'll go. But I'll be back. Come on, kids."

"You have a nice day now," the man called to their backs. It sounded as if he were hoping for something else.

Chapter Twenty-Nine

"THERE'S SOMETHING ABOUT being out here that makes you see things in a different way," Dominick said. He and Fiona were leaving the tiny town of Chimayo and climbing into the mountains again. To their left, the cliffs in the distance looked like abandoned dwellings. With a lyricism she hadn't known existed in him, Dominick had insisted they take the scenic road to Taos and had rhapsodized ever since.

"There's a whole different look out here," he continued, lifting his hands from the wheel to outline it. "All these orange buildings and flat roofs. Who knew there was anything like this in America? You start seeing details like carvings and—what did you call them?—vigas?"

Fiona nodded. He must be one of those people who could compartmentalize the different parts of their lives so that one thing did not spill over and color anything else. Dominick's worry about his daughter could be kept in one place while he enjoyed what he was seeing. It was true that Fiona had stopped checking her phone every few minutes—there had been nothing from Lee since that one message and her flurry of frantic responses—but she was seeing the world through a gray scrim.

"You don't seem very worried about your daughter."

He looked over, picking up the criticism in her voice. "What worries me is Coral in Mexico, with all the crime you hear about. I'm worried her mother might not send her home. Who knows where Eve's head is these days."

"But you're not worried about the plane? I know, I know." She held up a hand. "You don't think anything happened."

They were passing a tiny cemetery by the side of the road. White wooden crosses were crudely painted with black names and hung with artificial flowers and rosaries. A hot-pink plastic rabbit with a buck-toothed grin stood on one grave mound.

Death was everywhere.

Every few minutes she checked the side-view mirror. Leaving Santa Fe, there had been a black sedan behind them for several miles, but once they were on Route 84 it had disappeared. But she had already told Will Dunlea they were headed for Taos.

Dominick pointed out a small corrugated-roofed house, its plaster walls painted a garish pink, and marveled, "Can you imagine something like that on Long Island?"

"No, but it's okay out here. People use whatever's available."

"Even junk."

You've been servicing McMansions too long.

They passed through a series of tiny towns—Oja Sarco, Las Trampas, Chamisal—names Fiona didn't bother to translate to herself. The homes here were mostly trailers and one-story brick boxes, a few with stuffed chairs out front. No niceties of indoor-outdoor furniture.

The road began to wind through the mountains again, through green alpine meadows that made her think of New England.

Gradually, fields of yellow and white flowers and stalky pines gave way to hillsides of fat green junipers.

"I could live out here." Dominick glanced at his hands on the steering wheel as if to judge whether they would work as well in New Mexico. "At least for part of the year. If Eve wants to be out here, it could work."

What about the power mower? "How long have you been married?"

"Married?" He slowed for a blinking light. "Twelve years. Eve's my second wife."

Ah. "But you're separated now?"

"No!" He turned from the wheel, his ruddy face outraged. "What makes you think that?"

"I thought she lived out here."

"Just temporarily."

"Oh." *Sounds like you two need to have a conversation.*

"She's an artist, you know? She says she needs the light."

Then they were coming into Taos, passing through an area of big-box stores, headed for the older section of galleries and inns. Dominick turned right and followed the signs to the Pueblo. "The inn's owner was telling me that real adobe—not just plaster painted dark red—has to be resurfaced every year or so. And because the flat roofs get destroyed by standing water, that's a major industry too."

Was he thinking of changing professions?

"I think this is real adobe," Fiona said, pointing at the buildings as they stopped at a gate house.

"Oh, I'm sure."

"No photographs in the chapel." The young man was stocky and solemn.

They assured him they would not take any.

There was an entrance fee of sixteen dollars per person, which shocked Fiona. Dominick handed over a credit card.

"Park over there." The attendant handed an instruction sheet to Dominick, who passed it on to Fiona. She studied the rules governing their visit. They were advised to stay within the Pueblo walls and not wade in the water or pet any dogs.

"This is amazing," Dominick said enthusiastically as they crossed the dusty ground. He gestured appreciatively at the adobe structures set in a horseshoe around the open plaza, dwellings recessed back into two or three stories. The doors and windows were rectangular cutouts, the walls punctuated by the round ends of vigas. The deep russet of the clay was broken occasionally by a green or turquoise wooden door frame. "Who knew there was something like this in America!"

Fiona tried to concentrate on the architecture and ignore her spreading feeling of desolation. Through the gray filter, all she could see was the grassless plaza, several skinny dogs lying in the dirt, and a sign that read, "Private—Keep Out!" "They don't have running water or electricity here," she told Dominick. "It's against tribal regulations."

"Thank God for *that*. Can you imagine TV antennas sticking out of these buildings?"

"No, but they're people too, wanting what everyone has. They aren't just here to look picturesque."

"Maybe not, but they're making a buck off it." He patted the pocket where his wallet was, and Fiona laughed.

"Let's try over there." She pointed to an open doorway that had a sign, "Fry Bread," taped outside. Tourists should be welcome.

As they stepped into the tiny room, dark in the corners where the sunlight did not reach, Fiona noticed that canned goods, strings of silver necklaces, and children's handmade moccasins were also for sale. Near the door was an old-fashioned red metal Pepsi cooler. A woman in a navy cotton shift with a sailor collar looked up from a newspaper and smiled.

"Hi. Can we have two fry breads, please?" Fiona asked. She watched as the woman stood up and dropped twin circles of dough onto a griddle. The bread soon puffed into fragrant pillows. When the woman slid the bread onto white paper plates, she set a clear plastic teddy bear filled with honey in front of them. Fiona drizzled some over her bread, then took a bite. "Wonderful!"

The woman ducked her head as if pleased.

"You wouldn't happen to know a Black Arrow family here, would you?"

The woman frowned. "No," she said, drawing her answer out. "Not that name. I am Sylvia Black Hook."

Black Hook, that was it. But Fiona could not think what to say next.

Dominick rescued her. "We're looking for a Black Arrow or Black Hook who was on a flight from Taos to Denver last Sunday."

Fiona winced at what had to come next.

"Clayton?"

"It could be," Dominick said. "My daughter was on that plane, and she got upset when she found she hadn't brought any money with her. He gave her ten dollars, which was a kind thing to do. I wanted to repay him."

Fiona stared at him.

"Oh!" Sylvia Black Hook did not look at the bill he had placed on the counter. "I am pleased to know that he is generous."

"He didn't tell you about it?" Fiona asked, forgetting that it had probably not happened.

The faintest cloud crossed the woman's face. "I have not heard from him yet. He went off to the university in Boulder. Jackson said Clayton got off the plane and found the bus for Boulder."

"Who's Jackson?" Fiona worked to keep her voice steady.

"Jackson works on that plane. It was Clayton's first time to fly. I made sure that Jackson would be with him." Her round face creased with remembered anxiety. "I told him, take the bus, take the bus, don't go so far from the ground. But he said, 'No, Ma, it's time.'" She reached behind her and pointed to an 8 x 10 graduation photo, held by a red clothespin to a wire of photographs. "Clayton."

"He's so handsome," Fiona said softly. With his clipped hair and engaging smile, Clayton looked like the kind of young man who *would* give ten dollars to a girl in need.

"He even got a scholarship!" Then she reached behind her and unpinned a smaller photo of two smiling young men. Fiona recognized the young one as Clayton. But the other, with his delicate mustache . . .

"Is that *Jackson*?" *Keep calm.* "And you saw him after Sunday's flight?"

Mrs. Black Hook gave her a puzzled look.

"It's just—he was on my flight down here Tuesday, and I thought I recognized him. Does he live around here?"

The woman smiled at her enthusiasm. "He lives off-Pueblo now. He and Amanda have a house on the Taos Pueblo Road."

Fiona took a last bite of bread and turned to Dominick. She had found out what she wanted and needed to leave before she said something that would upset Clayton's mother.

Dominick got the message. Moving toward the door, he gave Mrs. Black Hook a warm smile. "Good luck to your boy in college."

"Thank you. But why doesn't he call me?"

When they were out of earshot, Fiona exploded. "Shit, shit, shit! Why do these things have to happen? Life is hard enough for people, but when they try to do something to make it better, they get killed."

"What are you talking about?" Dominick grabbed her arms tightly, and they faced off in the center of the square. "Why do you think he's dead? You're the most negative person I know. Maybe, just maybe, this Jackson did see Clayton get on the bus to college."

"Maybe. Anyway, we have to find Jackson! He can tell us what happened to everyone." The thought of an eyewitness, someone who could answer their questions, seemed like talking to someone who had died and come back with tales of the afterlife.

They started walking toward the parking area, but Dominick veered toward the adobe chapel, its steeple raised to the sky in a striking scalloped design. "Coral sent me a postcard of this. I want to take a look."

Fiona tamped down her impatience and followed him. As they skirted the chapel, she saw they were heading for the small churchyard. At one end, sunken into the earth was a mission belfry, a metal bell still enclosed in the center of its cutout arch. A few of the graves had upright white slabs, but many more were simply marked by wooden crosses painted white, standing guard over mounds of earth. Here and there small blue flowers grew over them.

She and Dominick stared silently.

Chapter Thirty

FIONA REMEMBERED THAT Jackson's name had been near the end of the alphabetical list. So when she saw Redhawk on a silver mailbox on the Taos Pueblo Road, she signaled Dominick to stop. The name had been neatly created by black vinyl letters, but the foundation of the small white house was covered with only a few scraggly shrubs that had succumbed to exhaustion.

She and Dominick climbed the worn brick stoop. When no one answered their knock, Fiona looked in the front window and was surprised to see that the living room was filled with cardboard cartons instead of furniture. "It looks like they're moving out."

"Really?" Dominick, holding her shoulder for balance, looked in too. "Or moving in."

"Do you usually put your name on the mailbox before you unpack?"

"You do if you want mail."

"Oh. Maybe we could ask the neighbors if it's Jackson's house."

They walked back to the Sentra. Across the road a very old man was sitting on a wooden chair in his yard. A worn panama hat was pulled down to his eyes and he sat upright, so still that Fiona feared he might be dead. A black dog, as bony as those on the reservation, lay at his feet. But when she and Dominick crossed the road, the dog's ears went up and he began to whine.

The ancient man lifted his head slowly.

"Excuse me," Fiona said, then remembered that in many cultures it was rude to ask direct questions. "We're wondering where to find Jackson Redhawk, who works for Day Star Airlines." *Please make it Jackson.*

The man looked across the road. "His car is not there."

"No…No one came to the door."

"She walks to work at the muffin shop."

"The muffin shop. Thank you." She motioned Dominick back to the car. As they drove away, she said, "How many muffin shops can there be? I don't even know of one at home."

"We have bagel shops."

"True." She glanced automatically in the side-view mirror. This time she saw a black sedan behind them. It looked the same as the one from Santa Fe. "Slow down! I want to get that car's license. I think it's the one that was following us before."

Dominick made an amused sound, but slowed. The car kept its distance, too far away for her to decipher its plate.

She was so intent on the license that Fiona almost missed the small, shingled house with a pink sign, "Mandy's Muffins." Dominick had to brake abruptly and make a U-turn. He waited in the car while Fiona went in.

But it seemed to be the wrong muffin shop. There were only two young women, both Anglo, working behind the counter, surrounded by a fragrant pastry cloud.

Fiona started to back out. They had no time to waste.

"Can't we help you?" The blonde straightened up from restocking the case. She was taller and thinner than her coworker but had on the same gingham pink-checked smock.

"I don't think so. But thanks." The fry bread had settled into the pit of her stomach.

"Twenty-seven varieties," the young woman teased, tossing her short clipped hair. "Mango pineapple to chocolate pecan chip. A muffin for every sign."

Fiona grinned. "Actually, I was looking for a Mrs. Redhawk. But I think I'm in the wrong place."

"Why?" The woman stepped around from behind the case. Beneath the smock she was wearing white capris.

"I don't see anyone who looks like her."

"What does she look like?"

Damn. "I'm not sure."

"I guess you aren't. I'm Amanda Redhawk."

"You look so…young." But it was fatal. Why had she assumed that Jackson's wife had to be Native American? "I—actually, I was trying to locate your husband."

"He's working." She was already less friendly.

Fiona damned herself for her stupidity. "I know. I mean, I know he works for the airline. Is he on a flight?"

"Why?" Cool blue eyes appraised her.

"I need to talk to him." *Close. You're so close. Don't blow it now.* "I need to find out about something."

"Who *are* you?"

Fiona knew she was losing it. "I just have to ask him one question."

Amanda stepped back behind the counter. "I don't have time to talk to noncustomers."

"Okay, give me something. Pineapple mango. Listen, I didn't mean to offend you. I'm not from around here. Can't we talk or something?"

"No."

"It's really important that I talk to Jackson."

"But he doesn't want to talk to you."

Fiona felt her temper rising. "How do you know? You don't even know who I am."

Amanda Redhawk smiled at someone behind her. Although Fiona hadn't heard the door, she realized other people must have come into the shop.

"*Please*. Will he be home later?"

"Not to you." Her eyes shifted. "You here for your blueberry fix?" she teased someone else.

Die of heartburn. Fiona stormed out.

Dominick looked over and smiled as she climbed into the car. "You find out?"

"No. She wouldn't talk to me." She was too embarrassed to tell him what had happened. It was her own damn fault for making assumptions. Why did she have to pay for every last mistake? And yet—hadn't Mandy or whoever she was overreacted? As soon as she knew Fiona was looking for Jackson, she had practically ordered her out of the shop. *Not all my fault.*

"We have to go to Eve's. That neighbor knows more than she's telling."

"Okay, but we've still got to find Jackson!"

It was a silent ride until they turned onto Valverde, and Dominick said, "I can't believe Eve's living like this. In a slum!"

"This isn't a slum. You've been doing pools in the Hamptons too long."

YET COMPARED TO their home by the water in Patchogue, Dominick thought, this neighborhood was grim. Before he came out here, his image of Taos had been of a gracious artists' colony, the kind of place to which Eve would aspire. Didn't a lot of movie stars live around here? Another postcard Coral sent showed the interior of Kit Carson's homestead. That was the type of place he had pictured Eve living in, a picturesque log or adobe house with azaleas and grass.

There was still no car in the driveway, but he went up the wooden stairs again. He knocked, then poked at the chile *ristra*. It was not doing well.

Nobody came to the door and it was still locked, so he turned and moved across the yard to the house next door. It was a dull brick square, smaller than normal but without the charm of a playhouse.

The woman he had spoken to last night opened the door so quickly that she might have been waiting for him. Today she was wearing a cotton housedress with turquoise and gold cattle-branding symbols printed on brown. She had poor people's hair, straggly and already turning gray.

Dominick smiled at her. "I'm back with more questions."

She grinned back and held open the metal screen door.

The inside of the house was as depressing as the yard, mostly overstuffed furniture under bedspreads. He identified the smell as collard greens and bacon. "You said Eve didn't leave you a phone number where you could reach her," he began.

"No, but I may know where she's staying," she hinted. "I'm the one who told her about the place."

Why didn't you tell me this last night?

"I stayed there once, before I was married." She winked at him. "When I was still a dish."

A dish of what? "You mean in Puerto Vallarta?"

She nodded her raggedy gray-brown head.

Last night he had been jet-lagged. Today he knew what to do. "I wanted to give you something for taking care of the cat." He extracted his wallet from his jeans and removed two twenties. "Buy him a treat."

The woman grinned confidingly. "I wasn't sure I should tell you, but since you're family and all..." She palmed the money. "It's called Casa del Dega."

"Casa del Dega. You wouldn't happen to have a phone number?"

"Sure! I still got the folder."

She moved back into the dimness and reappeared holding a creased brochure, white lines where it had been unfolded and refolded many times. Dominick looked at the photos of a small and charming hacienda. The woman wouldn't let him keep the brochure, of course, but he knew he could get the number from Siri.

"You're sure she's coming back after next week?"

"Sure I'm sure. She's got to get back to her job."

Her job? What was she talking about? "What kind of job?"

"Over at that Honda dealer. Secretary stuff, I think."

He sat frozen on the faded couch. *Admit it. Eve isn't coming back.*

When she had returned from her artists' residency in June, she arrived at Islip-MacArthur looking like a waif—skinny in black jeans and a black leather jacket, her long scraggly hair dyed a deep maroon, and those ridiculous emerald contact lenses. But Coral had scolded her for having three earring holes in each lobe. "That's so *yesterday*, Mom. Nobody does three holes anymore."

"They do in Taos, honey chile."

Eve had checked through two large paintings—"So that I can show you guys what I've been doing"—and brought a small carry-on filled with presents for Coral: a turquoise and silver bracelet, tooled cowboy boots, a pottery woman covered with children that Eve said was called a "storyteller." She had brought Dominick a silver bolo tie clasp in the shape of a coyote's head, something he could not imagine putting around his neck.

It turned out the paintings had actually made the trip so she could leave them with her gallery in Sag Harbor.

After they had made vigorous love—at least that hadn't changed—he'd asked, "What about your stuff? Are you having it shipped?"

"My stuff?"

"Your clothes and art supplies. I know you have more than you brought!"

"Oh. My stuff." She rolled away from him then and stared at the ceiling. "It's in Taos. In a house."

"In a *house?*"

She had given a kick with one leg, as if annoyed she had to spell it out. "I'm going back next week for a little while longer. I'm not finished out there yet. And I want Coral to come for a visit while I'm still living there."

He never should have let Coral go.

Back in the Sentra he took out his phone and requested the number for Casa del Dega. A moment later it was ringing.

A voice answered in Spanish, a language he knew from the day laborers he hired for big jobs.

"*Hola?* I'm looking for a guest, a woman named Eve." He hesitated. What last name would she use? "A woman with long reddish hair? From New Mexico?"

"*Sí, sí.*"

There was a long pause, and then finally a breathless Eve. "Hello?"

"Eve? It's me. Sorry to bother you on vacation." He wasn't, of course. "But I have to know if Coral's okay."

"How did you get this number?"

"Never mind that. You never should have taken Coral down there!"

"What are you talking about? She's not down here. I put her on the plane last Sunday."

"Eve, she wasn't on the plane. Or the one after that." *As you very well know.*

"She never got home? Is this one of your tricks?"

"I didn't come all the way to New Mexico for a *trick*. Listen to me! Is there anyone else she might be staying with? If she'd got-ten off the plane at the last minute?" *Give me the name of anyone, some boy she was enamored with, someone for whom she would miss the flight home.*

"Are you saying that Coral is missing?"

"Eve, she never got to New York." The heat of the sun through the windshield was making the sweat slide down his face.

"But how could that be? And you're in New Mexico? Have you been to the house?"

"That's how I found out where you are." For a moment he felt comforted that someone else cared as much about Coral as he did.

"Are you staying in my house?"

"Of course not. I'm at an inn in Santa Fe."

"Where? How can I get in touch with you?"

"You have my cell phone." *Even though you refused to give me your new number.*

"Dom, I don't get it! What if she's been kidnapped? I'm coming back."

"Back to Taos?"

"Of course back to Taos. There's no way I can stay here *now*." She calmed down enough to say, "Call me as soon as you find her!"

Chapter Thirty-One

IN THE NEXT block, Jackson watched the Sentra pull away from the curb.

He was reaching for the ignition to turn the Lexus on when his phone rang and he looked down at the screen instead. *Mandy.*

"Jack? That girl you're following was in the shop looking for you."

"For me? That's why she went in? I thought she was just..."

"She knows your name. That you work for Day Star."

He leaned back against the headrest and closed his eyes. "Oh, God. She was at the Pueblo too. I didn't go in, but—what if she was talking to Sylvia?"

"She could have been. Not that Sylvia knows anything to tell her." The reproof in her voice made him flinch.

"You're still blaming me for something I had to do."

"Had to?"

"You know she'd made me promise to let her know how it went. And the truth is so terrible it would kill her."

"Come on, Jack. You lied because Day Star told you to lie. You think if you go along with this, they'll let you fly. It's never going to happen."

"That's not true! They said as soon as all this dies down."

"What happens when Christmas comes and Sylvia is expecting her grandson to come home?"

He had no answer.

"Or before then, if she contacts the college and they say he never showed up. Maybe they'll send letters wanting to know where he is."

"But we won't be living here. Anyway, doesn't she have something wrong with her?"

"Emphysema. What—now you're hoping she'll die before she misses Clayton?"

"Of course I'm not. She's like my grandmother too! I'm the one who should have died. I never should have taken that money."

"But that was a bonus! For bravery, they said."

The money—the thirty thousand dollars—was the only thing Amanda understood. He knew she would not let him give it back.

"I have to go," he said.

"It won't be forever."

Wouldn't it? His bruised leg still ached, though he was fortunate not to have broken any bones, but he dreaded sleep because of the dreams. Heads without bodies placed in crevices in the mountains. One little girl's, which had been calling for soda, started screaming, "Blood! I want blood!"

Last night he had been on the plane again, but with everyone dancing in the aisles, laughing and happy, like they were at a party. He knew if they kept on moving that way, it would make the plane crash. He kept yelling at them to sit down in their seats, but it was as if they couldn't hear him.

Mandy kept telling him it was the nitrous oxide. "What you can't remember is trying to break through in your dreams."

"But why am *I* being punished? I didn't put dirt in the fuel line. It was sabotage, it had to be! Someone who doesn't want us to get that wilderness charter."

"It won't be forever," she said again now.

She didn't know the worst. And he was not going to tell her.

Chapter Thirty-Two

THEY MET FOR dinner at the Jackalope Café, a restaurant with dark pine walls and oil paintings of Western landscapes. Because it was early, they were able to get a table in the back where they could talk.

But no one had anything to say. They sat silent, exhausted and disheartened. Fiona had nothing to contribute. The ride back from Taos had been somber. No more talk about Territorial architecture or native building materials. Dominick seemed to have finally accepted that Coral was missing.

Coming into Santa Fe, he decided he had to file a missing person's report immediately.

Fiona pointed out that Santa Fe was not the place to do it. "She hasn't even been here, as far as you know. Taos would be more logical."

Then he wanted to turn the Sentra around, but Fiona would not let him. In part because she thought it would be hopeless, in part because she was tired of driving through mountains. "We'll talk about it at dinner. We'll make a plan."

He'd given her an outraged look. "This isn't a committee decision! This is my daughter we're talking about."

"And my—and Lee. Look, we'll try to reach Maggie and see what her father remembers. There has to be an explanation." Although Fiona had dialed Maggie's number numerous times during the day, there was never any answer. "You said yourself that all we've turned up are people who made the flight okay. Coral's probably fine."

"So where *is* she?"

Being held by terrorists, which none of you believe in. They had not talked for the rest of the trip.

THE GROUP ORDERED dinner listlessly.

"You look sunburnt," Rosa said to Dominick. "Even over your tan."

Fiona nodded. "The sun is closer to earth here." It sounded like a geography lesson. "Or maybe it's the thinner air."

"And it's dry," Greg put in. He was wearing his striped polo shirt. "It really dries out the snot in your nose. I've got to keep cleaning mine out."

"TMI, Greg."

"Fiona? Welcome to the real world."

If her Uncle Eimer had been there, he would have reassured them that it was always darkest before dawn. And over the carafe of white wine and pitcher of Dos Equis, the mood normalized slightly. Fiona told Rosa and Greg what they had learned at the Taos Pueblo.

Rosa pulled out her electronic cigarette. "Do you think this Jackson actually exists?"

What kind of a question was that? "Well, his wife and Mrs. Black Hook seem to think so."

Rosa blinked at her patiently. "I mean, exists now. You couldn't find him, and his wife wasn't cooperative."

"Mrs. Black Hook said she saw him after the flight. He told her that her son had gotten on the bus to Boulder okay."

"See?" said Dominick. "It shows the plane got there just fine."

But Rosa leaned back in her chair and looked wise. "Maybe if you were struggling to eke out a living on an Indian reservation, and someone offered you, say, ten thousand dollars to tell people something, you might figure, what's the harm?"

"Ten thousand dollars usually means harm to *someone*." Fiona was suddenly furious at Rosa's cynicism. "And she hardly seemed like the type to lie. You met her, Dominick."

"I thought she was very nice."

Rosa raised her hands in surrender. "Okay, she wasn't bribed. But I have to tell you something else." She put it off for a moment while she dipped a newly served shrimp into a green sauce. "I went to Susan's today, as you know. There didn't seem to be anyone inside so I talked to her next-door neighbors, and they told me she was very ill with liver cancer, stage four."

Fiona sucked in her breath.

"But the neighbors thought she had left for New York anyway. I told them she had never arrived, so we went in her house to look."

"And you found her?"

"Well, she wasn't in the house. So then we checked her garage. She was in the car. She'd turned on the gas because of the pain, because she was dying anyway."

"*What?* She killed herself? And you were the one who found her?" Fiona couldn't make it seem real.

"We called the police, and they came right away. I was there most of the day. Frank—the neighbor—drove the Explorer back, and I came with his wife in their car. They were so nice; they took care of everything. They knew her better than I did, of course." She stared at the tabletop, morose.

Fiona reached over and squeezed her hand. "Had you ever met her before?"

"Not in person. But we talked on the phone a lot. Especially lately. I can't believe she never told me how sick she was."

Dominick learned forward urgently. "So she was never on the plane?"

"No. She never left Santa Fe."

"That's why her name was in parenthesis," Fiona said. "Because she never made the flight."

"Yeah, she was a no-show," Greg said.

"She's hardly a 'no-show.' It's not like she blew the flight off." Yet, in a way, that was what she had done. "How did you make out today?" Fiona asked.

Greg looked wary. "With what?"

"With whatever you were trying to find out."

"Yeah, you know what? Even if you know someone's post office box number, they won't tell you where he lives! And even if you have his cell phone number, the phone company won't give you the address. What kind of rinky-dink town is this?"

"A law-abiding one," Fiona said mildly. "Did you try finding him on Google?"

"Yeah, the usual shit. I'm looking for a place anyway, not a person. Dimitri's apartment. He's got some stuff I need."

"What kind of stuff?"

"Are you always this nosy?"

Fiona reached for one of the last two shrimp. "Let me get this straight: Your friend's missing, and you want to break into his apartment and take stuff?"

"Easy, Fiona," Dominick cautioned, lifting a hand.

"It just sounds strange to me." *No wonder no one would give you the information. I wouldn't either.*

"He's got something I need, okay?"

"Okay." Fiona closed her eyes for a moment. When she opened them again, there was more food on the table. She had ordered blackened redfish, but when she saw it she couldn't imagine picking up a fork and eating it.

"Tired?" Rosa asked sympathetically.

"I guess." Tomorrow it would be almost a week since she drove to MacArthur Airport to pick up Lee for a celebratory dinner—to celebrate his return to her and discuss their plans for finding an apartment. A *week*. She had been out here three days herself, and what did she have to show for it? Nothing but contradictions and lies. She was still no closer to knowing what had happened than she had been standing at the kiosk in Islip-McArthur Airport.

"Bon appétit!" Rosa announced. She seemed determinedly cheerful. Would she be leaving now that she had found out what had happened to Susan?

Fiona realized how abandoned she would feel.

They ate in silence for several minutes, but then she said, "We need a better approach. We need—"

"A psychic," Rosa said.

"We need to pull in the police and the FBI," Dominick corrected her. "We need them to find my daughter."

Fiona had been going to say, "To talk to people along the route and see if they've seen or heard about anything unusual." But she considered their suggestions. "Okay. First we use a psychic to tell us what happened. Then when we know, we go to the police."

Dominick shook his head. "I'm not waiting. I'm going to the police now."

"And you can ditch the psychic," Greg said.

"No, no, the police use them all the time." Rosa leaned forward earnestly, forearms on the deep red tablecloth. "A man in one of Susan's books could look at someone and see the rest of that person's life. The police used him to pick up information at murder scenes."

"Where does he live?" Fiona asked.

"Oh, nowhere around here. South Carolina, I think."

"But isn't Santa Fe supposed to be some kind of center for mystics?"

Greg snapped his fingers. "Right! We'll just look in the New Age yellow pages."

"You really think it works?" Fiona asked Rosa, ignoring him.

Rosa considered, sipping the last of her wine. "I think some people have an extraordinary way of grasping bits and pieces of things. It's uncanny. And sometimes a hint is all you need."

Greg put his head in his hands dramatically. "You really think some psychic is going to tell us what happened? What if she gives us bad information? That's worse than no information at all."

"Well, we don't know anything now, so what's the difference?" Fiona turned to Dominick, who was taking out his wallet to settle up, and reached into her purse for her own. "Day Star isn't going to admit anything. They'll point to people like Dr. Seelander and Maggie's father and Jackson and to the FAA, who says the plane came in. They'll give the police a doctored manifest that shows Coral and Lee weren't on the plane. I think we should go to the police, but they won't investigate a plane no one says is missing."

"But *people* are missing!" Dominick cried. "We haven't actually talked to anyone at the Denver airport to find out what happened when the plane got there. How many people were on it or anything else."

Fiona nodded. "Good point. We could get up early tomorrow morning and drive to Denver."

"And see a psychic tonight," Rosa insisted.

Greg looked as if he was going to object again, but then seemed to reconsider. "You think she could tell me where Dimitri's apartment is?"

"She'd probably tell you to look in the white pages." It was a bad joke; Fiona knew they didn't have a reverse directory for cell phones. She started to stand up, but was distracted by Rosa. She was waving at a woman in a fringed buckskin dress who was overseeing the tables, a woman in her fifties whose hair was pulled back in a gray braid that reached her waist. Fiona had identified her as the owner earlier.

"Is everything okay?" she asked when she reached them.

"Perfect," Rosa said. "But we need a good psychic."

Chapter Thirty-Three

PAOLO RECCHIA LIVED far up Canyon Road, past the galleries and artists' studios and cafés. By the time the two women reached the residential neighborhood, Rosa was out of breath. "I'm not used to this," she gasped.

"I thought you went to the gym."

"I do. For Stretch 'n' Sculpt and water aerobics—not mountain climbing."

Because the restaurant owner had assured them it was only a short walk, they had not gone back to the inn for the car. Fiona had imagined she meant five or six blocks.

"I'm so sorry about Susan," she said. "What a sad way to end."

"I think she had a different idea about dying. Maybe it was because she wrote so much about death, but she seemed to act as if it was no more than checking out of a hotel. That you just went on to your next destination."

Fiona shivered.

"What makes me feel so badly for her is that she was finally getting the recognition she deserved. Okay, part of it was the story—it's very dramatic. But Susan did a beautiful job writing it. And then her body betrayed her."

"How long had you known her?"

"I'd been her editor for seven years, and we had a very friendly relationship. She was going to stay at my house. It wasn't as though our publisher was rolling out any red carpets; I'd worked hard to get her the TV spot, and we hoped things would take off from there." Rosa stopped walking for a moment. "It can't be much farther. Have you ever been to a psychic?"

"Once. At a bridal shower. It was supposed to be light entertainment." She laughed. The woman, a tarot card reader, had smelled of musk and carried her cards wrapped in black velvet. During Fiona's five minutes, the reader had laid out the cards, then reared back a little. "You're not the bride, are you?"

"No."

"Good." She frowned at the layout. "You have an eventful life ahead of you."

"Lots of travel?"

"If you want."

"Am I going to be happy?"

"Who's happy?" The woman shrugged. "Better to keep busy like I do."

"What did she tell you?" Rosa asked.

"She was glad I wasn't the bride."

"Well, this man sounds impressive."

"I guess." She would have to try not to act skeptical. But she was no believer.

When they told the restaurant owner what they wanted, she had mentioned Paolo Recchia, then said, "But he's booked for months. Maybe for years. I can ask around for someone else."

"No," Rosa said firmly. "We need the best. Can't you just call and see if he's had any cancellations? We're very flexible as to time. And we'll *pay*."

She made it sound like a bribe, but the woman treated it good-humoredly and left to call. She returned with a slow smile creasing her face. "Nine fifteen. He said he was expecting you to call."

Despite herself, Fiona felt a chill. "How do you know?"

"He described you. In a general way, of course."

But now Fiona wondered if Day Star, anticipating they might look for a psychic in Santa Fe, had coached several of them to give out misinformation. No, that *was* truly paranoid. It was more likely that someone from Day Star would follow them, go in afterward, and demand to know what he had told them. What if they tortured or even killed him?

She whirled around and saw no one behind them. *Get a grip.*

But the thought of putting someone else's life in danger made her think about Egypt.

She had been there for two weeks when the instructor who had taken her hang gliding offered her an expedition by moonlight to the pyramids in Giza. The monuments were closed to tourists at night; they would be beautiful and deserted. Fiona had agreed right away and cajoled a French photojournalist from her hotel, Marcelle Delame, into coming along and taking pictures.

There was a reason for that. A newspaper travel editor had been questioning whether her *Eccentric Traveler* blogs were— uh—exaggerating just a little, and Fiona wanted the photographs to show him. The truth was that, once in a while, she veered into what *might* have happened.

"It will be awesome," Fiona promised Marcelle.

Three men had driven them the sixteen miles from Cairo in a jeep and then walked them in by flashlight for the last half mile. When they reached the Great Pyramid, Marcelle, excited, had decided to climb to the top to take photos. The moon was full, casting its magic. One of the Egyptian men had accompanied Marcelle—to protect her, Fiona assumed.

She stayed at the bottom herself, making notes on her iPhone. She needed to climb to the top as well, but wanted to detail the atmosphere first.

She had been describing the light on the sand when a voice cried out in protest, and Fiona jerked her head up to look. Marcelle was not at the summit yet, but the man had his arms around her and they were struggling.

"What's he doing?" Fiona cried to the men beside her.

But instead of answering, the younger of the two had grabbed her roughly around the waist from behind, and in a moment was pushing on top of her in the sand. Too late she realized how foolhardy she had been. He had her skirt up and was clawing at her underpants while trying to hold her down with his other forearm. She fought him bitterly, finally getting close enough to bite his shoulder through his shirt.

It wasn't his surprised outrage that saved her, but the scream that came from above them as Marcelle lost her footing and plunged to the lowest stones with a thud that echoed in the desert air.

The men had run then, dropping the flashlight on the sand as they raced toward the jeep. Fiona ran to Marcelle, gasping as she saw blood pulsing from the wound in her forehead. She grabbed her wrist for a pulse, then put her face down next to Marcelle's, her hand on her chest. She was not breathing. The pyramid was several stories high but recessed enough so that she should not have reached the bottom. Unless she had been pushed . . .

Fiona had taken the flashlight and fought her way through the sand, wondering if the men were lying in wait to kill her for what she had seen. But when she reached the parking area, the jeep was gone. She had finally been able to get a phone signal and dial 122 for the police. When she was connected to someone who spoke English, she reported that there had been an accident at the Great Pyramid in Giza, that a woman had fallen. Instinctively she had not identified herself. When they demanded her name, she broke the connection.

What happened next haunted Fiona months later. She waited for the police, sitting shakily on a low metal guardrail while she agonized over what to do. Could she find those men again and have them arrested? Would the police turn it around and blame her, like Amanda Knox? At the least they would arrest her for trespassing. Even in the best case, it could take weeks. When she heard the sirens, she hid in the brush. Then, dazed, she limped back to civilization and took a taxi to her hotel.

The next morning, she confronted the hang-glide instructor.

To her shock, he denied knowing the men or what she was talking about, denied making any arrangements for her to go to Giza. "You Americans are crazy," he'd said firmly. "No one will believe here what you say. They will put you in jail for a long time!"

So she had fled. Bruised, terrified, she had flown out of Cairo that night and not looked back.

The Eccentric Traveler disappeared.

Chapter Thirty-Four

As Rosa unfastened the gate lock, Fiona looked down the road again. She could not see anyone else on the street or the headlights of any cars. They had found the house by the number on its enameled tiles, but there were no business signs anywhere.

The man who came to the front door was charm itself. He was wearing a white silk shirt with billowing sleeves that emphasized his Mediterranean darkness and made his hips in black pants look even smaller. He could have been a tango dancer, but for the large wooden cross around his neck covered with tiny silver body parts: arms, legs, eyes, hearts, even a kneeling woman. *Milagros,* Fiona knew. People afflicted in those areas bought them and left them in church as prayers for relief.

She recognized the fluttering in her stomach as hope. Could this man tell her where Lee was? But psychics weren't real.

"Let's sit outside," he suggested.

They followed him around to a small patio, its slatted top covered by vines. Torch lights illuminated the area and showed tubs of evening primrose. Since the landscape itself was so arid, any flowers seemed to be in pots where they could be watered. Fiona settled herself into a white metal chair and identified the strongest scent as gardenias. The place seemed mysterious and magical, but she was too anxious to enjoy it.

"Juice?" Paolo Recchia asked.

Fiona shook her head.

"I'd love some!" Rosa said flirtatiously, tilting her head up to look at him. Fiona remembered the piano player; at Rosa's age, was it all innocent again?

Fiona capitulated. "Oh, I'll take some too. What kind is it?"

"My own blend."

As soon as he left, Rosa leaned over and whispered, "He seems very down to earth."

Fiona nodded.

Paolo Recchia came back holding a tray with three cut-glass tumblers filled with an apricot-colored liquid. After setting the glasses down in front of the women, he took a sip from his own. Fiona noticed that he had put on round, rimless glasses, giving him the look of a scholar. She had no idea how old he was.

"You've come a long way to get here," he observed.

You'll have to do better than that.

He must have read her expression, because he added, "But you're not here on vacation. You have a darker mission."

"You can tell that?" Rosa gasped.

He laughed and waved a hand toward Fiona's forehead. "Anybody could. The lines between her eyebrows are very deep. And you were insistent about seeing me tonight."

"That's true. But I'm insistent about everything."

He smiled at them both. "How can I help you?"

Fiona looked to Rosa, but the older woman gestured at her to talk. "We need to find out more about something that happened last Sunday." When she finished telling him the story, she added, "We brought a map of the area. And things belonging to the missing people." That had been Rosa's idea. They had borrowed a New Mexico-Colorado map from her hotel and then pooled whatever personal items they could find.

"That's good." But instead of putting out his hand to take the objects, he sat back in his chair and studied the women.

Was he waiting for them to feed him more information? Perversely, Fiona kept quiet. Then she remembered her vision of Lee in the library that first afternoon. Should she ask him about that?

Rosa was fishing around in her Guatemalan bag. "Don't you want to see?" Her voice shook a little.

"If you want," he said gently.

She brought out an envelope and a wallet-sized photograph and laid them side by side on the glass table. The envelope was from Dimitri to Greg, with his P.O. box address in the corner. Fiona had looked inside, but Greg had taken out the letter. The photograph showed a girl with long brown hair and lush features. She had an energetic, turned-up nose and full rosy lips. Wide blue eyes. Dominick's eyes, though his were brown.

Fiona reached in her purse and extracted a small earring shaped like a shell. It was one of the pair that Lee had given her after they'd flown to Nantucket on a whim. She placed it on the table with the other object, making certain it did not roll.

Paolo picked up the earring first. It disappeared into his fist.

"My friend—the man I'm in love with—gave it to me about a month ago. I don't know if it still counts."

He picked up the photograph and studied it, looked at the envelope. "These people are together."

"They are?" Fiona felt as shocked as if he had reached across the table and shoved her. "But where? Or are you talking about their spirits?"

He gave a small wave to show that he did not believe in the artificial boundaries between life and death. "They may still be as you knew them."

May. She clung to that. "But where are they?" Her voice was a croak.

You don't believe in psychics, remember?

Rosa dug into her bag again and brought out the map. "Show us where!"

"It is not where they are. There is something larger that you must find." He rested his elbows on the table and looked beyond Fiona. "The mountains, yes, but also sand."

"Sand?" He must be picking up that they were from Long Island. Or maybe it was the shell-shaped earring.

"But what town is this large thing near?" Rosa cried.

"There is no town. A green sign, a signpost, but not a place. Mountains with snow and roads, but—" He slumped in his chair and looked at Fiona. "You should not go on with this. There is great danger."

Rosa gave him a smile. "Oh, we're pretty tough."

But Paolo would not be drawn in. "This is not a game to play. I don't mean a game, it is not just something for you to find out. It is dark, darker than you know."

"But we have to find these people!" Fiona insisted. *Tell me where Lee is!*

He sighed. "You may." He handed her back the earring, then rubbed his hands together, his wide sleeves moving like wings in the darkness. "A young man will help you," he murmured. "A young woman has betrayed you."

They waited, but he did not say anything else. To give him time, Fiona picked up her glass of juice and took a sip. She put it down, shocked. She had been expecting something like nectar, perhaps an apricot blend. Instead it was tangy, not sweet at all, some kind of vegetable drink.

"What do we owe you?" Rosa asked finally, bringing her woven bag back up to her lap. She slipped the envelope and the photograph back inside.

"I have no set fee. I want my gift to be helpful. People leave what they think it is worth to them. But I implore you to think about it, to retreat from a dangerous quest is not shameful."

"But how dangerous is it, really?" Rosa's question seemed to echo in the dark, fragrant garden. "I mean, is it life threatening?"

"Dangerous means life threatening." There was reproof in his voice.

"Well, we'll certainly take care, won't we, Fiona?"

"Yes." Her body felt too heavy to move. She was sorry now they had come.

"Here." Rosa took out her wallet, removed several bills, and left them under her empty juice glass. "And thank you for seeing us on such short notice!"

Before he could say anything, before Fiona could push to her feet, Rosa was down the path and out the gate.

As Fiona finally stood up, the psychic touched her shoulder. "Take care of your friends," he pleaded.

"They're really in danger?"

"And especially yourself."

"What's going to happen?"

But he was closing the garden gate.

When Fiona caught up with her on Canyon Road, Rosa apologized. "Sorry I ran out; he was giving me the willies."

"He hinted at a lot of things."

"They love to talk in riddles! All that stuff about dark men."

"Young men. Maybe he was the young man who would help us." Maybe he said that to everyone.

Rosa stopped walking under a streetlight. "No, that sounded as if it was in the future. The young woman who betrays us was in the past."

"Probably Mandy Muffin. She'll do everything to keep Jackson away from us. Or maybe it was the young woman in Taos who gave Day Star my car rental information. Speaking of young women, let me try Maggie again."

She took out her phone and retrieved Maggie's number. She pressed it in, expecting to hear the usual ringing. But this time it was answered immediately.

"Yes?"

"Maggie, it's Fiona."

"Fiona! Thank *God.* Thank God, thank God! It must be telepathy."

"I've been trying all day."

"I was at the hospital with my father."

Fiona felt Maggie's anxiety as an electric shock, whipping through her own body. "Is he okay?"

"He died!" It came out as a wail.

"What? How?"

"It's still so unreal. Last night after dinner he started coughing up blood. Then this morning he was very disoriented, more than usual, and he couldn't move his arm. So I got him to the hospital and—" She couldn't go on.

Fiona palmed her phone. "Her father *died.*"

"My Lord!" Rosa reared back, steadying herself against the lamppost.

"They saw him right away; they admitted him and said he was bleeding internally." Maggie's voice was ragged in her ear. "They tried to do what they could, but tonight he just stopped breathing."

"Oh, God. I'm so sorry. What was he bleeding from?"

"They're not sure; they're doing an autopsy. But in a man his age they said something probably ulcerated in his stomach or bowel."

"Maybe the plane stopped suddenly and he was thrown against his seat belt."

"I don't think it was anything with the plane. It's so hard on the kids; they can't understand. But you know what? I'm really glad they sent him here, even this way. It gave us a chance to say good-bye. And he was slipping away—his mind, I mean. But lying there in the hospital he looked so bewildered, as if he just didn't understand what was happening to him—my poor daddy." She was sobbing now.

Fiona felt herself start to cry.

Rosa reached over and took the phone out of her hand. "Maggie," she said briskly. "Do you need anything? Any help with the arrangements? Anything at all?" She listened for a while, then said, "Well, we'll be home in a day or two. And we'll call you tomorrow."

She turned to Fiona, who had finished wiping her face. "He'll be cremated there and she'll fly out when she can with the ashes. Her mother's buried out here."

"What about the kids?"

"Her ex-husband will take them."

"Oh." So he hadn't died in the car crash after all. It was the marriage that had not survived.

Chapter Thirty-Five

THEY MOVED QUICKLY down Canyon Road. The windows of the shops along the road were dark, the signs on the doors turned around to "Closed." A Mexican gallery on the left was deceptively lit, its spotlight focusing on rain sticks and hand-dyed silk scarves, but a carved wooden plaque on the door announced "Shut."

Where were all the people who had been here before? It didn't feel safe to be walking there alone. "Do you think he was just trying to scare us off?" Fiona asked in a low voice.

"No. Do you?"

"No."

They walked even faster, and Fiona was cheered to finally see the lights of a restaurant ahead with people at tables on the patio. Thank God!

Yet once they had passed El Farol, the road grew dark again. On the way up, she had not noticed how closed off the buildings were, protected by stone walls or iron gates. A long white-picket fence glowed eerily ahead of them like a false trail. The road twisted just enough so she could not see very far ahead of them—or behind them.

Without discussing it, they had stepped up their pace nearly to a run. "You okay?" Fiona asked as Rosa's panting increased.

"Hanging in. Look how menacing that animal seems now."

Fiona looked. The huge carved, painted cat's head above a shop, an animal that had seemed whimsical when they were going up Canyon Road, now stared at them like a malevolent deity.

"We should have called a cab," Rosa gasped. "But the woman at your inn said they were hopeless here. We'd probably still be waiting."

"I haven't seen any driving around," Fiona agreed.

IT SEEMED MIRACULOUS to finally come upon Rosa's hotel. "I need to stop for a moment," she said, and Fiona followed her obediently in.

As they approached the bank of elevators, Fiona could hear "Smoke Gets in Your Eyes" from the piano lounge. Rosa gave the entryway a quick, wistful glance, and Fiona supposed she would be there later on, cradling a piña colada and singing.

Indeed, when she came back downstairs, Rosa almost succumbed. "How about a quick one? My nerves are *shot*. This has been a terrible day."

"I think we have to talk to the others first. Make plans." Yet as she said it, she remembered Paolo Recchia's caution. Rosa was the one he had seemed most worried about. "Or maybe not. You deserve a drink. I'll go back and tell them what we found out."

Rosa gave her a knowing smile, creating pathways around her mouth. "If we're making plans, I need to be there."

"Well—some of us should leave for Denver tonight. To see if we can see anything large in the mountains and talk to the airport."

"You mean you and Mr. Charming?"

"I think I'd feel better if Dominick was along."

"Ah. Everybody but me. Is it my age—or my unfiltered cigarettes?"

"You aren't looking for Susan anymore."

"And if you find something important, you'll come back for me?"

Fiona looked away. "You could always drive the other car back to Albuquerque. It's not like we all have to be there every minute."

"But you do?" Rosa turned toward the door.

"Well, I'm the one who got us into this. And," she looked at Rosa directly, "I'm scared for you. Paolo Recchia scared me. He made it sound as if we're a bunch of clueless Easterners here on a lark. That we don't understand how nasty things can get."

Rosa put her hand on Fiona's arm. "It's sweet of you to worry about me. But I'm tough as a dried-up cactus. I should be worried about you, you're so young. C'mon, let's go break it to the others."

When they approached the Turquoise Trail Inn, most of the windows were dark. "Maybe they're already in bed," Rosa said.

"They better not be!"

"Just an impression."

"Sorry, I guess I'm on edge. And PMS is worse when the air is thin. Just when I should be super alert, I'm not thinking straight. I don't want to take everyone else down with me."

Rosa looked amused. "We're all consenting adults."

Dominick and Greg weren't in bed. They were in a side sitting room, the one area of the inn with no historical pretense. It had fake wood-paneled walls and furniture stuffed into too-tight floral slipcovers. There was a table stacked with battered board games and shelves of DVDs.

The two men were watching *Terminator 2*, focusing on the screen with the intensity of recruits watching a training film.

Greg looked over finally and gave a slow wave, and Dominick smiled. But neither of them moved toward the control to pause the film.

Fiona went over and stood in front of the large screen. "We have to talk."

"This is the best part, right at the end," Greg protested.

"Get a life. And not Arnold Schwarzenegger's." She still did not move.

"Are you this much of a pain to your boyfriend?" But he clicked the remote, and the picture disappeared.

"We can talk in my room," Fiona said.

"*Now* she invites me to her room."

"Did you find out anything?" Dominick asked her quietly as they funneled into the hall.

"I don't know. It was interesting. I'm not into supernatural stuff, but he scared the hell out of us."

"Really? What did he say?" For the first time, Dominick looked frightened.

Instead of answering, Fiona unlocked the door to her room and switched on the overhead light. The bed had been made, but everything else looked the same. She and Dominick sat down on the end of the bed, and Greg and Rosa took the director's chairs.

"Did you show him the map?" Greg asked. His earlier skepticism seemed to have dissipated.

"He said it didn't work that way. Or he doesn't. He said we should be looking for something big. He mentioned mountains, but no town."

Rosa brought the map out and handed it to Fiona.

"My God. There are mountains everywhere! And not that many towns." Then something else caught her attention, something that made her feel as if she had been scooped into the air and dropped down hard. "What is the Great Sand Dunes Monument?" she demanded, lowering the map so everyone could see and pointing to a rectangular shape.

"Just what it says," Greg told her. "It's a little desert. You don't expect to find it in the middle of mountains."

But she was already turning to Rosa. "That's what he said, that it happened near sand. I thought he was picking that up from Long Island. But it's between here and Denver."

Dominick gestured at the map. "There are a lot of mountains around it."

"Mount Lindsey, Little Bear, Blanca Peak," Greg recited without looking. "All fourteen-thousand footers."

"But did he say what had happened there?"

Fiona shook her head. "Just to look for something big."

"Well, it couldn't be the plane. That landed in Denver."

"They said it made a stop to refuel. Do you see any airports around there?"

Dominick looked at the map. "No. There's one farther east, but it's not that close."

"Oh, God." Fiona pressed against Dominick, stricken, needing his comforting bulk. "We forgot to tell you. Maggie's father died."

"He *died*? When?" Dominick's voice was as shocked as hers had been.

"This afternoon. Or this evening."

"This happened in New York? How old was he?"

Why did people always ask that? "It doesn't matter. He had dementia. But he died from internal bleeding. It started this morning, and she took him to the hospital. That's why she was never home."

"My Lord."

"I brought a map book of Southwestern mountains I can loan you," Greg said suddenly. "But I need it back."

"Why would you loan it to us?" Fiona asked. "Aren't you coming?"

He shook his head. "Nah. What I need is right around here."

"But in the restaurant it sounded as if you were going with us."

"I'll get the guidebook. I'll show you what to look for."

As soon as Greg was gone, Dominick asked anxiously, "Did the psychic say anything about Coral?"

Fiona and Rosa looked at each other.

"He didn't talk about anyone specifically," Rosa said. "He just said the people we're looking for are together now."

"What the hell did he mean by that? Did he think it was good or bad?"

"He didn't say."

"There seems to be a lot he didn't say."

It was uncharacteristic of Dominick to complain, but he had been stressed since leaving Taos.

"What happened at the police station?" Fiona asked.

"I don't know why I bothered! All they did was have me file a missing person's report, which they faxed to Taos. They took my cell number in case they find out anything. That was it."

"But she's just a child. What about an Amber Alert?"

"They don't believe Eve ever put her on the plane. They thought it was impossible that Coral got on the plane and didn't get off in Denver."

"Did you tell them what we thought about the terrorists?"

"No."

"No?"

He turned on Fiona, exasperated. "Because I don't believe anything like that ever happened. I want the police to take Coral's being gone seriously, not think I'm a whack job. Maybe I should have said she was abducted by aliens!"

"That's very disappointing," Rosa said quickly, before Fiona could answer. "They should have taken you much more seriously."

Elbows on his knees, he put his head in his hands. Finally he looked up. "When Eve gets back, we'll go to the police in Taos. That's what I should have done."

Greg came in then and handed Fiona a small, leather-bound guide, open to a mass of swirls. It was a thumbprint she could not hope to read. Silently she handed the book to Dominick, though she doubted he could understand it either. Then she turned on Greg. "When did you decide not to come?"

"I told you, I don't have time. What I'm looking for is in Santa Fe. I'm not part of your little expedition."

"But you owe it to us!"

"*What?* How?"

"Well, Dominick let you stay with him." She could not think of anything else. "Please, Greg, we *need* you. What if we left right away and got back before noon? That would give you time to do what you have to do."

"We can't go now," Dominick warned. "It's too easy to make mistakes when you're tired and it's dark. We won't be able to see anything for hours."

In the end, they decided to get up and leave at five in the morning. And Greg agreed to go.

But as Rosa was pushing herself out of the canvas chair, she said to Greg, "Will you drive Fiona and me to my hotel? I don't think it's safe for us to be walking around."

When Fiona turned to stare at her, she added, "You're not staying in here by yourself." She gestured at the flimsy brass lock on the patio doors. "That wouldn't stop a squirrel. You're on the ground floor, where anyone could break in."

"Okay."

"You'll come?"

Fiona saw that the others expected her to protest. So she said, "Just let me get my stuff."

"Good girl!"

Safe girl.

Chapter Thirty-Six

THE EXPLORER WAS waiting by the curb with its lights off when she and Rosa crept out of the Inn of the Kachinas at five the next morning. They climbed into the backseat, and Dominick inched out into the street. He seemed to assume that he would be doing the driving, and no one had challenged him.

As they turned the corner toward Route 64 and Dominick finally switched on the headlights, there was a surge of relief. *We made it!* Armed with maps, intelligence, and hope, they were on their way.

"When Coral was a little kid," Dominick said, "Eve wouldn't let her have any toys."

Fiona leaned forward. She couldn't imagine him allowing that.

"She felt that she should only have *real* stuff. She bought her art-store paints and a working camera, and planted vegetable seeds with her so they could watch things grow." It was hard to tell if he was complaining or reminiscing. "From having books read to her instead of watching TV, she could read by herself at three."

Rosa made a satisfied sound.

"But it all fell apart when she started school."

"No doubt she was bored," Rosa said wisely.

"When she was in first grade," Dominick went on relentlessly, "she was invited to this birthday party, and Eve suggested she make a painting or write a poem. So she painted a picture and took it. And when she saw the presents everyone else had brought, she felt really terrible. Especially when she was given a My Little Pony and a bracelet set as a favor. Eve was furious; she wanted to yank her out of school. But that's not the answer. You have to live in your world."

"There's something so pure about that though," Fiona said. "Maybe if everybody did it…"

"Yeah, but they don't. So she gave up on Coral. 'She's *your* kid,' she used to tell me when Coral wanted a princess costume or to eat at McDonald's. Of course that's past now; she's into gymnastics."

"Is that *the* Los Alamos?" Greg demanded, pointing to a road sign. They all leaned to look.

"Those were fascinating men," Rosa said. "Misguided, eccentric, but brilliant."

Greg turned in his seat. "They weren't misguided. Without them we wouldn't have the technology we do now."

"You think you have to invent certain things before you can invent others? I mean, in a straight line?" Fiona asked. It was an interesting idea.

"Naw, it's not that linear. A thousand people jump off a sinking ship and try to swim for land, but most of them drown. The ones who make it to an island already see things differently. Then a few of them swim to another island, and so on. But no one ever goes back to the ship." He shrugged. "The islands are always there, waiting to be discovered."

"So we didn't really need Einstein."

"Uh-uh. Someone else would have reached that island, just called it something different."

"Oh, look at the camel!" cried Rosa.

It was a rock formation in the shape of a humped animal. Evidently it was natural; there were no concessions built around it. Across the way the Tesuque Indian Reservation was offering bingo and something called "Pull Tabs."

Without asking anyone's permission, Rosa pulled out her onyx cigarette holder and inserted a real cigarette, a Camel, and then fished out a matching lighter. Evidently she reserved her electronic cigarettes for public spaces.

Fiona opened her mouth to protest but then closed it again. "That's a neat holder."

"You'll never guess who it belonged to."

"Who?"

"Dorothy Parker."

"Really?"

The flame flared briefly in the darkness, and Rosa inhaled. "Someone who knew I admired her writing gave it to me. Dorothy never got enough respect. Her ashes sat on her lawyer's desk for years."

"Dorothy who?" Greg asked from the front seat.

"You kids," Rosa scolded, exhaling through her nose. " 'Men seldom make passes at girls who wear glasses.' "

" 'Guns aren't lawful, nooses give. Gas smells awful, you might as well live,' " Fiona agreed, then pressed her hand to her mouth. "I'm sorry, I wasn't thinking about—"

"No, that's fine. One of my favorites is, 'It serves me right for putting all my eggs in one bastard.' Anyway," Rosa said, addressing

Greg, "Dorothy Parker was a great wit and short-story writer. She spent her last years in Hollywood working on films."

"I didn't know that," Fiona said.

It was growing light outside, and she saw produce trucks loaded with melons and corn on their way to Santa Fe.

Then she closed her eyes.

FIONA WAS FINALLY awakened by a rumbling. Catty-cornered to her in the front, Greg was snoring. The noise was getting louder.

She gave her head a shake to wake up and leaned toward Dominick. "Where are we?"

"We just left Taos. I'm gonna need coffee soon."

"Me too. Stop anywhere you see. Have you seen signs for Questa yet?"

"Believe me, there's been *nothing*."

"Look!" said Rosa. Fiona had not realized she was awake. "There's a sign for D. H. Lawrence's ranch. He traded the rights to *Sons and Lovers* for it. His ashes are up on the mountain in a chapel. Frieda was smart enough to be buried outside with a view of the valley."

"Who's Frieda?" Greg asked.

Both women laughed. "Go back to sleep," Fiona advised.

"How come you know where everybody's ashes are?" she asked Rosa.

Rosa smiled cryptically and glanced out the window. " 'Golden lads and lassies must, as chimney sweepers, come to dust.' Shakespeare."

"Pleasant thought."

"Oh, there's more." But Rosa looked thoughtful and stared out the window instead.

The green-carpeted mountains that had been close to the high-way started to recede as the ground flattened out. There were signs for deer and "Dangerous Crosswinds," and several notices that ski areas were closed. Fiona could see lights going on in the houses scattered on the prairie and thought about the people inside. An ordinary Saturday morning with a list of tasks to accomplish. She envied those people.

When they came to Questa, it was no more than a collection of drowsy motels, gift shops, and a "Wash-o-Mat." In another moment there was a sign bidding them *"Via con Dios,"* and they were over the Colorado line.

Chapter Thirty-Seven

"SAN JACKSON—OLDEST TOWN in Colorado" was spelled out by white stones on a hillside. Fiona saw a mural of mules pulling a covered wagon on the side of a building, a sign for "Liquor to Go," and that town was over. Finally, a few miles later, there was a lighted café ringed with pickups.

"There!" Fiona cried, but Dominick was already pulling into the crowded lot.

Rosa stirred and read the sign: "Powderbush Restaurant. Do we have time to go inside?"

"Might as well," Dominick said. "We've got to eat."

The Powderbush was like the luncheonettes of Lamb's Tongue: red-vinyl chairs with aluminum-tube legs, battered maple tables, and white plastic doilies under skinny vases. Taped to the glass front door was a notice advertising a rodeo. Fiona paused at the bulletin board inside the door, which was papered with handwritten ads selling rifles, pickup trucks, and a satellite dish. The notices nearly buried a calendar of a little girl hugging a Saint Bernard.

They waited uncertainly in the doorway, breathing in the odors of disinfectant and fried food.

"Sit anywhere!" a waitress advised them. Except for her and a family of parents with three children, the patrons were all men. Fiona felt eyes tracking them as they found a table near the crowded counter. In contrast to the ethnic mix of Santa Fe, these men all seemed Anglo, ranchers and farmers, friends who called back and forth to each other as if they were in their own homes. The only exception was a Mexican in a tan park ranger's uniform who was hunched over coffee at the counter.

"And how are y'all this beautiful morning?" The waitress, tanned and with long golden braids, seemed younger than she had across the room. Seeing her at first, noticing her rounded stomach in jeans, Fiona had fantasized that she was a single mother trying to make ends meet. But this woman looked barely twenty.

"We don't know yet. We need coffee," Fiona told her.

"Coming right up! What else can I git you?"

No menus here, of course.

Dominick gave her his open smile. "What do you recommend?"

"Just whatever you want."

"Well—how about three eggs, scrambled, and some of that bacon I keep smelling?"

"Fries with that?"

"Why not?"

Rosa, who was delicately picking the sand from her eyes with a fingernail, said she would have the same and the others agreed, though Fiona subtracted an egg and added grapefruit juice.

"Oh, honey, none of that here. Orange, tomato, papaya. And they come large or small."

It seemed an impossible decision so early in the morning. "Orange. Small," she said finally. Then she got up to find the rest-rooms. Two adjoining hollow-wood doors were labeled "Dukes" and "Duchesses," with crowned silhouettes on toilet thrones. Inside the Duchesses was a plaque with a happy face that admonished

If you sprinkle
When you tinkle,
Please be neat
And wipe the seat!

Back at the table, she recited the poem to the others. Rosa shook her head as if at the demise of literature, but Greg grinned. "They've got one in the Dukes too:

No matter how
You shake or dance,
The last few drops
Go down your pants."

"That's disgusting!" Rosa cried. "I'm glad I'm from New York."

" 'Thank God I'm a country girl,' " Fiona teased.

The men laughed, but Rosa said, "God save me from local humor."

"It's not Dorothy Parker," Dominick agreed.

"Where do you think that park ranger is from?" Fiona asked suddenly.

"Mexico?" said Greg.

"No, I mean where he works. He might be a good one to ask if there's been anything unusual going on around here."

"But we're not there yet, are we?" Rosa asked.

Not if you believed in psychics. Fiona sipped her coffee restlessly.

In the next moment, a strong odor of cooking oil spread across the table. Looking up as her plate was lowered, Fiona saw that it was not from the home-fried potatoes and onions she had envisioned, but a pile of golden French fries. Her stomach turned over.

"Catsup?"

Greg grinned at the waitress. "Sure thing, honeycakes."

Oh, please. Fiona hoped she would slap him down, but when she returned with the red plastic bottle she was all smiles. "Y'all staying at the lodge?"

"Which lodge?" Fiona asked.

The waitress met her eyes, surprised. "You know, that hunting and fishing place over on the lake. That's where everybody stays. The motels and campgrounds are up around Fort Garland."

Greg preened at her. "Any motels you especially like?"

At that moment Fiona became aware of a thumping sound that seemed to be coming from everywhere. Turning, she saw that the men at the counter had begun banging their coffee cups in unison again the wood. They were unsmiling, and her heart began to thump along with them.

But the waitress grinned. "More java, guys?" she called, moving toward the coffee urn.

"I'm glad I'm from the East," Rosa said firmly.

"Leaving early was smart," Dominick said. "If anyone's following us, they won't know where to look."

"They will if we're lucky," Fiona said.

"What the hell does that mean?" Greg demanded.

"It means," Dominick said with a sigh, buttering a biscuit half, "that it doesn't matter to them where we are as long as we're not where we shouldn't be."

"Well, shit!" Dark eyes wild, Greg looked close to a tantrum. "That means we're shooting fish in a barrel. Leave me off; I'll make my own way back."

"It's not like that," Fiona reassured him. "We just have to be careful."

"I knew I should have stayed in Santa Fe." His scowl didn't lift until the waitress returned, and even then his smile was forced.

"Y'all want anything else?"

"Maybe. What have you got?" But his heart wasn't in it.

She slid a green rectangle onto the table as if it contained a secret message.

Everyone's hands reached for it. But when Fiona turned it over, it was only the check. "I've got this," she said. Then, noticing the line at the cash register, she said, "I guess you pay over there."

"The locals probably just tell them what they had," Rosa agreed.

The locals. She imagined how conspicuous her group must look.

As SHE WAITED for change, Fiona saw the tourist father approaching the ranger. She had not paid much attention to the family who had looked, to her morning-jaded eyes, like models from a JCPenney catalog, but now she decided to speak to the ranger too.

When she finished paying, she approached them. The father had flip-up sunglasses and thinning hair with large freckles on the dome of his head. "But when we got there," he was continuing, "they chased us away. They said it was private property, so we didn't get to see anything. They wouldn't even let me take pictures!" He had an earnest, educated voice that was now a whine.

"And that was for the whole town? It's possible someone bought up the old buildings; they're not worth much. News to me though." The ranger's white teeth flashed in his mahogany face. "Maybe they want to build condos." The smile widened. "Ghost town condos—that's a thought."

The tourist looked as if he had suggested destroying the Grand Canyon. "They can't do that! That town is history. Marysville is important. To think of destroying it…" He straightened up, the short wide sleeves on his cotton shirt flapping. "I'm not leaving till I see that church. Who can I contact about this?"

The ranger, ducking his head for a last swallow of coffee, looked back up with his engaging smile. "It's north of my area, but I wouldn't worry about it, sir. Probably they're shooting a movie or some commercial. There are lots of good ghost towns north of here. If you stop at the Fort, they have literature about them."

He turned his gaze skillfully on Fiona, signaling the end of the conversation. "Are you worried about Marysville too? Have a good vacation, sir," he called as the man edged unhappily away.

"Oh, no," Fiona told him. "I just wondered if you'd heard about anything unusual happening—a plane in trouble around here, anything like that. Not a 747 or anything," she added, seeing his incredulous expression. "Just something different, not quite right."

The ranger gave her his wonderful smile. It made him seem pleased simply to be in the world. "So you're *looking* for trouble."

"In a way."

"Nothing I can think of," he said cheerfully. "That's oh for two. I'd better get back to the Fort, where I know what I'm talking about."

Fiona laughed and went back to her table where the others were standing, waiting for her.

"We need to get up high and look for something big," Greg was saying. "Maybe something silver that shines in the sun."

Which of them was he expecting to sprout wings?

"What we need is to rent a helicopter."

"Do you know how much that costs?" Fiona asked. "It's hundreds of dollars when Lee has to rent one for aerial shots. Not that he's the one paying. Maybe when we get closer to the Sand Dunes we can think about it."

"It might be cheaper out here than New York," Rosa said. "Lots of people out here seem to have their own small planes."

How in the world did she know that? It made sense, but still . . .

Rosa bought two packs of Camels at the register, and they left.

Perhaps because it was on the driver's side, Dominick was the first one to notice the flat tire.

Chapter Thirty-Eight

CHANGING THE TIRE cost them valuable time. Greg was furious. "Who's fucking idea was this anyway?" He kept complaining until Fiona told him to just shut up and help. First they had to grapple with an unfamiliar jack and overtightened lug nuts, then look for a place to have the old tire repaired. Even Rosa admitted it would take too long for AAA or the rental car company to send someone.

They found a filling station back in San Jackson, a yellow stucco structure with three pumps holding an unfamiliar brand of gas. Next to it was a small weathered house, its porch crammed with discards. As they pulled in, Fiona saw that it was a second-hand furniture shop, opening at noon. Would anyone really buy a dresser missing its bottom drawer?

But at least the mechanic knew what he was doing. He showed them where a metal butterfly had been pressed into the tread, a time bomb designed to expand against the inner tube and cause a slow leak. He also found an identical device in the left rear tire.

Dominick shook his head. "God help us if both tires had gone at once."

Rosa shuddered. "We would have been stuck in the mountains miles from anywhere. And probably without cell phone coverage."

While they waited for the patching equipment to heat up, Rosa and Fiona walked down the road. "Look at that." Rosa pointed to an oversized statue of two bronze figures rising out of the rock, staggering under the weight of a massive cross. "Centuries of symbolism from one strange image."

Fiona sighed. "I know how they feel."

Somehow, without her realizing exactly when, her hope of finding Lee alive had quietly slipped away. Now she only wanted the truth.

THEY SET OUT for Fort Garland again, with Rosa reading the map. "Las Animas de Purgatoire. That means 'Souls Lost in Purgatory.'"

It did not cheer anyone up.

"Northeast of here used to be the Goodnight Cattle Trail from Texas," she continued. "They had such marvelous names for things."

Marvelous names, but the country they were driving through was desolate.

Greg ducked to see out the front windshield and gestured at the mountains ahead of them. He was finally animated again. "That's Little Bear! Blanca Peak is just behind it."

"Greg, that couldn't be." Rosa pressed her finger to the map. "It's miles from here."

"I don't know how far away it is, but I'm telling you, that's Little Bear. I've seen too many photos not to know it when I see it. Is Penitente Canyon anywhere around here?"

"Penitente?" Rosa frowned through her reading glasses.

He turned around to look at the map with her. "It's near La Garita. There!"

"But that's west of here. I wonder what *garita* means anyway."

Fiona slumped back against her seat and closed her eyes. *So much fun traveling with you two.* It was mean to begrudge them any pleasure, but she was starting to believe that the search was hopeless. All they had to go on were hints and murmurs about mountains and "something happening." What if the note from the receptionist had just been another Day Star ploy to send them down a wrong track?

You couldn't trust anyone.

She shifted as the motion of the road collided with her breakfast and made her nauseous. Maybe Greg was right to suggest chartering a helicopter. Even if it cost thousands of dollars, they could buzz the mountains day and night until they found something—if there was anything to find. That way they would have an outside witness and not be in any danger themselves.

"So where are these Sand Dunes?" she demanded, opening her eyes again.

Rosa looked. "They're just north of the mountains and the Fort."

"We should be asking more people more questions." Residents in these one-traffic-light towns would certainly be sensitive to anything unusual. Assuming the worst had happened and people had somehow died on the plane, what could an airline do with a collection of bodies? Would they take them to local funeral homes and make up a cover story—or dig a mass grave and leave them? Maybe they should be looking for a large mound of disturbed earth.

"You know what?" she said. "I think we *should* rent a helicopter and fly over the area."

Greg shifted in his seat, resting his chin on his knuckles as if to see her better. "When I said that, you shot the idea down. Let me remind you that we already have a plan. Not my plan; some psychic's plan. You insisted I come along because of the mountains, and I finally agreed. The Great Sand Dunes. Little Bear. Blanca Peak. Do any of those names ring a bell?"

"Yes, Quasimodo, they do, but it's not like they're the only mountains around. Paolo Recchia didn't use any of those names. Colorado is *littered* with mountains." She held out her hand. "Let me see that climbing book."

"Nah." He shook his head. "It'll just make you sad."

"Fiona, we have to start somewhere," Dominick said reasonably, tilting his head to try to engage her in the mirror. "This is what you suggested last night."

"I know, but—that was before I saw how big everything is. We could spend months hiking around here." It hadn't seemed this daunting when she had flown over it on the Day Star plane.

"You're too much, you know that?" Greg raised his head. "Now that you've had an epiphany—'It's all so bi-ig'—you expect us to drop everything and change course. Who made you Alpha Dog?"

To her surprise, she laughed. "It's that bad?"

"Worse."

"It is overwhelming country," Rosa defended her.

"No, it's not that. I mean it is, but we don't know what we're looking for or even the right place to look. All we know is that people are missing and 'something happened' between Taos and Denver. Supposedly around here."

"Because a *psychic* said so," Greg broke in.

Dominick turned to look at Fiona. "I say we just go on to Denver and ask questions there."

"Wait a minute. What about the mountain? I didn't come all the way up here not to summit. I'm not just here for your delightful company," Greg said.

"Which mountain were you thinking of?" Fiona asked. "I guess the tallest would have the best view."

"They're all about the same, fourteen thousand feet. Blanca's the tallest. But pick one."

"How do we get to them?"

Next to her, Rosa crinkled the map. "We go through Fort Garland and pick up 150 North."

Fort Garland was dominated by the military post that had been built by Kit Carson as a defense against the Ute Indians. Fiona was reassured by the large American flag sticking out of the adobe. It was a reminder that even here the laws she had grown up with were still in effect. They were laws that made covering up wrongful death a crime.

They turned left. The mountains were on their right now, with flat range land in between. Fiona was chilled by the sight of so much unforgiving stone, but this time she said nothing. The tree line ended two-thirds of the way up, giving a clear view of the mountain tops. Any plane landing here would be seen from the highway.

"We want Route 150," Greg told Dominick. "It's probably the next right. Okay," he added, checking his guide after Dominick had made the turn, "clock about nine miles."

Dominick shook his head but kept driving.

Most of the dirt roads they passed had swinging triangular fences with locks. Then, across the way from a sign identifying a bison ranch, Greg said, "Stop! Turn in here."

The road sloped slightly downward, sheltered by trees. At the base of the mountain, it turned right and started to rise. *Maybe we could drive to the top*, Fiona thought hopefully. She had seen those bumper stickers, "This car climbed Mt. Washington."

Just after the three-mile marker a dirt road cut off to the right. "This should be Lake Como Road," Greg said.

Dominick signaled unnecessarily and turned onto it.

The road was a nightmare. Uneven and cratered, it jounced the Explorer hard. The shape of the small tan boulders along its sides reminded Fiona uncomfortably of strewn luggage. As the map slid off her lap, Rosa clutched the grip on the door and the back of the front seat to steady herself. She sucked in her breath noisily as Dominick, avoiding a boulder shaped like a hatbox, scraped the front tire against granite.

Fiona, eyes now closed, was focused on keeping her stomach calm.

"I don't think we're supposed to be driving on this," Rosa gasped. "I've been on mountain roads in Italy, but nothing like this!"

After another few minutes of inching along, careful not to let the truck slide into the dense green underbrush, Dominick stopped. Shifting into Park, he removed the key. "This is as far as we go."

"Are you kidding?" Greg said in protest. "This baby's a four-wheel drive."

Dominick gave him a look. "And what happens when we slice open the radiator? Or another tire gives way? I'm not going to try to explain why we drove a rental car up this mountain!"

"Obviously they thought of that when they mined the tires," Fiona said. "They knew we couldn't risk it with only one spare." It would be even worse trying to back out. They never should have come in this far.

"You think the airline did that?" Greg asked skeptically.

"Well, it wasn't some cowpoke pissed off because his java was late."

"No? I kinda thought it was. They're pretty touchy out here." He consulted his guide. "We've got about a mile hike in to the lake, then level on a pack trail. Another two miles up the west face."

Rosa groaned.

Greg looked up. "I guess we're not all going."

There was a thoughtful silence.

"Only one of us has to get up high and look around," he said finally.

"But you shouldn't go by yourself," Fiona said.

"So come with me."

She turned to Dominick. She was probably relying on him too much.

"Don't worry about me," Rosa said briskly. She made a sweeping motion with her hand. "Go! I brought plenty with me to read. I'll be fine."

As if it were just a matter of whether or not she would get bored.

"No." Fiona remembered Paolo Recchia's warnings. "None of us should be alone."

"I'll stay," said Dominick. "I'm no climber."

Later, Fiona would be haunted by how casually they had made the decision of who would go up the mountain and who would stay behind.

Chapter Thirty-Nine

"HAND ME MY pack," Greg commanded and Fiona reached into the luggage well behind her. She wrested the red backpack up to him, shocked by how heavy it was. When they got outside, she said, "You're bringing this whole thing?"

"I always do."

"But why?"

"It's got what I need." Flipping back the top, he loosened the drawstring and tilted the pack so she could peer in. "Rope, runners, chalk bag, harness, hammer, chocks, and 'biners. Climbing boots, camera. Clothes for heavy dates in Santa Fe."

"I don't see the boots."

He pulled out something that looked like laced dance slippers, with black rubber covering the top and far up the heel.

"But I don't have anything like that!"

"You won't need it for here. You've got on sneakers, and that's fine."

So why are you taking your fancy shoes along? But she realized it was a matter of security, to prevent possible loss if he left them behind. *As if you could prevent losing anything*, she thought, shaken by sudden fury.

The noon sun burned as if radiating off metal. As soon as she and Greg started along the path, she had to strip away her sweatshirt. But that gave more territory to the tiny irritants that buzzed her face annoyingly. Maybe once they reached the snow on the mountain it would be cooler and insect free.

Greg reached out to a low bush and pulled off a needle. Cracking it open, he handed it to her. "Smell."

She did. It was fragrant and fruity.

"Pinion." He started to move again. "You've never climbed?"

"No."

"Scared of heights?"

"No."

"Good."

She swiped at the insects nearest her eyes and said, "Sounds like you do this a lot."

"Whenever I can. Climbing's the only thing that matters to me. Besides pizza and beer. And fucking. Two out of three on this trip ain't bad."

"But what about your job?"

"It pays for my trips. Money means climbing. Period."

"Is that why you're so cheap?"

He laughed. "When Dimitri and this other guy from Oregon and I go, we're *really* cheap. We take a tub of peanut butter and some loaves of day-old bread. And lots of apples. Chocolate too; it tightens you up. But none of this fancy freeze-dried shit." He hitched up his pack to even it.

"You have a steady girlfriend?" Fiona asked him, more to pass the time than caring.

Greg gave her a grin. "She thinks so. But I don't need anyone telling me what to do, how to spend my money. My college girl-friend—when we got engaged, she wanted me to give up climb-ing. 'Too dangerous.'" He imitated a querulous soprano. "Like I'm ever going to do *that*. I might as well be dead."

"So you gave her up instead."

"Damn straight."

Nearly stumbling on a rock and then righting herself, Fiona asked, "Have you ever had any accidents?"

He turned on her, their rapport instantly gone. "Why? Why do you ask that?"

Taken aback, she said, "Just curious. I wondered why she was so worried. Accidents do happen."

"Not if you're any good, they don't."

They went on in silence until, ascending a small rise, Fiona stumbled against a hidden boulder and started to fall.

Hearing the scrape of her shoe on dirt, Greg turned around and steadied her. "Want to go first?"

"No, I'll be okay."

"This guy you're looking for—you been with him long?"

"About six months."

"That's good. That it's not that long, I mean. Like I'm not expecting Dimitri to jump off this mountain any minute yelling, 'Hey, dude!'"

A preposterous image. "I haven't given up hope yet."

He made a noncommittal sound.

FINALLY THEY WERE approaching water. Fiona was thinking about how unusual it seemed to find a lake on a mountain when her left foot caught in a root, and she stumbled. She clutched at a stand of tall green plants—Indian pipes?—but could not right herself and landed hard on her knees.

Greg, ahead of her, didn't see what had happened. When he finally sensed her absence, he turned around and came back. "You okay?"

"I think so."

She let him pull her up, but her ankle was unexpectedly sore, and she felt unable to put her full weight on her foot. She tapped her foot once or twice experimentally on the path, feeling a pain shoot up her calf. "I'll be okay."

He squinted up at the peak doubtfully. "I don't know, Fiona. This mountain, it's like a kindergarten outing. Rosa could probably do it. But no way am I going to have your ankle giving way and you sliding off a ledge. And me getting blamed."

"I'll be okay! Just—why don't you go ahead? I'll catch up." She lowered herself to the ground to inspect her ankle and felt hard stalks of grass pressing against her jeans. Inside her shirt, lines of sweat pooled and meandered down her back. "I just need to rest for a minute."

"Catch you on the way back. I'll tell you one thing, though."

"What's that?"

"If I ever settled down—and I'm so not ready to do that—I'd look for someone like you."

Before she could say anything, he was gone.

THE BEST THING was that it was always faster going alone. But it was weird that there were no other climbers. No voices, nothing but the back-and-forth calls of a few birds. And, of course, the usual constant cracklings in the underbrush. He had relied on Dimitri to identify the rustlings of everything out here, to tell the difference between foxes and bobcats, jackrabbits and snakes. Dimitri wasn't even spooked by rattlers. Greg reminded himself that they usually nested in flatter, hotter areas, not on mountains.

Why the hell had Fiona asked him about accidents; did he have some kind of mark of Cain on his forehead? Only one accident in his whole life, and that had been years ago with the Outing Club. He'd been a kid then, showing off a little, but even when the report was made, no one blamed him. It was understood that rock climbing was dangerous.

He caught sight of the aspens that signaled more water and wondered if it was potable. He had filled up his canteen back in Santa Fe, but only had the one with him. Not that the hike up would take very long, but he was already sweating like a sumo wrestler. He reached back and eased the pack away from his shoulders to let the air circulate under his soaked shirt.

It had been a fall day when the accident happened, the trees that brilliant New England rust though the sky was overcast. He couldn't even remember the name of the mountain now. Although they were belaying, he had used very few chocks, trying to impress Dimitri by depending on his own hand holds and his own balance. And it would have been fine if Ben hadn't slipped and panicked, hadn't ripped them all off the mountain like someone peeling away a Band-Aid.

Overhead a hawk wheeled slowly as if keeping an eye on his progress to report back. Ben had punctured the wrong part of his spine on some jagged edge—every climber's nightmare—and wasn't able to walk anymore. Dimitri had complained of headaches afterward and that he couldn't concentrate on anything. Was that when his failing at everything started? Still, if the data-compression program was as good as he claimed it was, it would make up for years of failure.

A droning began somewhere above his head and it only took Greg a moment to realize that it was not an insect, but man-made. Instinctively he pressed himself into the shade. When he and Dimitri climbed on Navajo land, on monuments like Spider Rock in Canyon de Chelly, they had been alert for aircraft or jeeps on the canyon floor. The Indians got picky about outsiders on their sacred land.

The noise turned staccato as the copter swooped lower and then moved away. Surveillance, but so what? This wasn't private land. As he paused on the climbing trail, something black overhead caught his eye. Squatting, he let his pack slip off to one side, then rooted around for his camera. He didn't carry binoculars; the telephoto lens usually brought things close enough.

Bringing his Nikon out, he focused up on the dark glint, then caught his breath. There was definitely something up there, something that did not belong. The trouble was, it was hard to see. Hints of color gleamed in some places, but they looked more like reflections on plastic. No, not plastic. What was the thing it reminded him of? Rainbows—rainbow slicks on oil.

Straightening, he leaned back to assess how to get up there.

It was tempting to leave the trail and go straight up the mountain. But he was alone, and pulling out his equipment was a hassle. For a moment he did nothing. Wiping the sweat away with his fist, he wondered if he should go back and tell Fiona. But what could she do? No, that would take too long. He would check it out, snap some photos, and then get the hell out of Dodge.

A shadow crossed the ledge before he actually heard—or saw— the helicopter again. It passed over him, then continued to the top of the peak. He let out his breath. It was painted a rich blue with yellow trim. Probably some kind of ranger patrol.

He raised the camera again. A breeze must have rippled the black cover, because he could now see glinting silver edges like the frosting on Rosa's black hair. He replaced the pack firmly on his shoulders and started to move again.

Chapter Forty

FIONA UNFASTENED HER sweatshirt from her waist, stuffed it under her head, and lay back gingerly on the rough grass. Beneath the plant spikes the ground was stony. Lying on her right side, she protected her face with her arm. The world smelled like her childhood, flowers turning to syrup in the sun, the sharp scent of earth waiting to foam up when the rain hit it. There was a different, cleaner scent too, something of the way sliced cactus might smell.

So close to the ground, she was no longer troubled by flying mites. She thought about Greg and his girlfriend. Would Lee have given up photography for her? But she would never have asked him to, any more than he would have made similar demands of her. They were who they were. She would never stop traveling. And Lee . . .

Closing her eyes, she moved her left ankle experimentally, wriggling it from side to side. It still felt sore, but she supposed she could walk on it. She would be able to make it to the Explorer when Greg came back. It was peaceful here, with only the constant low buzz of nature and the drone of what she assumed was a crop duster, coming closer then fading away.

Surveillance…She thought of something she had only seen in movies. The police were always planting tracking devices on criminals' cars to monitor where they went. Day Star knew the cars they were driving. It would have been easy for them to plant something when they were mining the tires. Why hadn't any of them thought of it?

They would have to look when she got back. If only they had thought of it when they were with the mechanic.

She had a sudden sense that this was not a safe place to fall asleep. No black car had been following them from Santa Fe, but if they were anywhere close to where they shouldn't be…Twisting her body around slowly, she was finally able to stand up. She brushed off her jeans and T-shirt, pulling away a few stubborn brambles from her sweatshirt. She looked up toward Blanca Peak but could not see Greg.

He would be annoyed, she knew, if she went back to the truck. But it seemed safer than waiting on this path by herself. She could leave him a note, but she had nothing to write with. He would know, though, when he did not see her.

There was irony here—that he was doing the hard work when he had not even wanted to come.

As GREG MOVED closer, still hugging the cliff, he saw that whatever it was was further away than it first appeared. It almost made sense to go back to the truck and try to drive up another road, except that there was the problem of locked gates and private property. He calculated the time it would take to get back to the others and decided to push on.

Searching for a cliff face with some natural footholds, he wondered if the helicopter could have been hired by relatives of other people who had never arrived. Someone smart enough to actually implement *his* idea. They must have seen the same thing he was heading toward. Had they stopped on the top? Was that why he no longer heard the copter? Stepping up onto a narrow ledge, he swayed for a moment under the weight of his pack. He considered bivouacking it, then decided against that. He might want to go down a faster way.

Greg kept moving laterally until he felt he must be directly under what he had seen, but the overhanging cliff face prevented him from looking that far up. It was the kind of climbing he least liked to do by himself. Still, there was a vertical crack of several inches that would lend itself to liebacking. Letting the pack slide off, he fished around inside and pulled out his climbing boots, his camera, and his canteen. After taking a long swallow, he laced and tied the boots, then closed up the pack tightly and pressed it against the stone. Much as he hated to leave it, he had no choice.

Pull with your arms, push with your feet. But instead of moving, he stood there for a minute, arms crossed against his chest. Listening. A fall from here, eventually landing in the brush, would be painful but not deadly, though there was always the chance of a freak accident like Ben's.

He ran his hand back and forth over the rock, assessing it. There was enough unevenness to guarantee points of contact along the way. If not, he could always use a few wedging chocks. But it didn't look that hard. What worried him, he acknowledged finally, was hanging out in open air like a bug on a thread. He shoved away the image that came right after that, a giant pair of scissors snipping the thread.

What the fuck—just get on with it.

The rock was firm under his embrace. When he scraped at it with his nails, it barely flaked and he found himself moving more rapidly than usual. His shoes worked perfectly, holding him without slipping. Justifying their outrageous price, he thought, as he let himself hang off toward the right. The problem was always money, enough money to go where the real challenges were.

As he reached the top of the cliff, he grabbed at its stony surface with his hands, then swung his leg up to anchor his heel on a boulder that slanted backward. With a final, awkward push, he was over the top gracelessly, panting like a winded dog, his legs shaking. Never again, not alone, not with helicopters buzzing the trees.

But for now he was home free. He moved his head to clear it, then looked around. The blackness he had seen from below was actually an immense sheet of vinyl pulled tightly over something. It looked like the black plastic covers you could buy for cars. In a few places the seams had ripped and gaped, revealing the silver he had seen.

As he moved around, he saw something extended like the wing of a plane. But how could it be a plane? The plane hadn't crashed, and even if it had there would be luggage, stuff, *people* strewn around. But who would store a plane on top of a mountain?

Pulling himself to a crouch, he moved closer. A spike had been pounded into the ground to hold the cover down, and he wiggled it until it became unpegged. Cautiously he lifted the vinyl and saw a pair of blue fabric seats sitting incongruously upright. They were splashed with something dark, their metal feet twisted. Airplane seats, definitely.

There was an odor of fuel mixed with something sweeter, something decayed. Quickly he let the cover drop and moved back, still on his knees. No way was he getting any closer, no way would he stumble over someone's fucking *leg*. It was time to take a photo, to show he had been here and what he had seen, though he would have to pull up the vinyl again to do that. He was reaching out his hand when he heard the chop-chop of helicopter blades. It sounded as if it was landing on the other side of the destroyed plane.

Shit. He stayed still, trying not to breathe until he heard the cruel crunch of brush as if someone was walking toward him. To hell with souvenirs, to hell with photos. He had to get away. But not by dangling over the cliff face again. He would have to go down the long way through the trees and meet up with the path. Except that his pack was on the ledge and no way was he leaving without his stuff. He would have to hide and wait them out.

Flattening himself behind a juniper tree, he felt his heart whacking in his chest like a moving army. *It doesn't matter to them where we are, as long as we're not where we shouldn't be.* He had had no idea what he would see from the mountain top, had secretly thought he would see nothing, but had been desperate for the climb. But this was proof that Dimitri could actually be dead, this incredible, smelly scene. He needed to get as far from it as he could, back to Santa Fe to find Dimitri's apartment and the program. Why had he let himself be sidetracked?

The others could do what they wanted. He was heading back to the rest of his life.

Chapter Forty-One

It took Fiona almost an hour to make her way back to the truck. The trail was not difficult, but it was uneven, and she had to protect her twisted ankle. Once, hearing a noise like a rattle, she froze and looked around for the snake. She stayed poised without moving for several minutes. But the sound did not come again, and she finally moved on. A little later down the path, she saw a gray hen coming toward her. She stopped, surprised, and it turned into a boulder. Only the tiny lavender flowers on stalks surrounding it were what they seemed.

When she saw the Explorer waiting up ahead like a faithful pack animal, its white sides streaked with dust, she almost cried. Her own body was sweaty and prickling with exhaustion, but she had had no more trouble walking. She was ferociously thirsty though; they should have thought to buy bottled water. *A bunch of city slickers under Western skies.*

Reaching the truck, she saw that the driver's side was reclined back and Dominick was asleep. Rosa had climbed into the front seat beside him and was reading. She peered at Fiona over red-framed half-glasses. "Back so soon?"

"Well, I didn't go all the way." She climbed into the backseat and left the door ajar so that closing it would not wake Dominick. Then she told Rosa what had happened. "It'll be a while till Greg gets back."

"Have a book." Rosa handed her *Examination in Blood*.

"Thanks, but I already bought it."

"Did you really? Bless you." Rosa looked delighted, but then her smile turned wistful and Fiona knew she was thinking of Susan.

"I brought it along, but I haven't had time to read it yet." She considered telling Rosa the story of how she had been prompted to buy it for Karen Jensen, but Dominick stirred and mumbled and they stopped talking.

Keeping quiet so he could sleep turned out not to matter. Less than a minute later there was an explosion from the mountain, a sharp report that Fiona's jumping heart identified as gunfire. A pause, another shot, and immediately after it a third.

Dominick jerked awake, banging his stomach against the steering wheel. Catching sight of Fiona in the rearview mirror, he seemed to relax.

"Greg's still up there!" she cried.

"It's just hunters," he said reassuringly, returning his seat to upright.

"Is it hunting season out here?" she asked doubtfully. At the farm, Eimer Jensen did not bring out his fluorescent orange vest and funny hat until nearly Thanksgiving. She had never heard of a license to hunt game in August.

"There are always poachers. Greg didn't come back with you?"

"He's climbing the mountain. He wouldn't let me; I hurt my ankle. But I was thinking, he'll need water when he comes down. I'm *dying* of thirst too. Maybe we could make a quick water run."

Dominick grimaced. "Once I get out of here, I'm not driving back in. As it is, we'll have to back up."

"Want me to get out and direct you around the boulders?"

He considered it and then nodded. "Good idea. The way this road curves, it's hard to see very far back. Just stop me if there's anything terrible."

Fiona climbed out but walked a few yards down the road instead to look for Greg.

When she did not see him, she came back to the truck and circled behind it, trying to direct Dominick away from the worst rocks. It was a minefield. She winced as he had to scrape the truck bottom over a boulder shaped like a sleeping guard dog and narrowly avoided hitting a large upright triangle.

He was definitely right about not driving back in. Sighing, almost stumbling backward over a high rock herself, she stuffed down the memory of gunfire. It had definitely come from the top of the mountain. What kind of game would they have up there?

As she turned the bend that led to the better road, she realized that something larger than a boulder was blocking the way. Putting her palm up to stop the Explorer, she looked again.

Slanted across the good road, filling it completely, was a huge black four-wheeler that stood high off the ground. It was outlined in lights like an off-season Christmas tree and on the door was a painting of a frenzied horse's head, red lips open in a frothing scream. Painted below it in white script was "The Death Squad."

Wonderful. The Death Squad. If the truck had been parked facing ahead instead of across the road like a slash, there would have been the possibility of asking the owners to move so they could get by. But there was a different message here.

Fiona squinted at the windows, but they were tinted too dark to be able to see inside. The best she could hope for, she understood suddenly, was that the truck would be empty, the Death Squad off on business elsewhere. But as she started back to the Explorer, she heard the metal hinge of a door creak open behind her. Unwilling to look, she kept walking, then ran the last few feet to the truck. This time after climbing in, she banged the door shut.

"Lock the doors!" she screamed. She realized she was shaking and wrapped her arms around her knees to stop the motion.

"What is it?" Dominick asked, moving his eyes from the rearview mirror to look at her. "You mean those guys?" But as he said it he pressed the master lock. Rosa sighed deeply.

The men appeared at Dominick's window, one several inches taller than the other. Both were blond, both dressed in fringed black leather vests with Western tooling, white shirts, and jeans. They were even featured and could have been handsome, but their eyes were brown beads, their jaws too long for their faces.

The taller twin motioned at them with a small silver gun to get out of the truck.

"Stay inside; I'll handle this," Dominick commanded. As he opened his door the two men moved to the front of the truck. Dominick stayed behind the door, using it as a body shield. "What's the problem?"

The man waved the gun again. "I mean all of you!"

"Oh, for God's sake," said Rosa, shoving the woven bag off her lap as if this were in the same league as the bathroom jingles at the Powderbush.

Wasn't she afraid? Fiona's own heart was beating a frantic tattoo. But after Rosa got out and moved around to the front grille of the Explorer, she slowly opened the door and climbed out too.

"You from around here?" the gunslinger asked, smacking his gun rhythmically against his thigh.

"No," Dominick said. "We're from New York. Is something wrong?"

"They got private property back where you come from?"

"Of course. But we didn't see any signs posted."

He turned to his brother. "Hey, Jake, you forget to put up the signs again?"

Jake looked amazed. "You put up signs where you come from? Like in your driveways and stuff?"

"How can a *mountain* be private property?" Fiona asked as calmly as she could.

"We didn't know we were trespassing," Dominick said quickly. "We'll be glad to leave."

But the Death Squad grinned at that. They had beautiful teeth, Fiona had to admit, then thought how absurd it was to think about teeth *when they were about to be murdered by the Double-mint twins.*

"You from New York too?" Jake was addressing her.

"Uh-huh. Iowa, originally."

"That's right, you got that funny accent. Say *Long Island* for me."

"What?"

"Not *what*. Long Island."

What was going on? "Long Island."

The pair nudged each other. "You don't say it right. *Lon-guyland*. If you're living there now, you're supposed to say *Lon-guyland!*" Then the gunslinger waved his weapon at Rosa. "Say 'toilet.'"

Rosa looked disgusted. "Toilet."

Jake wiggled a roguish finger at her. "I bet that's not how you really say it. I bet you say *terlet*, don't you? *Erl* and *terlet*. Now say it right." He reached into his holster and pulled out his own gun, a gun that Fiona had not allowed herself to notice.

"Toilet," said Rosa stubbornly. "I'm not from Brooklyn!"

She's going to get us killed. Fiona opened her mouth to give them what they wanted, but it was swallowed up in gunfire as Jake aimed his pistol at the ground near Rosa's feet. A rock shattered, a cyclone of dust spiraling up. He raised the gun to Rosa's chest.

"What the hell are you *doing*?" Dominick demanded, hoarse. He stepped around, blocking Rosa.

From the road came a siren.

The brothers turned on each other. "Shit!" Jake yelled. "You had to play games with them instead of—"

"You're the one who kept it up."

"If you're shooting, shoot to *kill*."

"Now what're you boys up to?" The small, dried-up character stepping around their truck looked less like a sheriff than an Appalachian apple-head doll, but Fiona knew from the set of his mouth that he was the law. Dressed in a turquoise-and-black checked shirt, his air of authority replaced a badge.

"Just having some fun with our new friends," Jake smirked.

"Looks like they don't got the same toys as you. That's not fair." He might have been talking to a pair of eight-year-olds.

The taller brother spat on the ground. "What gives you the right to keep on our ass this way? My lawyer says it's harassment!"

"Just happened to hear gunfire and came to investigate."

"You're tailing us!"

"Not hunting season yet."

Fiona's heart fell miles. If it wasn't hunting season, then what were the shots on the mountain about?

"You git on now," he added, gesturing at the brothers, "or these good people may decide to make a complaint."

Jake's brother spat again, a gob that landed on a yellow bush and hung, glistening. Everyone watched it, mesmerized.

The pair turned and stomped away.

The sheriff looked at Dominick. "No telling what they might have done. Glad I came along."

"So are we!"

"But who are they?" Fiona gasped. She felt as if her body were dissolving.

He twisted his mouth. "They call themselves 'The Death Squad.'"

"I know, but who are they? Are they from around here?"

The sheriff looked uncertain as to how much he should tell her, then said, "They're Jesse Wilcox's boys. Jesse and Ginger Lee are decent enough folk, but they should have kicked these kids' butts years ago. Tried some of that tough love stuff."

Another Day Star connection. "Would they do things like flatten your tires?"

He peered at the Explorer. "You got a flat?"

"No, I just—"

"Honey, they'd do worse things than that. They used to like to lasso kids on bikes, pull them off the bike and drag them along the ground. For fun. Then they grew up and got this Death Squad idea. Going around, righting wrongs. Only their idea of right and wrong…It's what happens when you got too much money, too much time, and no good reason for being alive."

But if they had been waiting for them in the truck, they couldn't have been up on the mountain shooting Greg.

"Don't know what set them off, but you don't want to go messing with them."

There was the sound of an engine revving, a crash of broken shrubbery. It sounded deliberate, one last temper tantrum.

The sheriff opened his mouth, then closed it again.

Dominick held out his hand. "How can we thank you?"

"Just glad to help out."

But Fiona wasn't ready to let him go. "Have you heard anything about a plane having problems around here?"

He pulled at his wrinkled chin. "A little two-seater banged into Mount Lindsay last week. That kind of thing?"

"No, bigger than that. There hasn't been anything unusual happening?"

"No…" But then he brightened. "Up north around Monarch, a friend of mine's been complaining about a lot of mysterious comings and goings. Strange people in the area. He was thinking maybe drugs. Something like that?"

"Maybe." But she felt excited. "What's the town again?"

"Monarch. Right in the mountains about fifty miles up." He folded his arms. "If you don't have stuff to do around here, I suggest you get on out. I can't watch the Death Squad twenty-four hours, and they're mean dudes. I'll watch, make sure you get outta here and onto the highway."

"That'd be great," Dominick told him.

Hands were shaken all around.

"You have a good day now."

"You too." But Rosa, though restored to good humor, seemed to be studying the man as if he didn't fit into her scheme of things.

They climbed back into the Explorer and Dominick locked the doors.

"I'm too old for this." Rosa exhaled, letting herself collapse against the seat. "I've never almost been shot before."

Dominick nodded vigorously. "I think he just saved our lives. Don't get out again; I can make it from here," he told Fiona. "The road wasn't that bad in the beginning."

She nodded, troubled by something she could not yet define. It had to do with Rosa. And more urgently, Greg. "But what about Greg? One of us should go back and look if we can't drive back in."

"Well, we certainly can't stay around here! That sheriff already warned us."

"I know. But—"

"We'll come right back and wait for him on the road. Nothing can happen to us on a main road," Dominick said.

"Okay." But she vowed privately that she would walk back in. With water.

When Dominick finally reached the highway, he asked, "Which way?"

"Back the way we came," Rosa said. "We know there are places not far away."

"Yeah, there's that gas station." Dominick waved to the sheriff, who was sitting in a white car opposite the mountain road, and signaled left. Then he gave them a stern look. "Next time, don't get out. That's the way mass murders happen. We could have all gotten killed."

"But if they'd shot you, they wouldn't have let us just drive off," Fiona said.

"You'd still have been safer locked in the truck. Keeping down and leaning on the horn. If the sheriff hadn't been right there…"

"But why would perfect strangers decide to kill us?" Rosa asked.

"Because they're not," Fiona told her. "They're Jesse Wilcox's sons. Day Star?"

"You think they knew who we were?"

"Of course. Why else would they mention Long Island? They knew exactly who we were."

"You think they were sent to warn us off?"

"I do."

DOMINICK PULLED INTO the gas station with the small grocery store attached. Fiona found a water fountain by the restrooms and drank for a long time. The others did too. Then, moving quickly, they picked out two gallon jugs of water.

"Let's get food," Fiona said. "We won't have time to stop again."

Quickly they assembled a pound of sliced Jack cheese, bread, tomatoes, tortilla chips, and grapes. When Fiona picked up a jar of Creole mustard, she saw that her hand was shaking.

In the dusty parking lot, two little boys in chaps and red felt cowboy hats ran around next to a van shooting each other as their parents shopped inside. They fell dead, then pushed back up out of the dust, again and again.

Climbing into the Explorer, Rosa gave a sudden amazed laugh. "It was a skit," she cried, pointing at the boys. "It was just a show."

Dominick, back in the driver's seat, gave her a tolerant look. "Kids like to shoot at each other. It's only a game."

"I liked the guy playing the sheriff best," Fiona said, catching on immediately. "The other two overdid it. The way he kept slapping his gun against his thigh…"

Dominick included her in a frown that was turning cross. "What are you talking about?"

"Rosa means, what happened to us wasn't real. The shot was the cue for the sheriff to turn on the siren and come in and 'rescue' us. That's one of the things that bothered me, that help was so conveniently waiting in the wings."

"But he was—"

"No, he wasn't," she interrupted. "He never said."

"He never said he was a sheriff? Are you sure? They sure acted like he was."

"*Acted.* I rest my case." It was not that she was eager to prove Dominick wrong. It was that she felt relieved that what had happened made sense.

He turned to Rosa.

"Look at it this way." The same relief made her jovial. "If someone who has just saved your life warns you that you'd better leave town for your own safety, and if he tells you that what you are looking for is fifty miles up the road, what are you going to do? If you're smart you'll leave town and go fifty miles up the road."

"You're saying there's nothing going on up in Monarch?"

"I think it's going on right here in River City," Fiona said. "The good news is that we're getting close." *The bad news is that we may not live to figure it out.*

Dominick started the SUV, looking truculent. "Next you'll tell me that those guys aren't even brothers."

"No, I think that part's true. And I definitely think they're from Day Star. Jesse's sons. Remember, he wasn't sure about giving us that information. Unless that was part of the act."

"Well I don't get it, and I'm a pretty good judge of character. I have to be. I can tell you, I was mighty relieved when that sheriff happened along."

"We all were. Then." Fiona exchanged a look with Rosa.

"So you don't want to go to Monarch after we pick up Greg?" He sounded as if they had already discussed it and made that plan. Turning to Fiona, he added, "That was your idea, wasn't it, to go around asking people if they'd noticed anything suspicious? Then when someone does, you ignore it."

"If you can believe him." She sat back, exhausted, unable to discuss it anymore.

"You can't. He was an unreliable narrator," Rosa said firmly. "You don't listen to someone who's trying to con you."

Dominick made a disgusted sound and pulled into traffic.

"Do you think Greg will know to come out and find us?" Rosa looked at her watch. "Four thirty? It can't be!"

"I think he'd keep walking till he found the truck," Fiona said with more hope than she felt. If he had found anything on the mountain, anything at all, they would go straight to the police and report it. No more sleuthing around on their own in the shadow of the Death Squad. If Greg hadn't seen anything, they could head on to Denver.

Chapter Forty-Two

GOING BACK, IT seemed shorter to get to the entrance road than it had to the convenience store.

Greg wasn't there. Where he and his red backpack should have been standing was only a backdrop of cottonwood trees.

The sheriff's white car was gone.

Dominick slid the Explorer onto a narrow shoulder, close to the road that led into the mountain. "I thought he'd be here by now."

Fiona stared out the window, silent. The others had heard the shots on the mountain as clearly as she had. Were they still denying the danger they were in? *These people are hiding something. They'll do anything to keep us from finding out.*

"I'm going to walk in and find him," Dominick said.

"No!"

He looked at Fiona in the mirror, surprised.

"It's one thing to be out here on the road." She gestured at the line of cars coming from the other direction, evidently leaving the Great Sand Dunes Monument. "But it's not safe to go back in there alone."

"You're the one who said it was all a play."

"That doesn't mean they weren't serious about warning us away." *Next time, shoot to kill.* "When we left here before, I was going to go in and find him myself once we got back. Now it feels too dangerous."

"I'll just go in a little way and yell for him," Dominick promised, opening his door.

"Eat something first."

"I'm not hungry."

"You don't know how long you'll be in there. Here, I'll make you a sandwich."

Rosa was looking at her, surprised.

"We don't have time. He may be hurt and need our help." And with that, Dominick was out the door and moving around the front of the Explorer.

"What was that about?" Rosa asked her. "Why don't you come up here and keep me company?"

"I don't think he should be out there alone. What if it gets dark early and he gets lost?" Grayish clouds already obscured the tops of the mountains. Fiona got out and climbed into the front, pressing the door lock button. Dominick had left the keys in the ignition.

"He'll be okay," Rosa promised, then said grimly, "What an exciting day. All we need now are piña coladas and a piano bar."

"Well, we could sip the water and sing 'New York, New York.' Make a kick line on the road. Listen, Rosa: the next time someone asks, the word is *terlet*."

"Terlet."

Eimer Jensen would have said they were whistling in the dark. *Eimer.* She wished her uncle were there now, holding the rifle he had insisted she learn to use. She had drawn the line at going into the woods with him to kill animals, but was a crack shot at tin cans.

The line of cars coming toward them had thinned to one every several minutes. It seemed too early for twilight, but the sun had disappeared from the sky, leaving only a few cool streaks of rose. Fiona could feel the chill seeping through the window cracks.

"This is *bad*," Rosa said, all pretense gone. "How did we get ourselves in such a bad situation?"

"I don't know. The worst thing is, you and Greg don't even have to be here. I feel like I made him come." And then she told Rosa what had happened to her in Egypt.

When she was done, when she'd told her about Marcelle's death and fleeing the country, Rosa reached over and stroked her arm. "What a terrible thing for you!"

"At least I got out alive. And this time I'm sure we will too. But it's—"

She was interrupted by a screech of tires on the gravel behind them, the wheeze of a truck braking.

Both woman turned to look at the same time.

The black truck had "The Death Squad" painted in white script on the front hood.

No. Fiona looked frantically down the dirt road, praying for Dominick and Greg to appear. She imagined them running to the Explorer and jumping in as she turned the key and they sped off. But the darkening area was as empty as when they had driven up. She was reaching toward the ignition when she felt the truck ram the back of the Explorer insolently.

The jolt was electric and shook her into action. She felt around for the emergency brake, found it, and released it as she turned the key and shifted into Drive. Cutting the wheel hard toward the asphalt road, she pumped the gas pedal. The Explorer jerked forward, breaking clear, jouncing Fiona and Rosa hard. This time, there would be no phony sheriff to rescue them.

Rosa craned her neck to look through the opening between the seats, and Fiona tried to yell at her to get down. But no words came out.

She heard the ping of metal hitting the truck before the explosion of gunfire. The back window splintering sent glass shards everywhere. Rosa slumped against the door, blood pouring from her forehead. Her eyes and mouth were half open.

Jesus, help us. Every word Paolo Recchia had said, every warning had been true. First, stop the bleeding. Reaching toward the floor, trying to drive fast at the same time, she groped in Rosa's bag until she pulled out a navy flowered scarf. Frantically she pushed it against Rosa's head, pressing as hard as she could. There was no time to do anything else but look for help.

Find the nearest hospital. She had not seen any signs for one on the drive up, and the Death Squad would never let them turn around. Better to keep going straight ahead and find help. Maybe there would be a house she could call from. Park in the driveway and press on the horn until someone came outside. But what if the Death Squad shot *them* too? Her phone was in her bag, somewhere in the backseat on the floor, but she could not take her eyes off the road to find it. A look in her mirror told her the truck was right behind her, though they hadn't fired any more shots.

Fiona streaked past a sign for the Sand Dunes in the shape of an arrowhead and realized, horrified, that this highway must dead-end there. But was that so bad? There would be rangers at the headquarters, someone who could help them. "Rosa?"

There was no answer. Fiona put her hand on Rosa's arm and shook her. She was still warm, still breathing . . .

A childhood prayer: *God, if you get me out of this, I'll never ask you for anything again.*

The black truck had switched on its high beams, illuminating the interior of the Explorer.

Fiona kept reassuring Rosa, trying to keep her conscious. "Rosa, you're going to be fine. You said you were tough; you can do this. I'm getting help right up the road."

What if Rosa lived, but her brain had been damaged?

As both vehicles screeched around a new curve, Fiona saw the flat, one-storied visitor center at the same moment she noticed the chain across the road. Helplessly she crashed through the metal, ripping it away. There was an interior light burning from somewhere inside the building, and she saw two official jeeps parked to one side. *Thank God.* Beyond the visitor center rose huge mounds of sand.

Veering in at the circular drive, she braked, banging the curb. Then Fiona leaned down on the horn. Even if no one was in the building, help had to be *somewhere.*

She honked continuously, but nothing stirred. Finally, pushing open the door of the Explorer, she leapt down and raced toward the dark building, in the direction of the huge white sea.

Chapter Forty-Three

THE MAIN ROOM of the visitor center was as dark as it had looked from the road. There was no one behind the reception desk, no one anywhere that she could see, but she banged on the glass, pounded on it. Someone had to be in a back office, closing up for the night. No one came.

She heard the slam of a truck door and knew it was not Rosa.

Then she was running for her life, around to the back of the building where she had imagined the light was coming from. It was from a security spotlight. She knew it would be futile to try to get inside and kept moving into the sand, into a world of her nightmares. Her legs were once again too heavy to run, the desert-like quicksand pulling her down. She felt her arms flailing, knew she would soon lose her balance, and struggled to keep going. She seemed to be back in Egypt, the peak of the tallest dune as high as a pyramid.

I should have died there.

An explosion of gunfire behind her brought her whirling back into her life, made her trip and go sprawling. The sand gleamed white, its coolness like a gentle hand against her face.

"Fiona, stop!"

She lay there as if she had been hit.

How did the Death Squad know her name? But of course they would know it; they would know everything about her.

"Fiona! Just where do you think you're running off to?"

She knew that voice. By the time she turned to look, Will Dunlea had caught up with her. Slowly she pressed herself to her knees. "Will, thank God! I thought it was your brothers."

Yet this was a subtly different Will from the one she'd met in Santa Fe. Instead of his carefully sporty clothes, the smooth red shirt and white slacks, he had on work jeans and a threadbare plaid flannel shirt. In his hand was something that glinted only slightly in the darkening light. It was as if an animal she had imagined tame had bared its teeth at her.

"Why did you shoot at me?" she gasped.

"I was trying to get your attention. But why are you still here? I thought you'd left for New York."

"No, you didn't." This was no time for "Let's Pretend." "Listen, you shot Rosa! We have to get her to a hospital."

He gave her a slight smile. "Collateral damage—isn't that what you lawyers call it? You took advantage of my kindness, you know."

"What kindness?" She pushed herself to her feet. "You lied to me about Lee. When I went to your office to pick up the voucher, someone told me there had been a problem with the plane between Taos and Denver. How could I go home after that?"

"Who told you that?" Even in the dusk she saw the shock in his eyes.

"I don't know her name." But as soon as she said that, she thought, *Priss*. It didn't matter; she would never tell him. "Anyway, that doesn't matter. We have to get Rosa help!" Every minute they wasted talking was making things more desperate.

He shook his blond head slowly, his lips pursed in a bemused smile. "For a smart woman, for a *lawyer*, you're not seeing the bigger picture."

"What—"

He leaned over and tapped her shoulder with the side of the gun. "This way." He pointed deeper into the sand.

"No! Rosa's—"

"Shut up! I'm tired of hearing you talk about Rosa. I'm really disappointed in you." His sudden grip was a leather cuff around her arm; she had to walk quickly to keep from being dragged. As it was, her feet caught in the long black footprints left by daytime tourists.

"We're going the wrong way." But she already knew. He was not her savior. He was the bigger threat hidden behind his brothers. He was the second car making a left turn when you'd congratulated yourself on avoiding the first.

"Here is good." He indicated the large dune they had circled behind and stopped.

Standing so close to him, she saw more lines in his face than she had noticed before. Sun lines. *Son lines.* Did Ginger Lee know what he was going to do? Should she try to grab the gun?

And then Will was twisting her arm, jerking her down so quickly that she lost her balance and pitched into the sand. Before she could right herself, she felt something heavy in the small of her back—a knee—and then his hand was spreading across the back of her neck. He was pressing her face down roughly into the grit.

"I'm not going to shoot you and make it look like murder," he said softly. "You're just going to go to sleep."

Terrified, sputtering, Fiona jerked back, trying to turn over, but found she could not move her head at all. Her eyes—she must have closed them instinctively; everything was black. Gasping, she opened her mouth for air and sucked in sand. Air pockets...but there were few air pockets; he had twisted her head back and forth to destroy any.

How had he known to do that?

She was drowning in sand, sand as warm as another body against hers. She was with Lee. No, it was death. The sky would blacken after a while, the moon would rise, the air get deeply cold. But she would not feel it. She and Rosa would be left here, one more layer of the disappeared.

No one would come looking for her. No anxious parents, no brothers or sisters, no determined best friend. Only Lee, but he was gone now himself. Rosa, at least, had sons. Would Maggie think to come to their aid?

She tried to breathe lightly, barely inhaling, but only took in more sand. One of her legs was jerking convulsively. She had not taken care of Rosa, despite Paolo Recchia's warnings.

Will was speaking to her softly. "I'm not enjoying this, you know. I really liked you."

It's not too late.

"But sometimes you have no choice. When my mom was growing up on the farm, they had to shoot animals that were sick or wounded for their own good. I know you won't see it that way, but this will help a lot of other people."

She tried to control her leg, to stop its motion and make it push her up. She tried scissoring her legs, but the pressure on her back was unyielding. How long could she hold out? *This can't be the end of my life.* Except that it was. In stories people relaxed and faced the moment of death with grace. *Stories.* How had her mother felt when the waters of Packer Lake closed over her?

"I gave you every chance to go back to New York." His voice was harsher now.

Who is he trying to convince? If only she could talk to him. But the blackness in front of her eyes was dissolving into spots, white, then red and yellow, blue, violet, white again, pulsing, pulsating, now attacking her, now retreating. No, not attacking, it was beautiful, a multicolored universe she had never known about. The spots made noise too, buzzing and humming. Even squeaking, like leather on sand.

The pressure on her neck eased slightly. "Jesus! You startled me, sneaking up on me. I told you to stay in the truck to keep an eye on the other one."

"What are you doing to her?"

Help me. Help me, whoever you are. Don't let him kill me.

"She was going to ruin everything. We go into bankruptcy, you'll never get to fly."

She felt something drop heavily onto her upper back, pressing her face deeper into the sand. Then suddenly there was no weight at all. This was how it felt to die.

But someone was grabbing her by her sweatshirt sleeve and flopping her over on her back. "Breathe!"

She tried, but all she could do was sputter and choke sand.

Then a mouth was on hers, sucking everything out, then breathing it all back in. She thrashed her head, trying to get away, but fingers were scrabbling at her nose, scraping away sand. "I said, breathe!"

She tried to inhale and pulled in some air, but it ended in a coughing spasm. Opening her mouth, she finally felt air rush in.

She opened her eyes and stared at the man holding the gun. She knew that face, that delicate mustache. *These planes are really very safe . . .*

"Come on!" He was trying to jerk her to her feet. "We have to get out of here!" He indicated the shape of Will crumpled in the sand.

But there were still too many colors and shapes pulsing against her face for Fiona to stand up on her own. "Jackson?"

The body sprawled in the sand stirred, turned over, and took in the scene. "Jackson, you can give me back my gun now."

"You were going to kill her!"

"I told you why. Don't be any stupider than you are."

Fiona saw Jackson's face tighten, then go bland. "Stupid? I know you think I'm stupid. I'm stupid, but I can shoot."

He moved the gun closer to Will's chest and fired.

Will, eyes wide, jerked back down.

"This is for all the promises about flying." He squinted and shot Will in the head. "And this is for—"

"Stop! You're wasting bullets!" Was it a bad joke? She didn't know.

"You're right." His arm dropped until the gun was pointed toward the sand. "Let's go. No, wait! Get his phone."

"His phone?"

"He keeps it in his front pocket."

You want me to kneel down and take his phone? When he's dead? But maybe he wasn't. She imagined Will jerking to life, grabbing her arm and pulling her down on his bloody chest. Jackson still had the gun, but it would be terrible.

Still, she sank to her knees, trying to keep from looking at the network of red lines across Will's face. Roads going nowhere. It spooked her that his eyes were still open. She made herself pretend he wasn't real. Don't think that he'll never eat at La Cantina again or sit behind his beautiful desk. *Stop. This man was trying to kill you. It was almost your body lying here in the sand.*

She put her hand on his jeans' pocket and felt the bulge beneath. But her fingers were shaking so much it was impossible to extract the plastic case. The smell of blood made her nauseated, and she wanted to turn away and collapse. If Jackson weren't so insistent… She made herself grasp the end of the hard plastic case and inch it out.

"Take it."

Fiona pushed back up, swaying as Jackson grabbed her. Then they were floundering through the sand, coming around the dune and toward the faraway visitor center.

"The rest of them think I'm stupid too." He was on a mission now.

"First we have to help Rosa. Please?" Belatedly she realized what it meant to be with Jackson Redhawk. "You know what really happened on the plane."

He kept pressing forward without answering.

"*Tell* me," she begged.

"Later."

They reached the asphalt and started to run, Jackson awkwardly as if favoring one leg, but when Fiona saw the screaming horse's head on the door she lurched back. "Are they in there?"

Jackson has a gun. Jackson will protect us from them.

"Who?"

"Those—Jesse's sons." She pointed at the truck.

"No…" Then he understood. "That's not their truck. There's a whole fleet of them."

"My God! And they just drive around terrorizing everyone?"

"Who's to stop them? This family owns everything."

They reached the Explorer, and Fiona yanked open the driver's side door.

"Rosa?" she cried.

Rosa was slumped in the same position as before. Her skin was gray in the overhead light, the scarf on her forehead clotted around the hole. Was it good that the bleeding had stopped—or did it mean there was no longer any hope? She leaned her face over Rosa's. There was shallow breathing.

"She's alive!"

Jackson had pulled open the backseat door and climbed in. Then he leaned over and assessed Rosa, tugging the silk scarf away from her forehead so he could see. Fiona was afraid he would make the wound start bleeding again, but he said, "It's okay. I think it just grazed her."

"Are you sure?"

"How old is she?"

"Not old enough to die!"

"Okay. We'll take her to Magdalena. Turn right on the main road."

Fiona started the engine and skidded out of the parking lot, shivering as she passed the Death Squad truck. Ahead, snaked on the asphalt, was the chain she had torn down. She clattered over it, driving as fast as she thought safe.

"Have you ever shot anyone before?" she asked.

"No." She assessed his voice for meaning but couldn't find any.

"Turn right up there; it's the cutoff for Mosca."

The Explorer's headlights played over flat grazing land, shining on the empty road. Crossing a cattle grate in the road, the tires made a deep moan. "Will you at least tell me what happened to Greg?"

"He's the climber?"

"Is he okay?"

"Will shot him."

"Oh my God. But *why?*"

"He was upset that he found the plane."

"The plane?" Fiona sought his eyes in the rearview mirror. "What plane do you mean? At least tell me if he's alive so we can go back and get him."

"We don't need to go back."

Chapter Forty-Four

FIONA GRIPPED THE steering wheel dizzily. It wasn't possible that Greg could be dead. She had been terrified when she heard the shots from the mountain but hadn't accepted what they might have meant. Not really. And it was her fault. If she hadn't begged him to come, he would be in Santa Fe right now, drinking a beer and planning his next climbing expedition. Maybe he would have found Dimitri's apartment and what he was looking for.

Now he never would. Tears burned her eyes as she remembered his last comment before he started up the mountain.

And then Jackson's other words flashed through her fog.

"The plane was on top of the mountain? But how could it be? It landed in Denver!"

"See those lights? We're almost there."

"At least tell me what happened to Lee Pienaar. Is he...still alive?"

"He's alive. That's why we have to hurry!"

Then they were entering a small town and driving into the parking lot of a two-story stucco hospital. Lighted arrows in the cement pointed to the emergency entrance. Instead of parking, Fiona drove up the ramp.

Jackson leaned forward as if to stop her.

She braked with a squeal and began honking the horn. Two orderlies in pale green cotton suits came running out. By the time they got to the Explorer, Fiona had reached across and opened Rosa's door. Then she opened her own door. She didn't see where Jackson went.

"What's the problem?" The first orderly was a grizzle-haired man in black-framed glasses.

"She was shot." Her voice was hoarse.

"Okay." The man stepped forward and put his hand on Rosa. "Oh boy."

Oh boy? What did oh boy mean?

The second orderly had already bolted back into the hospital.

Fiona sank back in the driver's seat. Greg was gone—was Dominick still alive, or had they gotten him too? *Like shooting fish in a barrel.* Rosa was—who knew. Half an hour ago she had been almost dead herself. The line between living and dying was fluid, as if you could cross it again and again.

As the men edged Rosa onto the stretcher, Fiona pressed her hand over her mouth. She had always thought of Rosa as tall, but that had probably been her personality. Her legs, slightly bent at the knees, looked thin in her black sweatpants. Her hair was matted, and she still wasn't moving. As the canvas dipped in transit, one of her arms swayed and Fiona admitted the truth to herself: Rosa was the one she was most desperate to have live.

"They have a few questions, miss, if you'll come inside," the younger man called to her.

"Oh. Sure." She picked up Rosa's bag and followed him through the entrance. At the nurses' station she handed over Rosa's license and a pristine Medicare card.

"How did she get shot?" The nurse, a woman her age with curly brown hair, gave her a stern look.

Fiona hesitated but then told her the truth. "This crazy truck called the Death Squad rammed the back of our SUV. We tried to get away, but they shot into our car as they passed."

"You're *tourists?*"

"Um…"

"And they shot at you?" She gave her head a shake. "Those two—their father *founded* this hospital. Just tell the police everything. Wait over there."

But Jackson was shaking his head at her. "We have to go while there's still time. When someone is shot, they tie you up for hours."

"Won't the police help us?"

"If you're coming, come on."

They moved rapidly out of the emergency room and to the Explorer, which was still on the ramp.

Inside, Jackson asked, "Where's the phone?"

"There. In my bag. On the floor." Fiona did not want to take her hands off the wheel. "Back the way we came?"

"No. Go right at that light."

Jackson found the phone and was switching it on. "Miss Lee?" A pause. "No, this is Jackson. Will can't come to the phone right now. He wanted me to call you to see what's going on."

He listened. "But you can't do that!"

More talk from a woman's voice that Fiona could not understand.

"You're at Marysville *now?* Don't do anything; we're on our way."
He pressed off. "Damn. *Damn.* Can't you drive any faster?"

"I don't even know where I'm going!"

"Go straight, and I'll tell you when to turn." He was pressing
numbers in again. "There's an emergency in Marysville. People
are locked in the church—they're going to be burned alive!" He
listened. "Any minute now. That's not important." He ended the
call. "She wanted me to tell her who was going to do it. If I'd said
Ginger Lee, she'd have thought it was a prank."

"She's burning people alive? The *passengers?* Oh my God, oh
my God." Fiona knew she was wailing, but she couldn't stop herself. "How much farther *is* it?"

"Three miles. Less. Stay calm and I'll tell you about the plane."

"O-okay." She made herself breathe slowly and look at the
field they were passing. Dark shapes of bison swayed like moving
haystacks.

"The plane that landed in Denver wasn't the one that left Taos.
It was at the Ranch. We were headed there, but we didn't make it;
we ended on the mountain. They helicoptered out anyone who
was okay and put them on that plane for Denver. It had the same
numbers, so traffic control didn't realize the difference."

Fiona caught her breath but kept from interrupting him.

"Because of the nitrous oxide, no one remembered what had
happened—a benefit they hadn't counted on. Small planes land
out on the tarmac and people are bussed to the terminal. When
the first bus got out there, they said they weren't ready. When the
next came ten minutes later, a few people and Day Star staff got
on, as if everyone else had been picked up."

"How could they do it all so fast?" Fiona braked for a dark
shape, but nothing was there.

"Everything was planned since the last time. They thought they could get our plane to the Ranch, but it crashed on the mountain. It was a hard landing, but most people didn't die. Some did. Like the man visiting his daughter. He—"

"You mean Maggie's father? But he *did* get there."

"That's what she told you?" Jackson laughed softly. "Money talks."

"You mean she just said that? They paid her to say that?" *A young woman will betray you.*

"Turn left here."

Chapter Forty-Five

IN THE SHINE of the headlights, Fiona could see the remains of a ghost town. The shell of a log cabin, other houses open to the sky, then several stone foundations where the wood had fallen away.

"Is this *Marysville*?"

"Turn the lights off," Jackson commanded. His hand rested on her thigh, but there was no erotic current.

"But I—okay."

She strained to stay on the road in the blackness, the dashboard lights the brightest thing to navigate by. Yet there seemed to be some light up ahead, an odd, not-quite-earthly glow. Her heart thudded—had they lit the fire already? Was Lee locked inside? To come so close to finding him—but she couldn't think about that. As the road angled sharply, a Milky Way of sparks was rising into the sky.

"Stop here!" Jackson said. "We'll walk. Take this." He handed her Will's gun. "You know how to shoot?"

Only tin cans. "What will you do?"

"You'll have to cover me."

Oh, God.

Jackson ran toward the lighted square, Fiona racing to keep up with him. The strongest light came from flames licking at the bottom of a battered white church, glowing upward like footlights. It took a moment for her to see the black truck with the frenzied, squealing horse's head, outlined with white lights, a horror movie where the dead kept coming back to life, a hand reaching out to grab your ankle.

But it *couldn't* be Will.

Then she saw Ginger Lee and the two men who had stopped them on the mountain road standing near the truck.

Jackson stopped between them and the church. "Are they inside?" he demanded.

"Leave it alone," Ginger said. "They won't feel anything."

"Yeah, shut up, Indian," the shorter brother yelled.

Jackson whirled to where she stood in the shadows. "Fiona, now!"

As the trio focused on her, startled, Jackson took off toward the church.

Fiona braced herself and pointed the gun at them.

The taller one—she couldn't remember his name—began to laugh. "Well, what have we got us here, Pocahontas?"

"Oh, for God sake," Ginger Lee said, sighing. "Will was supposed to take care of her."

Fiona startled at her voice and the dead weight of the pistol dipped in her hand. She righted it immediately.

I wanted you for my mother.

"For heaven's sake. Mickey, take care of this."

His hand moved toward the holster on his belt, and Fiona sucked in her breath. Then she fired and hit him in the thigh.

He howled and fell to the ground.

Say terlet, sucker.

She heard the bang of a wooden door from the church, but she knew she couldn't look and see. "Like you said," she yelled at Mickey. "Next time *I'll* shoot to kill." She felt like an animal trying to make herself look larger, fiercer, but her hand was shaking. How much longer could she keep them at bay? With Mickey on the ground, she had to keep watching everywhere. Soon they would think of a better way to fight back.

Ginger Lee paid no attention to her injured son.

Something inside the building cracked sharply, sending a panoply of sparks into the air and then raining them down. The Death Squad's truck glittered like a carnival float.

Do something.

"I grew up on a farm like you," she said to Ginger. "As I think I told you. But how did you move from killing sick animals to *people*?"

"Don't compare yourself to me, you little nothing. You're not like me at all. Jake, do something!"

But she was distracted by someone running around the truck and stopping in front of them.

Fiona gasped. It was the tourist from the café who had complained about Marysville.

He looked at the gun she was holding, shocked. "What are you doing?"

"They're burning the church down with people inside! They won't let us rescue them!"

"People are in there? I already called the fire department!"

Without waiting, he turned and was running toward the church.

Almost immediately there was a siren, its wail startling in the empty countryside.

"Come on!" Ginger snapped at Jake. "We can't be here."

They turned and ran toward the Death Squad truck. Fiona kept the pistol trained on Mickey, who was ignoring her, propelling himself with his arms as he dragged his leg along the ground. He yelled at them to wait.

They didn't wait. The Death Squad truck passed the first fire engine and skirted the ambulances and two sheriff's sedans. Fiona lowered the pistol as vehicle doors opened and a collection of men and women raced toward the burning church. Then she collapsed on the ground, put her head on her knees, and sobbed.

Chapter Forty-Six

SHE WAS STILL weeping when she heard Jackson say, "It's okay, stop; we got them all. Take care of her."

Fiona looked up then and saw him supporting a young girl with long brown hair, her arm in a grimy cast. *Coral?*

Coral. They had found Coral.

"She's been drugged—they all were. She's groggy, but okay."

Pushing to her feet, Fiona held out her arms and embraced the girl. "But why didn't they send her home with a story?"

Jackson gave a grim laugh. "They wanted to. But there was never any answer at her mother's house and no answering machine. By the time they knew about her father, he was already out here looking for her."

Dominick. Where was Dominick?

"And the others in the church?" She almost couldn't form the words.

"Okay. They're okay. They're taking them to the hospital. Your—he's fine, he was in the first ambulance. He'll be conscious soon."

"You mean he was unconscious all this time?"

Jackson sighed. "In and out. They couldn't risk sending him home. And then you were out here." He remembered something. "Who was that man who helped?"

That mystery man? The Lone Ranger? She fought down a hysterical laugh but didn't answer.

"Let's go to the hospital. The same one, in Magdalena."

Yes, I have to see Lee. But she wavered. "I have to find Dominick." She glanced at the girl pressed against her. "You know your father's cell number, don't you?"

"Uh-huh."

"I'll see you there." Jackson ran quickly toward the last ambulance.

"Can you walk?" Fiona asked Coral. "My phone's back in the truck."

"If you help me."

They passed the remains of ruined church, the fire finally extinguished. Its white paint had blistered and darkened completely.

"I hate this hospital!" Coral said suddenly. "I hurt my arm, and they wouldn't let me go home."

"It wasn't exactly a hospital," Fiona said gently.

"And this little German boy who hurt his leg, he died, and they left him lying there! And then they put him in a *bag* and took him outside." She started to cry.

"It's okay, it's okay." Fiona hugged her more tightly. "You're safe now. They'll arrest the people who did this. We'll call your dad and go get him."

Please, God, make Dominick okay.

She checked the passenger seat for Rosa's blood, then helped Coral in. Before she turned on the Explorer, Fiona asked, "What's his cell number?"

Coral, small in the passenger seat, looked very tired but recited it.

Dominick answered on the second ring. "Fiona? Where *are* you?"

"I'm fine. I have someone who wants to talk to you." She handed the phone to Coral, who took it awkwardly with her free hand. "Daddy?"

She couldn't hear his response and couldn't see Coral very well. Tears welled in her own eyes. She'd probably collapse when she saw Lee.

"I know. But I broke my arm and it hurts!"

"Tell him we'll pick him up," Fiona said urgently. "Ask him where he is."

Instead, Coral handed the phone to her and slumped against the seat.

"Dominick? Are you still at the mountain?"

"Was that really *Coral*?"

"Yes, it's okay. We're going to pick you up."

"I'm at that gas station where we got water. I didn't know where else to go."

"Is there an address?" It sounded silly as she said it. "For the GPS. I don't know where the hell I am."

"I'll ask."

A moment later he told her.

Chapter Forty-Seven

FIONA THOUGHT CORAL and Dominick would fall into each other's arms, sobbing. Instead, Dominick cuffed her on the chin and said, "Hey, kid," and she said, "Why didn't you come get me? I hated it there!"

"Believe me, I was trying."

They climbed into the backseat and began talking in a low murmur.

Fiona set the GPS for Magdalena, and they were off.

The hospital blazed with lights as if there was a party going on. This time Fiona went into a lobby that was furnished in 1960s style, turquoise and bright orange vinyl. A few ragged magazines lay on a kidney-shaped coffee table, and there were prints on the walls by an R. C. Gorman wannabe.

Lee was in a second-floor private room. She stood in the doorway for a moment and took in the IV drip and tubes, almost not recognizing him. His fair hair was shaggy and a light beard covered his face—Lee, who was more meticulous than anyone she knew. He gave her a groggy smile, his lips twitching.

To her surprise she did not break down, just went over and kissed his forehead hard, then hugged him tightly.

"I'm not letting you out of my sight again," she murmured.

"Good. Obviously I can't be trusted."

THE SURVIVORS MET two weeks later at an Indian restaurant in Patchogue—a place that Rosa had chosen. When Fiona pushed open the heavy wooden door, the waft of heat and spices stunned her. Tandoori was elegant, lit subtly like a cave, with carved rosewood panels that showed scenes of daily life in India. At the back of the restaurant was an open, black-walled oven; to its right a man in a white robe stroked a long-necked sitar. The mingled odors of sandalwood and spices took Fiona back to New Delhi.

Rosa had asked Fiona and Lee to come before the others so they could talk privately. She was waiting at the bar in a far corner, under an overhead drape of dark blue silk. An apricot-colored drink stood on the counter, and she laughed when she saw them. "Can I interest you in a piña colada, Fiona?"

"Oh, God. You know what happened the last time I had one." She leaned over and kissed Rosa, careful not to touch the white gauze pad on her forehead. "How *are* you?"

"I'm fine. I'm tough."

"You remember Lee from the hospital." She pushed him forward like a proud mother. Although his recovery from his concussion had been good, he was quieter, more pensive than before.

"Of course I do." She leaned forward for a kiss. "You're feeling okay?"

"Better every day. Fiona worries too much. My vision's still blurry sometimes, but the doctor says that should improve. Funny thing is, I still can't remember the flight."

"That's what everyone says. Order what you want and let's sit at a table."

"How do you know no one can remember the flight?" Fiona asked when they joined her.

"Ah." Rosa looked complacent. Tonight she was wearing an emerald-green cotton dress, embroidered and mirrored, with long jade earrings. "That's one of the things I want to tell you."

Lee lifted his glass and the other two clinked theirs against it. He had decided to keep the beard and looked to Fiona like a Viking explorer.

"I've been in touch with the others because—okay, Susan's gone. I accept that. It's tragic that she never enjoyed the recognition she should have gotten. But I'm not looking for someone to replace her. This is a wonderful story, and *I'm* writing it."

"No! Really?"

"To paraphrase Samuel Johnson: When a man knows he will be hanged in two weeks, it focuses the mind wonderfully. When I was in the hospital I realized I've been part of the backstage crew all my life when what I really wanted to do was write. And this story has everything. Drama, twists, the Jesse-Ginger Lee connection."

Fiona didn't know what to say. She looked at Lee, but he was smiling and nodding at Rosa. For a moment she felt a sense of regret that she wouldn't be the one doing the writing. Then she opened her hand over the table as if to let it go.

"Will you help me?" Rosa was asking. "Tell me everything you remember?"

"Of course."

"I've contacted Ginger Lee, but she hasn't responded, of course. Do people get mail in jail? Those sons of hers are cretins; I'd never talk to them."

"They're in jail too?"

"Of course they are, for attempted murder. The plane scam was bad, but trying to get rid of the last passengers was worse. No bail. Lots of publicity because of who they are."

"I know." An ashen-faced Ginger Lee, looking older and furious, had been all over news sites. "But they're not blaming Jesse Wilcox?"

"Oh no. They did an evaluation and interviewed his caretakers and decided he couldn't have known what was going on. I tracked down that Day Star receptionist who gave you the note, Priss Fields—she's a key witness. She knew about the identical plane at the Ranch, always kept ready. Sometimes they had parties on it."

Lee shuddered. "These are evil people."

"And they almost got away with it. If you're not looking for small discrepancies, you won't see them. It's a huge airport, the Day Star plane with the right numbers landed, nobody paid attention. They even loaded it up with passengers and flew it back to Taos. A new flight crew was scheduled, and they didn't even know what had happened." Rosa waved her glass. "So much human drama. The way that grandmother came all the way from Germany for the little girl…it's got everything!"

"You've already done so much research," Fiona said admiringly.

"Well, I won't live forever. But there's something I wanted to tell *you*, Fiona." Rosa's brown eyes were focused on hers; the white bandage accentuated the wrinkles around them. "Before I got shot you were telling me about what happened to you in Egypt. I've been thinking about that a lot, the way you seemed to be blaming yourself. You shouldn't. Those men were *criminals*. You did the right thing to leave Egypt when you did."

Fiona drank a sip of merlot, stalling for time. She had not been expecting this. "But it still feels like I ran away. And nobody knew the truth of what happened to Marcelle."

Lee put his hand over hers. "Marcelle was dead. You were in danger of being incarcerated permanently." He smiled at Rosa. "We've had this conversation before, obviously."

"Post-traumatic stress," Rosa said wisely, then turned to Fiona. "You think the Egyptian authorities would have believed you? You could have been another Amanda Knox, locked up for years!"

"She thinks the authorities are looking for her. That she can't fly internationally anymore."

"No, I don't." Fiona said, embarrassed. This was going to be hard to admit. "I checked, and I'm not on any list. But I—I couldn't face living on a farm again for a year, even in Africa. I was going to tell you. Soon."

Lee took a sip of wine. "I've been thinking about that. Could you stand it for a month? Maybe a year is unrealistic. I can take all the photos I need to in a few weeks. We wouldn't even have to give up the apartment."

"Are you sure? You're not just saying that because I—"

"Saved my life?" He put his arm around her and squeezed her. "No, but it made me realize I can't risk losing you. Ever."

"*Aww.*" Rosa beamed at them.

"Hey, you!" Dominick was coming toward them, his hand on Coral's shoulder. "I should have known I'd find you in the bar."

"Just killing time." Rosa stood up and let Dominick enfold her in a hug.

Fiona hugged Dominick and Coral too and watched the men shake hands. "You look great!" she told Coral. The cast on her arm looked professional and new.

"I'm back in school. What kind of place *is* this?"

"It's Indian; you'll love it," Rosa told her. "Our table's in the other room."

Fiona watched Dominick guide his daughter toward the entrance. He had always believed it would work out, that nothing terrible had happened. Was that the secret? To believe life wouldn't let you down?

Except it sometimes did.

The table was set for eight, a lush white tablecloth and napkins, dark red plates. She knew who two of the other plates were for, but had a symbolic place been set for Greg, like Elijah at a Passover Seder? She didn't need a reminder that his life had been unfinished; she thought about him at odd times every day. The irony was that Dimitri was one of the people rescued from the church. It was doubtful he would walk again, but the program he had been bringing Greg was brilliant.

And then Amanda, blonde and chic, was standing in the doorway with Jackson, looking around. Fiona waved at them and they came over.

No more pink smock. Amanda was crisp in a stylish black outfit, accented by a heavy turquoise-and-silver neckband. Jackson wore narrow-hipped jeans with a silver concha belt and a white dress shirt. On his feet were the same style of Western boots that Will wore. Fiona had a terrible image of him going back and wresting them off Will's feet. But she was sure he hadn't.

Jackson knew everyone from the hospital, but Fiona said to the others, "This is Amanda Redhawk."

"Really?" Dominick stared at her a moment, then stood up to embrace her. "Your husband was a hero. He saved my daughter's life!"

Amanda smiled over at Jackson "In the end, he was."

"You came all the way to New York to have dinner with us?" he continued, amazed.

Now Amanda laughed and looked at Fiona. "No, I'm trying to get into the Fashion Institute if they'll have me. Fiona's been a big help with everything. And Jack—well, I'll let him tell you."

But Jackson sat down next to his wife, looking grave. "First of all, it wasn't just me. If Fiona hadn't kept on looking, none of this would have come out. At the church she kept the family away from me so I could go inside. She saved *my* life."

And suddenly, led by Rosa, the people at the table began applauding. It was picked up quickly by the wait staff and then everyone in the room. "Speech, speech!" someone in the corner with no idea what was happening called out.

Fiona wiped at her eyes. "*Everyone* was brave." She looked at Dominick. "The way you stood up to those guys? And went off to find Greg?"

At the hospital she found out that Dominick had gone up and down the path, calling Greg's name, until it was too dark to see anything. Then he'd hiked out to the road and managed to flag down a pickup truck. Not knowing where anyone else was, he'd gone back to the gas station.

"A lot's happened," Dominick said. "Eve's staying in Taos; it's what she wants. She says she's living her dream." He looked disgruntled at that, then recovered. "At least I still have Coral. We thought she should stay up here because of her gymnastics, but the doctor doesn't think her arm will heal in the right way. They really botched it up."

"Oh, I'm so sorry!" Rosa cried.

"It's okay," Coral told her, "I was getting too tall anyway. My dad's getting me riding lessons. When I was out in Taos, I found this great horse!" But her face changed. "I want my mom to come back."

"I know, sweetheart, but it will be okay. I'm going to lease you a horse!"

Fiona started to laugh, but was saved by the waiter coming back. He had been there several times, seen them talking, and moved discreetly away.

"Can I have a Caesar salad?" Coral asked him quickly. "I don't think I'd like anything else here."

Rosa shook her head, but the waiter promised to see what he could do.

"Jackson, you never told us what you were going to do," Rosa said.

"Oh." He ducked his head, embarrassed. "There are a lot of airlines here. Because of what happened in Taos, they've offered me a job. Two of them."

"More than that. He's just being modest," Amanda told them.

In the aftermath of the Day Star collapse, Jackson had been recognized as a hero. He had been credited as saving the lives of the passengers in the burning church, seven people. Eight people, if you counted Jackson rescuing her from Will earlier. The police had accepted Fiona's version that he shot Will while defending her. They didn't seem to care about the second bullet.

Fiona gestured at the empty chair. "Is that for the mystery tourist?"

Rosa laughed. "Nobody knows who he was. No one has come forward. But I'll have to find him. He's part of the story too."

"Is it for—Greg?"

Rosa looked sad. "I guess it should be." She raised her wine glass, filled from the carafes that had been waiting on the table for them. "He was a hero too."

They drank to him somberly.

"I can't get over feeling guilty about him," Fiona said. "It's like the movie *Hair* where that hippie accidentally gets sent to Vietnam and dies. He didn't even believe in the war, but got caught up in it because of his friends."

Rosa reached across the table and grasped her wrist. "Fiona, stop! You're not responsible for everything that happens to other adults. He insisted on climbing the mountain that day."

"I know."

"But who is the chair for?" Dominick asked. "I can't think of anyone else."

"Maggie," Rosa said. "But I doubt she'll come. She was feeling terrible when I spoke to her."

"She should." Fiona felt outraged. "She almost made us give up!"

"They promised her forty thousand dollars. That older man who said he had been on the shuttle went to see her. He told her that her father had had a heart attack during the flight and died. She thought her father would want her to use the money to get Derek more help."

"Wait a minute," Dominick demanded. "Her father never got to Long Island? It was a lie?"

"She's a good actress," Fiona said. "*I* believed her."

"You mean she did it for the money?"

"Well, we're all still finding our way," Rosa told him. "But as Dorothy Parker once said—"

Fiona laughed. " 'Gas smells awful. You might as well live!' "

Acknowledgments

THE CHARACTERS IN my books may come and go, but my support staff remains constant:

Chelsey Emmelhainz, my wonderful editor, who infuses the entire process with hope and good sense.

Agnes Birnbaum, who can always see the next possibility on the horizon.

My trusted first readers, who approach my first drafts with love and invaluable critical sense: Tom Randall, amazing husband and poet; Adele Glimm, dear friend and writer herself; Robin Culbertson, insightful reader/writer and wonderful daughter-in-law. This year, Susan Uttendorfsky turned her accomplished editorial eye on the book as well.

To all my wonderful friends, who allow us to inflict our literary party games on them, and my Goddesses. To Liz Randall and her Retired Teachers Book Club, and always to the Setauket Meadows Book Club, who are welcoming and enthusiastic and even listened to the first chapter of this book!

To my New York City book group, who work hard to foster literary excellence and fascinating conversation.

A nod to my longtime friend Wes Craven, who left us all too soon.

Finally, my stimulating and creative family, who make life worthwhile: Tom Randall, Andy and Robin Culbertson, John Chaffee and Heide Lange, David Chaffee, Jessie Chaffee and Brendan Kiely, Joshua Chaffee, Caroline Chaffee, Katie and Dave Bennett, Dave and Liz Randall, Deborah Hess. And, of course, our hopes for the future: Andrew and Emily Culbertson, Charlotte and Reagan Bennett, and others yet to come.

To the world itself: Thanks for the memory.

Want more from Judi Culbertson?

Be sure to check out her Delhi Laine mysteries:

An Illustrated Death

A Photographic Death

A Bookmarked Death

Now available from Witness Impulse.

About the Author

JUDI CULBERTSON draws on her experience as a used-and-rare book dealer, social worker, and world traveler to create her mysteries. No stranger to cemeteries, she also coauthored five biographical illustrated guides with her husband, Tom Randall, starting with *Permanent Parisians*. When she is not feeding family, friends, and cats, Judi creates artwork for her company, Red Sled Ornaments.

Discover great authors, exclusive offers, and more at hc.com.